THE MISPLACED PHYSICIAN

Also by Jeri Westerson

The King's Fool Mysteries

COURTING DRAGONS *
THE TWILIGHT QUEEN *
REBELLIOUS GRACE *

The Irregular Detective Mysteries

THE ISOLATED SÉANCE *
THE MUMMY OF MAYFAIR *

The Crispin Guest Medieval Noir Series

VEIL OF LIES
SERPENT IN THE THORNS
THE DEMON'S PARCHMENT
TROUBLED BONES
BLOOD LANCE
SHADOW OF THE ALCHEMIST
CUP OF BLOOD
THE SILENCE OF STONES *
A MAIDEN WEEPING *
SEASON OF BLOOD *
THE DEEPEST GRAVE *
TRAITOR'S CODEX *
SWORD OF SHADOWS *
SPITEFUL BONES *
THE DEADLIEST SIN *

Other Titles

THOUGH HEAVEN FALL
ROSES IN THE TEMPEST
OSWALD THE THIEF

* *available from Severn House*

THE MISPLACED PHYSICIAN

Jeri Westerson

SEVERN HOUSE

First world edition published in Great Britain and the USA in 2025
by Severn House, an imprint of Canongate Books Ltd,
14 High Street, Edinburgh EH1 1TE.

severnhouse.com

Copyright © Jeri Westerson, 2025

Cover and jacket design by Piers Tilbury

All rights reserved including the right of reproduction in whole or in part in any form. The right of Jeri Westerson to be identified as the author of this work has been asserted in accordance with the Copyright, Designs & Patents Act 1988.

British Library Cataloguing-in-Publication Data
A CIP catalogue record for this title is available from the British Library.

ISBN-13: 978-1-4483-1481-2 (cased)
ISBN-13: 978-1-4483-1681-6 (e-book)

This is a work of fiction. Names, characters, places and incidents are either the product of the author's imagination or are used fictitiously. Except where actual historical events and characters are being described for the storyline of this novel, all situations in this publication are fictitious and any resemblance to actual persons, living or dead, business establishments, events or locales is purely coincidental.

No part of this book may be used or reproduced in any manner for the purpose of training artificial intelligence technologies or systems. This work is reserved from text and data mining (Article 4(3) Directive (EU) 2019/790).

All Severn House titles are printed on acid-free paper.

Typeset by Palimpsest Book Production Ltd.,
Falkirk, Stirlingshire, Scotland.
Printed and bound in Great Britain by
TJ Books, Padstow, Cornwall.

The manufacturer's authorised representative in the EU for product safety is Authorised Rep Compliance Ltd, 71 Lower Baggot Street, Dublin D02 P593 Ireland (arccompliance.com)

Praise for the Irregular Detective Mysteries

"Westerson is a commanding author, who handles plot, setting, character and humour with equal polish . . . A thoroughly engaging read for the casual mystery buff and dedicated Sherlockian alike"
Bonnie MacBird, bestselling author of the Sherlock Holmes Adventures

"Original, unique and inventive . . . pitch perfect!"
James R. Benn, bestselling author of the Billy Boyle World War II Mysteries, on *The Mummy of Mayfair*

"A heartwarming tale"
Booklist on *The Mummy of Mayfair*

"Highly enjoyable"
Kirkus Reviews on *The Mummy of Mayfair*

"Westerson is an imaginative storyteller who brings history, humor, hubris, and humanity to this inventive mystery"
Booklist on *The Isolated Séance*

"An enjoyable Holmes pastiche whose many twists are complemented by pointed social commentary"
Kirkus Reviews on *The Isolated Séance*

About the author

Jeri Westerson was born and raised in Los Angeles. She is the author of the Crispin Guest Medieval Noir Mysteries, the King's Fool Tudor Mysteries featuring Will Somers, three paranormal series and several historical novels. Her books have been nominated for the Shamus, the Macavity and the Agatha awards.

www.jeriwesterson.com

To Craig: Never misplaced. He's much too valuable.

GLOSSARY

Architrave – a moulded frame or beam resting atop the capitals of columns in Greek or Greek revival architecture.
Ballast – the broken rocks and gravel that surround railway sleepers and track.
Barouche – A four-wheeled horse-drawn carriage, where the driver sits in front and passengers sit facing each other in the carriage under a collapsible covering.
Bloaters – smoked fish in the herring family.
Boater – a straw hat typical of the period for men and women, with a flat top and a wide brim.
Bradshaw – *Bradshaw's Monthly Railway Guide* was the ultimate if not weighty compendium of all the railway schedules and prices in Britain and Ireland in the mid- to late 1800s. Its only competition was the ABC or *Alphabetical Railway Guide* with an expanded version of sights of interest in Great Britain used into modern times (there's an Agatha Christie mystery that uses it as a major clue!) before it ceased publication in 2007.
Bricky – brave, fearless.
Castor set – a turntable/silver container for a cut-glass or crystal set of bottles and cruets not just common on the Victorian table but indispensable into the 1940s in the United States as well, consisting of a matching set of cruets with stoppers each of vinegar and oil, a mustard jar with a lid and spoon, salt and pepper, and often powdered sugar.
Copper – slang for a policeman. See Rozzer.
Crawlers – destitute women who are usually too weak to beg on the streets and spend their time in a twilight stupor in doorways.
Custodian helmet – the traditional headgear worn by British police constables (Bobbies) and sergeants on foot patrol, a tall hat with a garter style badge worn on the front of it designating the individual constable's number and city.
Drummer boy hat – a small, round 'pill box' sort of hat with a chin strap that drummer boys, warrant officers, sergeants, and

other ranks wore in the military in this time period. Like a traditional bellboy's hat.

Esse – a particular brand of iron cook stoves still manufactured today.

Fingersmith – pickpocket or to perform the act of pickpocketing.

Friction ridge skin marks – fingerprints.

Gladstone Bag – or merely 'Gladstone'. Named after William Gladstone, an early nineteenth-century British prime minister. By the late nineteenth century doctors were using it to carry their medical equipment.

Hansom cab – a two-wheeled horse-drawn carriage, where the driver sits atop the carriage that is big enough for just two people, with a door that covers the lap.

Hessian – another term for burlap.

Injectors – control on a locomotive that injects water into the boiler.

J-pen – the nib for a dip pen (as opposed to a fountain pen that has the ink in a well inside it) with a sharp point with a flat edge.

Knickerbockers – short, loose/ballooned trousers that fit tightly below the knee with high socks usually stuffed into them for a sporting day in the country, or for golf.

Knifeboard bench – seating on the top of horse-drawn omnibuses, particular to the trolley-type carriages popular in London from 1875 to 1895. So-called for its resemblance to a utensil for sharpening knives. Enough room for about eight riders sitting back to back.

Mounting block – a block or step on the pavement near the kerb so that ladies could easily mount their horses on the street or to assist in their getting into or out of carriages. Also called a horse block or carriage stone.

Nick – noun, for prison, usually expressed as *the* nick. Or verb, to steal, or to arrest.

Norfolk jacket – a hunting/shooting jacket with full sewn-in belt, single-breasted tweed with two box pleats in the front, one in the back. Worn with shorter trousers – see Knickerbockers.

Omnibus – a horse-drawn conveyance for several people. Formerly abbreviated to 'bus as the apostrophe stands in for 'omni'.

Oriel window – a bay window or series of bay windows atop one another that protrudes from a building but does not reach the ground.

Penny dreadfuls or penny fiction – lurid tales of crime, romance or the supernatural, printed cheaply and for a penny each, and then later for a ha'penny each in the early nineteenth century, sometimes later appearing in book form.

Pepperpot or pepperbox revolver – an early revolver from the early to mid-1800s where the barrel revolved to shoot bullets instead of a cylinder chamber. Short and snubbed-nosed, it was good for easy concealment, much like a Derringer, only a bit larger and with more bullets.

Punter – customers, or marks; those who are tricked by con artists.

Regulator – control handle in a locomotive that will make the engine move faster when employed.

Rozzer – slang for police. See Coppers.

Sleepers – the wooden railway ties immediately beneath the tracks that holds them together.

Somers Town – a district in Northwest London bounded by three railway stations: Euston, St Pancras, and King's Cross.

Tender – the rail vehicle immediately behind the steam locomotive/engine that carries the coal.

Tripper – a tourist.

Union suit – men's underwear that included an attached undershirt and long-legged underwear, with a flap in the back and a slit in the front for ease in the loo. Also known as a 'combination'.

Vamp – in this instance, the upper part of a shoe or slipper.

Walking dress or walking suit – plain suits for women often with male collars and ties, consisting of jacket and skirts with straight lines and no train for ease of movement, for women to do their shopping, strolling, or work at a place of business or factory, usually made of sturdy materials. Upper-class women mimicked the same styles, with jackets with open lapels to show off embroidered shirtwaists with the addition of waistcoats.

Wotcher – British slang term for a greeting: 'How are you?' 'Good to meet you.'

Acknowledgments

Grateful thanks to Sue Millard for helping me with horsey questions; to my editor Sara Porter for driving the book on the right track and for being generous with the deadlines when a family emergency made it impossible to write; to my many copyeditors, cultivating all those additional U's and L's; to the cover designer who makes the books pick-upable (the copyeditors will love that word!); and to the rest of the crew at Severn House and Canongate for getting my books into your hands, dear reader.

'You have a grand gift for silence, Watson. It makes you quite invaluable as a companion.'

'The Man with the Twisted Lip' (1891),
Sir Arthur Conan Doyle

ONE
Badger

London, 1895

'Now, look here, lads,' said Tim Badger to the waifs surrounding him in his Soho flat. 'You're all about to become part of an extraordinary venture! The Dean Street Irregulars! It's you, my young fellows, who will go round all of London, listening, watching, finding out what me and my colleague need to know about certain people and things. We're going to fight the criminal world together!'

'What do we get paid?' said a dirty-faced boy by the name of Ned, wearing a tatty oversized coat and a dented bowler. 'You promised us we'd be paid.'

Tim laughed and tapped the boy's shoulder. 'That's good thinking, son. Always get the price upfront. You'll all make a shilling a day when you're on the job.'

They all gasped.

'And a bonus if you're the first to find the man or thing we're after. But listen good. I was in your shoes when I was your age. So don't think you can get the better of me by stretching out the days you're supposed to find the bloke we're looking for. Because I'll know. That's what being a detective is all about. And then you'll get nothing for your trouble. Get me?

'I used to be part of them Baker Street Irregulars that Mister Sherlock Holmes himself hired. Street boys like you lot. You know about Mister Holmes, don't you? He's a detective, but he don't work for no police force. Not a bit of it. He gets hired by ordinary folk to find things the rozzers can't find. And he was made famous by his own bosom friend, a doctor bloke, called Doctor John H. Watson, who writes down all their stories and sells them to *The Strand Magazine*. You can read about him and his adventures every so often. Well, *I* was one of them street lads just like you, from Shadwell, mind, so I know all the tricks. Mister Holmes called us his Baker Street Irregulars on account of that he lives on Baker Street. Now, if you run into any of those Baker Street lads, you leave them be. They're doing important work too, for Mister Holmes, so don't interfere. Because you'll be busy doing the same for me and my Mister Watson of Badger and Watson Detecting Agency.'

'Where is this Mister Watson?' said a ginger-haired boy called Seb.

'He ain't in right now, it being Sunday. He's a black bloke,' Tim said, sweeping his gaze over a black child standing nearly in front of him, 'and he's as smart as they come. That's why I just knew he'd be a great detective, like me.' He grinned. *Of course, his name being 'Watson' like Mister Holmes's Watson didn't hurt either*, he mused. 'He's like a scientist, he is,' Tim said aloud. 'Though he'd had a lot of different jobs before I met him.' He ticked them off on his fingers. 'He was a chimney sweep, a milkman, even worked in a *fun fair*.' The boys were all smiles at that as they looked at one another. 'And,' Tim went on, 'he also worked as a chemist's assistant. That's where he got a lot of his scientific knowledge. See all them scientific things back there.' He pointed, and all the boys turned to look at the table full of retorts, burners, beakers, and even a brass microscope with a cracked lens. 'He's self-taught, he is. Got it from reading books.'

Some of the boys guffawed, but Tim raised his hands to silence them. 'Now, now. Books, me lads. Reading books might be hard at first, but you get to know the words and what it's trying to tell you. As we get to know one another, I might see my way into loaning you some of them books, and you, too, can learn. And some are just for enjoyment. You'll find you like reading. I've got some penny dreadfuls lying about that some of you might like, about ghosts, and vampyres, and dastardly deeds. And the more you read, the better you are at it. Now. Just in keeping with the day and you being new and all, here's some brass for you.'

He took his coin purse from his inside coat pocket and opened the clasp. 'Don't push! You'll get your turn.' Each boy raised a dirty palm to him and he placed tuppence in each one. 'You're all going to have to learn to cooperate with each other. Maybe some of you are already mates, but I guarantee you that you'll all be bosom friends once we get on with it. That's the only way to accomplish anything. Oi! You boys in the back. Listen when I'm talking to you. You think I got this nice flat and these clothes all by m'self? No! I cooperated and got me a business partner, and then Mister Holmes himself stepped in to help us out with money to get started. We pay a portion of the rent here ourselves now, just from the jobs we've done.' The boys oohed and aahed. 'We're getting by,' he said, stuffing his thumbs proudly behind his lapels. He glanced at the carved wooden box on a side table they called the 'Magic Box', because it held coins for them to do their job of paying for hansom cabs, bribes, and other sundries. 'Magic' because they never saw Mister Holmes put the money in there, but there it was, every week. Now, because they worked hard and received more and more paying clients these days, the money in the box dwindled. And that also made him proud. 'And a good paying job might be in the future for any one of *you* if you listen and take care,' he added. 'Save your coins, lads, and you'll make something of yourselves. Now. Remember what I told you. Watch for the signal from Ned Wilkins, here. He's your unofficial boss now. He's the one who will report to us and gather the rest of you for training. Any questions? All right. Off with you, then!'

The boys, all of different ages and sizes, scrambled out of the door, rushing by Mrs Kelly, the landlady, as she tried to press herself against the wall.

'Oh my!' she said in her faint Irish brogue. 'Mister Badger, I didn't know we'd be playing host to a gang of ragamuffins.'

'Not ragamuffins, Mrs Kelly. The new Dean Street Irregulars. Our eyes and ears in London town.'

'My, my. You're certainly coming up in the world, Mister Badger.'

Smiling, Tim smoothed down the breast of his coat. 'Well, it's nothing really. Just a lot of hard work. Nose to the grindstone and all.'

'And where's Mister Watson today?'

'It's Sunday, Mrs Kelly. He's seeing his mum, so the both of us won't be here for dinner, remember?'

She shook her head. 'If I didn't have my head on tight, it would fall right off. Sunday, of course. You'll be joining him as usual.'

'I will. Mrs Watson has been like a mother to me for these last five years of my acquaintance with Ben. It's a lovely thing to have such a solicitous mum.'

She blinked hard, and that was Tim's cue that she was about

to start tearing up at his pitiful past, so he moved swiftly towards the fireplace to grab the mail from the mantel. 'Any other post, Mrs Kelly?'

'That's the lot. From yesterday, of course.'

'Of course. And where's Murphy?'

'It's her day off today, Mister Badger. Will there be anything else?'

'Her day off?' *Oh, so that's why Ben left early today*, he thought to himself. *Finally got up the nerve to call on our little Miss Murphy, did he?* Neither of them knew whether it was the best of ideas to socialize with one's maid, but when he and Watson had spent all their lives little more than servants themselves, it wasn't hard to fathom it. Except that Mister Holmes was still paying the lion's share of their upkeep *and* Miss Murphy's wages. 'I wonder what Mister Holmes would say to that!' he said aloud and then whipped his head around . . . but Mrs Kelly had already vanished.

He flopped into the green wingchair to the left of the fireplace that he had taken ownership of and tore open the letters, still satisfied enough with himself to grin at the idea of his new Dean Street Irregulars. 'And Ben said it wouldn't work. We'll see, my man.' He huffed a sigh and read the little piece of paper. Some woman from Somers Town was enquiring whether they could help her find a lost dog that barked too much. Rolling his eyes, he put that one aside, knowing well what Watson would say: 'Someone probably popped him one to keep his gob shut.' The other was a simple envelope with a penny lilac stamp and no return address. He tore the edge open and shook out the paper. On it was one word made from something cut from a newspaper and pasted on the page. It read, *Don't*.

He pinched open the envelope to look inside, even shook it out into his hand, but there was nothing else there.

'That's queer,' he muttered. 'Now, here's a thing that needs some deducting. Er . . . deducing.' He picked up the letter paper again and lifted it to the light of the window. It had a watermark and some lines, so he decided the paper was of a decent sort. Carrying it by its corner edge, he moved to Watson's chemistry table. He found the dusting powder and sprinkled it as Watson had shown him, shook off the excess, then grabbed a magnifying glass and looked at the friction ridge skin marks. Watson had told him about these marks that were evident on every person's fingers, and that they were permanent to the person and completely individual; no two were ever alike. They never changed, even when one aged. He had read the papers Watson gave him, one by a Sir William James Herschel and one by a Henry Faulds, but Watson's simple explanation had made more sense to him than those pages of dense writing.

He found the marks all over the paper and was quick to eliminate the new ones – his own – from the many more marks that appeared to be the same, meaning they were from one person. 'Amazing,' he whispered. Watson was always introducing him to amazing things. 'You truly are a scientist, Ben,' he muttered. Watson would certainly expect him to investigate further by figuring out from which newspaper or papers the stranger had created the message.

He lowered the magnifying glass. How was he ever to do that? Except . . .

'Hello. I recognize this "Don't".' He grabbed the discarded copy of the *Daily Chronicle* that lay by the fireplace. Licking his finger, he thumbed through the pages until he found it. 'Here it is.' He folded the pages back. It was an advert and the image of a dark lighthouse on a rocky island with the headline in its searching light that said, *Don't Cough. Save Yourself From Wreck. Use The Unrivalled Keating's Lozenges.*

He held the letter next to the advertisement and nodded. 'Same typeface, same advert, right enough. But probably used in many papers. Though I can certainly check that with Miss Littleton.' He was about to tear out the advert when he remembered Watson's words: *Don't be in such a hurry that you become sloppy. Take your time.* 'All right, all right,' he muttered and rose again to find the scissors and cut it out neatly, putting it with the letter in Watson's chemistry area.

'I suppose the next thing is to check with Miss Littleton . . . oh. Did she work on Sundays?' News still had to be gathered, he reckoned. As a journalist for the *Daily Chronicle* and the person who penned their cases as adventure stories for that same paper, they had all become friends. Though . . . Tim had tried hard not to think about becoming more than that to her. It was a foolish notion, after all. She was the daughter of a baronet – not just the upper class, but *nobility*. These days, however, she was as poor as he and Watson were. Her parents had died and had not left her much. She worked for a living as a reporter, but he rather thought that if she had the financial means to be independent, she would have done it anyway. She was that independent herself, one of those Modern Women.

He shook his head at it. Even though he appreciated the notoriety her reporting gave the Badger and Watson Detecting Agency, he believed it truly wasn't the place for a woman to work in a man's world, like a newspaper. On the other hand, what was she to do? He didn't like the idea of her being someone's governess or maid. That would be wrong for someone of her stature. Perhaps a private tutor? But then she would likely have to leave London . . . and he didn't like the thought of that at all. Of her leaving, that is. He . . . he liked seeing her on a regular basis, liked the glow on her face and the sparkle in her eyes when he and Watson recounted their adventures for her to pen. Even though Ben still didn't trust her. He could see she enjoyed the work and did a fine job for the Badger and Watson Detecting Agency, for they had received commissions from those stories. Just like Mister Holmes did from his own notoriety from *his* Watson in *The Strand Magazine*.

If only she weren't a baronet's daughter . . . He sighed.

His thoughts of Miss Littleton were interrupted by a persistent ringing of the doorbell. Who would call on a Sunday? He glanced at the clock. It was almost time for him to leave for Camden for that Sunday dinner with Mrs Watson, and then he wondered if Miss Murphy would also be in attendance. How Watson mooned over that girl! But having to listen to that Irish accent all his life . . . He shivered at the thought. Maybe Watson wouldn't be so jumpy now when she came into the room. He was all a-jitter whenever she made an appearance. Though it *was* rather funny.

Mrs Kelly's footfalls clomped across the tiled entry, and he could even just hear the door opening. Voices. A strident one from a woman, and Mrs Kelly's calm tones trying to assuage the other. Finally, two sets of footfalls clattered up the stairs to his flat and knocked harshly on the door.

'Come in, Mrs Kelly—' He barely got out before the door flung open. A woman pushed past the landlady before she could announce the caller, but there was no need for introductions. The flushed woman, with hair all askew, grabbed Tim by his arms. 'Oh, Tim!'

'Mrs . . . Mrs Hudson?' he said aghast.

TWO
Watson

Ben knew Badger was gathering his new Dean Street Irregulars in the morning, and he wanted to be out of the way for it. Not that he wasn't proud of Tim for the idea, but he wasn't comfortable with children. Not street children. Ben wondered if he would have befriended Badger if he had met him when Tim was still one of those Baker Street Irregulars with ragged clothes, fingersmithing on the streets, though he could still see that cagey boy with hubris in everything Badger attempted. Maybe he *would* have befriended him, though it was probably better that they had met when they did, when they were both young lads out in the world. All in all, the timing of their meeting didn't matter. They were good friends now.

Ben had left their flat early this Sunday morning, determined to follow their maid Katie Murphy to see what she got up to on her day off.

He had dressed, ate quickly when Mrs Kelly brought their breakfast, then threw an excuse to Badger and told him that if he was late, Badger should head over to his mother's without him. A baffled Badger didn't even have time to ask. Ben wanted to leave before he had to answer too many uncomfortable questions.

He waited on the corner, watching their flat behind the blind of a newspaper, when he saw Miss Murphy – pert with a pretty heart-shaped face, hazel eyes, and reddish-brown hair – emerge from the downstairs kitchen steps. Off she went, heading towards the omnibus stop on Oxford Street. *Blimey!* How was he to jump on the 'bus and her not notice?

There was nothing for it. He hated to spend the money – Badger was always telling him how tight he was with it – but this was an emergency! At least . . . that was how he reconciled it. He was going to have to get a cab to follow her.

He found a hansom waiting at the cab stand within view of the omnibus when it pulled up. 'This is an unusual request,' he told the cabby, 'but we're going to follow that 'bus.'

'It's your shilling, guv.'

He shook his head. He was mad. Mad to do this. And what if, in the end, she was going to meet a man? He hadn't reckoned on that. He'd never asked if she had a bloke that called upon her. But then again, why should she share so personal a thing? *I'm a ruddy detective! If I can't deduce from the scant information we have of her, then what am I doing in this detecting business?* But that still sounded hollow to his ears.

'This is mad,' he muttered again, leaning his head against the side of the cabriolet as the driver finally pulled away from the kerb to follow the slow pace of the omnibus horses.

Ben kept his eye glued to the 'bus, making sure at every stop that she didn't get off. But she seemed to stay with it, all the way to Regent's Park. She changed 'buses and got off again at Albert Road and seemed to be heading for the zoo.

He clambered out of the cab, paid the man, and walked on, keeping a good distance behind her. He noticed how different she looked when not dressed as a maid. She wore a simple walking dress in a light brown tweed with a little straw hat with a bird on it. She walked smartly as she did in the flat, with a sure gait and her chin high. She carried a little handbag, clutching it in her fingers, and when she walked up to the ticket booth, she opened it, took out a coin purse, and paid her entry fee.

Through the gate she went, and Ben sidled up to the other patrons in the queue, hoping to keep his eye on her. The people moved quickly forward, and he was able to snatch his ticket just as she disappeared around some hedges.

He scrambled after her and followed along the edge of the gravel walkway, throwing himself into the bushes every time she seemed to be turning to look behind her.

The first exhibit she came to was a collection of spotted deer behind a metal fence. People were feeding them from bags of peanuts they had bought from a vendor pushing a cart. The creatures nibbled in the palms of squealing children and giggling ladies.

The peanuts smelled good to Ben, so he carefully made his way to the vendor and paid his tuppence for a bag.

Murphy seemed entranced by the deer and, pressing her hand to the bars, one came over and mouthed her fingers. She smiled and drew her hand away. And thus she stood for a time, before she wandered further and went into the aquarium building. Ben battled with himself as to whether he should risk going in or waiting outside. There were reflective surfaces in an aquarium. She could spot him if she was observant, and he reckoned she *was* observant, always keeping in mind what her employers wanted of her.

Mindful also of the time – he'd have to meet his mother in the afternoon, so it was a good thing they were already in Camden – he couldn't help but consult his pocket watch, even though it was nowhere near time for him to go.

When he looked up, she had exited the aquarium and was heading towards the camel house. She took her time, strolling to each enclosure and looking up at the netted aviary rising above the zoo's grounds like a cathedral. She stopped to read the plate about the camels, going over each word, until she looked up at the gangly animal slowly striding towards her in hopes of a bite to eat.

It was then that she spun on her heel and, with arms folded over her chest and little cape shawl, she stared at Ben.

He almost dived into the hedges behind him . . . but gave it up as a bad job. He straightened, tucking the bag of peanuts into his coat pocket. He lifted his bowler. 'Good day to you, Miss Murphy. What a coincidence me finding you here.'

She hadn't relaxed her posture. 'It's no coincidence at all, Mister Watson, as you well know.' Her brogue seemed to get thicker the angrier she got, and, embarrassed, he finally conceded the point.

'Yes, well . . .'

'And just why is it you are you following me?'

'I'm not following you,' he blurted.

'You most certainly are. I spotted you getting into that hansom cab and watched it follow us.'

Crikey. Some detective I am. 'Er . . .'

'Just what is it you want, Mister Watson?'

What *did* he want? That would start a whole conversation he hadn't wanted to pursue. Or did he? What the deuce *did* he want?

He suddenly realized he had stood that way, frozen, for some time. Reaching into his pocket, he pulled out the bag of peanuts. He opened it and stretched his arm towards her. 'Peanut?'

He hadn't noticed she was wearing net gloves, but she reached into the sack and withdrew a peanut, cracked it, let the shell fall to the ground, and popped the nut meats into her mouth. She chewed, swallowed, and nodded her head in thanks.

'Please, take the bag.' He suddenly wasn't hungry.

'No, thank you.'

'You could feed the animals with it.'

'As could you.'

'But you seemed to be more interested in—'

'Mister Watson, I feel I must ask you again. Why are you following me?'

He suddenly felt awkward. His belly was too big, his arms were too fat, his hands hung like satchels. She was white, he was black. He could feel a trickle of sweat running down the back of his neck and hastily wiped at it with his outrageously large hand, or so he felt it to be.

'Very well,' he muttered. 'Erm . . . the truth of it is, Miss Murphy, I've been trying to get up the nerve to . . . to talk to you. To ask you . . . if it would be possible to . . . on your day off, that is . . . to share a . . . a meal. Or just some tea.'

'Oh.' Her arms finally relaxed at her sides, her little purse dangling from her wrist. 'I see. And this was your way of securing that situation, was it?'

She was so Irish in her way of speaking. It charmed him like the devil. But at the same time, he feared her. Feared what she would say next.

'Er . . . perhaps it wasn't as above board as some men could be. We are in . . . strange circumstances.'

'You're my employer.'

'Well, strictly speaking, Mister Holmes is still your employer. Mostly. We – Badger and I – didn't hire you.'

This, he discovered, did not seem to impress her as he had hoped it would. She wore a sceptical expression and even began to stare down her nose at him. This was not going according to plan . . . if plan there ever was.

'Look, Miss Murphy, I'll be plain. I think you are an exceptional woman. You work hard. You're industrious. Between you and Mrs Kelly, you lay a fine board. But simply put, if simply put it must be . . . I . . . I rather fancy you. I suppose that's the crux of it. Now there will be no ill will between us, miss, if you tell me truly whether you could consider my calling on you . . . Oh, I know

The Misplaced Physician

I've got faults, but I'm an honest man, gentle by nature, and honourable in my intentions. Erm . . . I suppose me being a black man may give you pause . . .'

She stepped forward then and pressed her hand to his, which stilled him. 'It doesn't give me pause at all. I don't think I've ever met a man as gentle as you are, Mister Watson. But . . . what does give me pause is our situation. For you are definitely my employer – Mister Holmes or no – and I am your maid.'

'I can see how that could . . . could be tricky for you. But I've never been a man to aspire to having servants. I'm as good as one myself, if it comes down to it.'

They stood that way for some time, she touching his hand, he looking down at her, concerned by the furrow between her brows . . . when all of a sudden that furrow fell away and she smiled. 'Shall we see the birds?' she said, taking back her hand.

The late morning soared as Ben walked slowly through the zoo, looking at the animals in the charming company of Miss Katie Murphy, who wouldn't say she would mind his calling on her and wouldn't say she wouldn't. She walked with him, pointing out the antics of the monkeys, the wingspans of some of the larger birds, the giraffes as they stretched their long necks into the trees beside their enclosure. He liked it best when she grabbed his arm when they ventured into the reptile house to squirm in discomfort at the snakes and giant lizards therein.

By noon, it seemed that they had seen all the animals on offer, and Ben finally turned to her. 'I would find it most satisfactory if you cared to take tea with me at a tearoom.'

And to his surprise, she agreed.

They found one not too far away on Hampstead Road. They settled in, and Ben found himself seated opposite her and ordering tea and sandwiches. There were a few gawkers – not the least of which was the girl taking receipts and payment at a tall front desk – and even a few of the servers. But their own server carried on with a smile and was most polite and efficient. Once the order was placed, and Murphy had removed her knitted net gloves and set them on her handbag perched on the edge of the table, she looked up at him in anticipation. And suddenly, Ben was struck by how their conversation, which had been so easy while looking at animals, commenting on this and that, had abruptly dried up.

With hazel eyes sparkling, Murphy smiled. 'Did you solve your case?'

'Oh yes. Yes, we did.'

'Was it who you thought it was?'

'Well . . . yes . . . and no.' And he proceeded to explain the strange case to her that took place after the mummy affair. And in so doing, he felt more at ease. He talked of the rescue of the woman – and her eyes grew wide and worried – and then to the fight in the tavern where they nabbed their culprit at last, and how Miss Littleton had written it all up, and that he seemed to lose the real memory of what happened in the reporter's daring account of it.

The tea and sandwiches had arrived, and he barely remembered pouring tea for her as they ate and talked, and he wondered how it had ever seemed difficult to do so.

They had finished long ago, ordering another pot of tea . . . and he didn't even think about the expense! He was having a jolly time, and she was so pretty to look at. He wondered what she saw when she looked at him, but he would never dare ask.

It was getting late, and he knew he would soon have to leave for his mother's.

'Badger and I always visit my mum for Sunday dinner. I don't suppose you could see yourself there this afternoon?'

She cocked her head and the motion reminded him of the bird on her hat. 'I can't, Mister Watson.'

'Oh, I see.' His heart fell. 'Well, it has been a most pleasant couple of hours and—'

'Mister Watson,' she said sternly, 'you mustn't jump to conclusions. And you must, in all courtesy, allow me to complete my thought!'

'My apologies, Miss Murphy. I mean . . . I know you were just being polite and all, but . . .'

'Mister Watson! Kindly let me speak.'

He closed his mouth with an audible click and sat straight-backed in his chair, hands in his lap.

She shook her head, composing herself. 'I only meant to say that I must be getting back to my work. I had the morning off, but it's back to my duties now. There's cleaning to be done. The rugs, the silver. I can't leave Mrs Kelly to it all.'

His smile came from pure relief. 'Oh. Work. S–so . . . the idea of having dinner with my mum sometime is not abhorrent to you?'

'Abhorrent? Shame on you, Mister Watson. I'd be very pleased to meet your mother. I'd like to hear all the stories about you when you were a mite.' Her smile betrayed her playfulness. And despite the fact that he dreaded that kind of exchange, he decided it would be worth it in the end.

Katie Murphy returned to Dean Street, and Ben moved on into Camden to Drummond Street and showed up just as Badger was rushing up from the other direction. 'Ben, we've got a job.'

'It can wait, can't it? My mum . . .'

'Crikey, Ben. Doctor Watson's been kidnapped!'

'*What?*'

'Mrs Hudson came to the flat in a dither. Doctor Watson's been taken, and Mister Holmes is out of the country again on government business – all very hush-hush – and can't be reached. It's up to us, old son.'

'Blimey. Oh . . . What about my mother?'

'We'll hurry on to tell her personally, and then I'm afraid we must go.'

'You're right, of course. Poor Mrs Hudson.'

They hurried all the way to his mother's door. It was a modest rented house, squeezed in between two taller blocks of flats. The outside could use some scrubbing, Ben noted, but he also noted how *her* steps were kept cleaned, and he knew his mother had been out there with a bucket and a scrubbing brush herself, even though she was merely a tenant.

When they rang the bell, the landlady bustled to the door – a round older woman, who was always pleased to see Ben.

'It's our Ben,' she said and hugged him. Mrs Pearl was less of a landlady and more of a friend to his mother, and he appreciated that the two of them weren't lonely, what with a good friend nearby to have tea with and to do a spot of knitting together to while away the time.

'Arlenis is waiting for you, and if I'm not mistaken, that's a roast duck I smell in the kitchen.'

Badger inhaled and made appreciative sounds. 'Ah, Mrs Pearl, did you have anything to do with that?'

'Well, I might have contributed a potato or two to it.'

'Marry me, Mrs P! How I love a woman who can cook!'

She squealed with delight, batting at him as he tried to embrace her. 'Now, you! You go in to see your mum now,' she said to Ben and, giggling, turned on her heel, leaving Ben feeling terrible that they couldn't stay.

Arlenis Watson had opened the drawing-room door and was waiting for them. 'What's all the ruckus?' she said, in her West Indies patois. 'Timothy Badger, you are getting more handsome every time I see you.'

'Aw, Mrs Watson. You are a one.'

'And Benjamin!' She took him into an embrace and pushed him back to look at him. 'There's something in your eyes today, my boy. You come in now and tell me all about it.'

'It's about a *girl*,' said Badger. Ben threw him a dark look, because, right on cue, his mother shrieked.

'A girl! Come in, sit down.' She hauled him over to her settee and shoved him into it. 'Who is this girl? Do I know her family? Where is she from?'

'Mum,' he muttered.

'She's an Irish *maid*,' said Badger with too much glee.

Arlenis Watson tilted her head, looking at him. 'Irish?' She turned her face to look down her nose at Ben. 'Is she a good girl, Benjamin? Some of those maids are flighty creatures.'

'She's not flighty,' said Ben. 'She's very efficient.'

'How did you meet her?'

'Tell her, Ben.' Badger smiled.

'Quiet, you,' he said out of the side of his mouth. He looked at his mother and resettled himself on the lumpy cushion. 'Well . . . she . . . she works for, er, Mister Holmes. Well . . . she *used* to . . .'

'Oh yes? That is interesting.'

'Tell her, Ben,' Badger said under his breath.

'If you don't shut it . . .'

'Benjamin! You got something to tell me?'

It was the tone. This was not a question. It was a demand. He cast a sharp look at Badger before facing his mother. 'In point of fact . . . she's *our* maid.'

'Benjamin Jameson Watson!'

Badger finally seemed to take pity on Ben and tugged him to his feet. 'Right now, Mrs W, he can't go into details. I'm afraid we have to leave you.'

'But you both just got here. And there's a duck waiting.'

'Mum,' said Ben, walking the weekly envelope of money to his mother's mantel and leaving it there next to the photograph of his father. 'We have to go. It's important. Someone we know is in danger.'

'Oh!' She approached him and took his face in her hands, hands that had worked hard all their life and were showing some wear. 'If it is a friend, you *must* go.'

'We must. Maybe you could come for supper sometime during the week to Dean Street, eh?'

'You just tell me when, Benjamin. But go help your friend first.'

They both kissed her cheek and hurried out of her flat. Ben gave a regretful sigh at the smell of the roast duck lingering on the breeze, before he followed Badger along the pavement to an omnibus back to Dean Street.

THREE
Badger

They arrived quickly to their flat on Dean Street and entered through the door marked with a 'B' in gold paint on the transom window. Mrs Hudson had waited. She jumped to her feet and whirled about with a worried expression etched on her face.

'Well?'

'Now, Mrs H,' said Tim, 'we haven't begun to investigate. I just went to fetch Ben. Please sit down and tell us *both* all you can.'

She scrabbled at the apron she still wore and tore out a note from its pocket, presenting it to them. It was Ben who snatched it first.

I HAVE DR WATSON, it said, spelled out in letters and words cut from the newspaper. *DON'T TRY TO FIND ME. DON'T CALL THE POLICE OR HE IS DONE FOR.*

Watson turned the paper over but that was all there was.

'We got one too,' said Tim. He scurried around the half wall that separated the sitting room from Watson's scientific kit and snatched up the other paper with a pair of tweezers. 'This is the one I opened only a few hours ago.'

Watson took the tweezers and looked over the paper, noting with a nod the dusting of the ridge marks on the page. 'That's good treatment there, Tim.'

'It looked too suspicious to me to merely let it go. That "Don't" is cut out from an advert for lozenges. See it attached to the letter.'

Watson lifted the page to look at the advertisement Tim cut from the newspaper and nodded again. 'Someone assumed Mrs Hudson would come to us.'

'And I'm right glad you did, Mrs H. Now, tell us what happened. First, how did you learn Doctor Watson had been kidnapped? What of his wife?'

'Oh dear, oh dear.' She sobbed into her handkerchief. 'Our dear

Doctor Watson moved back into the Baker Street flat only a few years ago when his wife died, just a bit before Mister Holmes . . .' She gave another sob but recovered herself. 'When Mister Holmes returned after the unfortunate events in Switzerland a year or so ago.'

Tim exchanged a look with Watson. *When Mister Holmes faked his own death, she means*, he wanted to say, but he reckoned Watson understood well enough. He was sorry the old doctor was widowed, but hadn't known he'd moved back in with his friend and colleague. They both must have been lonely.

'So he was in residence with Mister Holmes.' All the times Tim visited Mister Holmes as an adult, he seemed to be on his own. When he was a lad and visited Baker Street as an Irregular, he recognized how close the two were, willing to jump into a case at a moment's notice, to travel to distant places, to work closely together, Holmes doing the detecting and Doctor Watson assisting with medical things and offering suggestions. And, of course, the good doctor wrote up their adventures for *The Strand Magazine*. In a way, he and Ben were a mirror of them, though it was equal parts Badger and Watson doing the detecting. Tim never thought he was better at it than Ben. 'And you say Mister Holmes is out of the country?'

'Yes. I am unable to reach him, even through the Home Office. As you may remember, Badger, very often Mister Holmes has worked for the government in secret.'

Tim remembered. But this time, his mind fell blank. With Badger and Watson's other cases, a murder or a theft had already happened, primed to be investigated. Time was not of the essence as this was. Doctor Watson had been kidnapped. The danger was not over; it existed in every moment. And he *knew* Doctor Watson. This was no stranger or some client that had just arrived at their doorstep. His emotions were getting the better of him and he suddenly had no idea where to begin. He glanced desperately towards Watson who seemed to sense Tim's dilemma, and, in turn, Ben faced Mrs Hudson, leaned towards her, and asked, 'Mrs Hudson, when was the last time you saw the good doctor?'

That's right, Tim thought. He didn't feel alone in this. *Ben's always there right beside me. Good old Ben. Just like Doctor Watson to Sherlock Holmes.*

'It was quarter past nine last night,' she said in her light Scottish accent. 'I had just delivered to him the last post of the day, and he was having a sherry in the chair by the fire and smoking a cigar. I asked him if there was anything further he needed before I retired for the evening, and he was ever so polite like always. I have been used to Mister Holmes's abrupt ways for years, but Doctor Watson was always just as polite as you please.'

Watson ran a knuckle under his bearded chin in thought. 'Did you retire before he did?'

'Yes, I think so. I left him in his chair.'

'Did you hear anything? Any unusual sounds, bumping of furniture, feet stomping, voices arguing, any sort of struggle?'

She shook her head, her handkerchief still held to her nose and mouth. 'I heard not one thing, Mister Watson. I was dead asleep; I was just that weary. It was as if the will-o'-the-wisp spirited him away. I never heard him ring for breakfast or tea, and I began to wonder, so up I went. He took no hat or coat and even left one of the slippers he was wearing behind.'

'One slipper, eh?' said Tim. Then it wasn't any friends that took him away for a lark, and there was, of course, the note. 'Where did you find the note?'

'It was left on the table. I searched the flat once I read it, but I touched nothing and came running straight to you.'

'Very good, Mrs H. Ben and I will take care of things. We'll need to come to Baker Street to make our investigations, and I recommend you pack a bag and stay with a relative or friend.'

'No. Absolutely not! I will be there when Doctor Watson returns.'

'Mrs H . . .'

'Timothy, I will wait for his return.'

Stubborn. But he loved that determined woman. She hadn't liked the presence of the scruffy Irregulars at first, but she got used to all those wild boys, and was kind to Tim when he found himself coming to Mister Holmes after he had been slapped about by his father and had nowhere else to go. The two of them were like a solicitous aunt and uncle to him.

'Come on, Ben,' he said. 'Gather what scientific things you'll need and we'll be off.' Ben had acquired a Gladstone, and Tim grimly observed that there appeared to be *two* Doctor Watsons these days . . . and hoped it remained so.

Watson went downstairs to hail a cab and the three of them climbed in to go to Baker Street. No one spoke, and Watson wore a solemn expression as he gazed out of the cab over the folding door. Watson had never met *Doctor* Watson, and Tim knew that he had wanted to; to consult with a scientific man was Ben's greatest desire. Tim supposed Ben wondered if he would *ever* meet him now.

Tim felt out of sorts himself, thinking that maybe they weren't quite prepared for this sort of thing. But what kind of detectives would they be able to call themselves if they couldn't help out a friend in dire circumstances? They'd have to *make* themselves prepared. He straightened his shoulders, getting himself into the proper state of mind. It didn't matter that they'd never done anything of the kind before. This was just another case and there was Ben Watson by his side. Together, they could accomplish anything!

So consumed with these thoughts was he that he barely noticed when the cab came to a stop in front of 221 Baker Street and he was jolted from his meanderings as Watson said, 'Go on, Tim.'

He got out of the cab, Watson paid the driver, and Tim took Mrs Hudson by the arm and escorted her up the front stairs and through to the entry.

The woman began to weep again as she led the way up the stairs to the flat marked with a 'B' above the door, just like their own flat in Soho. She climbed each stair as if she bore a heavy burden and pulled herself up slowly by her grip on the banister. She unlocked the door and stepped aside to let them through. As they stood in the entry, Mrs Hudson lit the lamps and kept herself against the wall. Long was she used to Mister Holmes telling her to keep out of the way, and so she must do it naturally now.

Tim watched his friend as he surveyed the drawing room, not yet venturing further in. *Think, Tim. The method, man!* And so he did as Mister Holmes did, as Ben Watson was doing now: using Sherlock Holmes's method of deduction by observation, looking at the evidence with logic and intelligence. Ben was looking about the room dispassionately for clues or for anything amiss. And though this room was familiar to him from his years as a Baker Street Irregular – and he knew it rather well from going in and out and his occasional late nights there with Mister Holmes talking to him of some case or other until Tim had fallen asleep, because the man did not know how to comfort a crying child any other way – Tim felt the room settle about him. The messy desk with its ink-stained papers strewn about, even on to the floor where it met a pile of older newspapers. The Persian slipper nailed to the mantel with that foul tobacco inside it. His chemistry equipment set up outside his bedchamber, much like Ben Watson had his scientific equipment ensconced outside *his* room. And somehow, bullet holes in the floral wallpaper forming the letters 'V' and 'R' that he had not noticed previously. *For the queen, Victoria Regina,* he reasoned. Mister Holmes was prone to doing something outlandish to relieve his boredom. *Mrs H must have loved that,* he mused. The chair Holmes preferred. The table and desk that Doctor Watson liked to use to pen his stories. The curtains with their bold pattern, the oak filing drawers, the pictures on the walls.

You know the room, you fool. Look at what's out *of the ordinary.*

There was a slipper lying in the middle of the floor on the rug, upside down, as if it had fallen from the victim's foot. Something that looked like cigar ash strewn in a line after it. A glass lay tipped over on the side table that had contained a dark liquid puddling just at the rim, and another glass beside it drunk down . . . no. No lip marks, no 'legs' from the wine. Not yet filled to half. Interrupted, was he?

Tim moved into the room and stood just over the two glasses. 'Doctor Watson already had *his* sherry and had poured another. He knew his guest. Or thought he was a client. It's only logical to invite a client in so late.' He moved to the writing desk that Doctor Watson used and behind the chair there were scattered papers . . . with a muddy imprint of a hobnailed boot.

'Ruddy hellfire, Ben! Look here.'

His colleague joined him and looked down at it. Watson rubbed his beard over and over in thought. 'Hobnail boot,' he said quietly.

'A rough fella, then.'

Watson nodded. 'What do you make of that ash on the rug?'

Tim launched himself stomach first on to the rug as he'd seen Mister Holmes do many a time when investigating. He pinched some between his thumb and forefinger and brought it close to his nose for a sniff. 'Cigar.'

'What kind of cigar?'

'I rather think that's your part, Ben. You're the bloke with the ash collection. Just like Mister Holmes has.'

Watson rumbled a sound in his throat and stepped forward,

placing his scientific bag on the side table before the settee. 'You said that Doctor Watson partook of cigars, Mrs Hudson. Do you happen to know which brand he favoured?'

'He preferred the Punch brand.' She indicated a box on a side table.

Watson got down on his knees before the ashes next to Tim and took a bit between his fingers and sniffed. 'Not a Punch. But no cheap cigar either.' He rose and glanced across at the hobnail print.

'If it ain't a cheap cigar, what was this ruffian with that boot doing with it?'

'Maybe the cabby?' said Watson.

Tim snorted. This would require a think if the method wasn't reaping them any rewards.

Watson opened his Gladstone and retrieved a glass phial. He took a scrap of paper from the table, knelt again at the ashes, and used the paper to push some of the ash into the phial, corking it.

'So,' said Tim, gesturing towards the two glasses and decanter sitting on a small oriental table. 'Doctor Watson welcomed a guest. A guest who smoked a cigar – not a Punch. And during their discussion, when the good doctor was pouring spirits into the second glass, he was somehow stopped or hesitated for some reason. Possibly during the explanation by his kidnapper why he was there. Or when Mister Hobnail made an appearance. That could also be the moment that his glass got tipped over, leaving a stain on the carpet. Sorry, Mrs H.'

'I'll take a thousand stains if Doctor Watson could be returned unharmed.'

'Indeed. *Then* what happened, Ben?'

'We must assume a weapon was prevailed upon to urge Doctor Watson to leave his flat in a hurry. So hurriedly that he lost his slipper, or perhaps a bit of a tussle that dislodged that ash from the cigar of his assailant *and* the slipper.'

'Right you are. And then they left by carriage,' said Tim. 'Probably not hansom as it was too late to engage one. An enclosed coach would make more sense if one was maintaining discretion. I don't know that there is any way to discover what livery company would have been hired. Or perhaps it was *owned* by the kidnapper.'

'It would be near impossible. But we shall have to look at the street anyway, though it might be too late to find any clues.'

Tim turned to the landlady. 'Has the post arrived yet, Mrs H? We're looking for a ransom note.'

She scurried out of the room with heavy, hurried steps down the stairs before Tim could call her back. It was Sunday and there was no post. She was as addled as they were.

Watson grabbed Tim's arm. 'Courage, Tim. I can see how worried you are. Don't let it distract you from what must be done.'

'I'm trying, Ben. It's just . . . a lot of memories in this room. I remember Doctor Watson sitting there, taking notes. And Mister Holmes pacing the room, making his recitation of the facts. It was like a music hall, sometimes. Mister Holmes making pronouncements using the method with his arms waving about, and the doctor spinning in his chair to face him, telling him how extraordinary it was, and soon me and the other boys were quite forgot.'

'Just put yourself into Mister Holmes's shoes, my lad. Think like he'd think.'

'No one can think like he thinks,' Tim muttered.

Mrs Hudson's hurried steps pounded up the stairs and they turned at her entrance. 'No post today, of course, but I missed this one earlier! It has no return address and looks very like the writing from the last one.' She handed over a plain envelope with its penny lilac stamp in the corner, postmarked London.

'May we assume,' said Watson, 'that this postmark indicates our kidnapper is in London?'

'Not if he's a clever bloke,' said Tim. 'He could have any accomplice post these at various times. Mister Hobnail, perhaps.'

'Yes, it would do little good looking for finger ridge marks on the envelope. And you're right. We cannot assume anything from so bold an action. Let us take a look at the letter.' Watson donned a pair of gentleman's cotton gloves and used a pen knife to carefully cut through the envelope. He handed the envelope to Tim, who took it with his handkerchief. Unfolding the letter, Watson angled it so Tim could read it at the same time.

The words and letters were cut from newspapers again and read:

£500 MUST BE DELIVERED BY NOON TOMORROW.
AWAIT FURTHER INSTRUCTIONS.

'Blimey, Ben. Where are we going to get five hundred pounds?'
'No one's paying anything.'

'But Mister Watson!' cried Mrs Hudson.

'There's going to be no need for a ransom, Mrs Hudson. We will get the culprit or culprits before it becomes necessary. Now.' He reached into his bag for his ridge mark powder and dusted the paper, blowing off the excess. Badger noted the clear prints before Watson carefully folded the paper again and slid it back into the envelope and placed that in the bag.

Next, Watson moved to Doctor Watson's desk. 'Hello, what's this now?' He crouched and looked under the desk and found a leather-clad notebook. He opened it to the pages it had landed on under the desk.

Tim cringed. No one was supposed to touch Doctor Watson's casebook! But before he sprang forward to snatch it out of Ben's hands, he drew himself back. *This is an investigation, Tim, my lad. We need to touch everything.* He girded himself and walked more sedately to where Watson stood, chin raised.

'Find anything?'

'Notes on cases . . .'

'I didn't know the doctor was writing any more of those. We haven't seen any in *The Strand Magazine* for some time. Certainly not during the time Mister Holmes had faked his death. Even Doctor Watson hadn't known his friend was alive. I suppose they've resumed their investigations together.'

'Apparently, he is writing several. Or these could be old stories. Something about a "Dreadful Business" or the other. Can't quite read the writing.' He gestured with the casebook. 'Some of these might already be published by *The Strand Magazine*.'

'And he shall have his chance to write more,' said Tim with a determined flattening of his shoulders. He glanced over the desk and paused. 'Oi, Ben. Look here.'

'Look at what?'

'Don't look at what is there. Look at what isn't.'

Watson measured the desk but still looked puzzled.

Tim gestured towards his brass inkwell. 'No pen. No nibs. They're all missing.'

'What the deuce . . .' Watson pulled open the drawer and could find no extra nibs or other pens, or even any writing paper. 'What does that signify?'

'Don't know. Yet.' Tim stalked down the hallway into Doctor Watson's bedroom, first taking it all in as he'd seen Mister Holmes do, and then looking in drawers and side tables for anything that struck him. When he found nothing of note, he returned to the drawing room, a room mirroring his and Ben's on Dean Street, except that Mrs Kelly and Katie Murphy kept the rooms tidy, and woe betide Tim and Ben if they didn't stay that way.

'Mrs Hudson,' said Tim, 'do you recall any letters that the good doctor might have received of late or any visitors that seemed to upset him? Perhaps right after Mister Holmes left the country?'

'I do not recall anything of the kind. How I wish I did!'

'Very well. Ben? Are you finished here?'

'Just about,' he said, his head in a cupboard. He pulled out an empty folder and carefully collected the scattered papers with the muddy foot imprinted on them.

'Then I'm going round to the front and see if anyone across the street saw anything from quarter past nine onwards.'

'Good idea. I'll meet you out there presently.'

Tim took Mrs Hudson's hands. 'Don't you worry, Mrs H. Ben and me have it well in hand.'

'Tim, you are a good boy. I trust you, lad, just as the governor trusts you.' She reached up and kissed his cheek, bringing a hot flush of embarrassment to his face.

The words caught in his throat, and all he could do was nod at the teary-eyed woman before he left her. Down the stairs he went, clearing his throat, and out of the front door. He surveyed the street with its busy traffic, cart-sellers wheeling down the lane, and men and women walking along the pavement on both sides. He looked up to the building opposite – a tall structure, with six floors above the five shops below it – a tobacconist's, a haberdashery, and a few others he couldn't readily identify – limestone for the ground-floor shops, and brick above all the way up to two sets of oriel windows side by side and three pointed gables on top. 'That's a lot of windows,' he muttered, calculating how many doors he'd have to knock on. 'Well, best get to it, I reckon.'

'Oh, Mister Badger!'

He turned at the feminine voice he recognized. It was that charming Miss Edwina Lewis from the mummy case. He had met her at a party of Miss Littleton's rich friends. Her auburn hair was arranged on her head much like Miss Littleton's in a fluffy halo, with a smart hat with several pheasant feathers springing from it.

'How are you?' she said, striding forward, hand extended. 'Do you remember me from that dreadful party in Knightsbridge?'

He took her gloved hand and kissed it, as she seemed to expect. 'Of course I remember you. How are *you* doing today, Miss Edwina?'

'How sweet. You do recall my name. I am remarkable, Mister Badger! I must say, you seem to have completely charmed our Ellsie. No one talks of anything else.'

'Oh yes? Well . . .'

'Yes, it's quite the talk of our circles. But then again, Ellsie has always been one to go her own way. Gentlemen of the best breeding would line up at her door, and she never seemed to offer them any interest. It was quite a puzzle. But now I see that she simply wanted to try her hand with the lower classes. I'm sure it's all a lark to her.'

Absorbing her words, Tim's whole body seemed to droop. 'I . . . I beg your pardon?'

'Oh yes,' she went on, clutching a small beaded bag between her gloved fingers. 'She could have had her pick, to be sure, but I suppose someone like you . . . well.' She leaned in and whispered, 'When Ellsie tires of the game – as she surely will – I would be more than happy to step into her place.'

An uncomfortable niggling feeling crept up his neck. 'Eh?'

'I must run. Good afternoon, Mister Badger. I hope I shall see you again.' She smiled, allowing that dimple to dent her cheek as she winked and strode away.

'What the ruddy hellfire . . .' He watched her go with some amount of new anxiety. Was Miss Littleton merely toying with him? Slumming? It got his back up . . . until he truly thought on it. No, no, that wasn't possible. Though it was true that she liked to play a game or two, she had always been honest with them. At least, once they had all started working together. This was mere gossip, and by far the worst gossip there was.

He glanced back the way Miss Lewis had gone, and decided that none of it was true. He pulled taut his waistcoat and squared his shoulders. Not after that kiss he and Miss . . . that he and Ellsie had shared. That was sincere enough. In a sort of way. After all, she only kissed him to hide what they were doing in the suspect's library. Though . . . if she *were* playacting, it was a blooming good performance.

He stood on the pavement, blinking. Was it *only* a performance? He'd like to think there was more to it . . . *Hold a minute*. He didn't have time for this sort of nonsense! He had to get back to business. Doctor Watson was still in peril.

It gave him a good excuse not to think too closely about Ellsie Littleton.

Crossing the street, he skirted wagons and boys playing in the gutter and marched smartly up the front steps. He rang the bell which brought a young man in livery. 'Yes, sir?' he enquired.

Tim produced a calling card from his waistcoat pocket. 'Tim Badger from Badger and Watson Detecting Agency, my lad. I'm doing some investigating and need to enquire of the inhabitants with windows facing Baker Street.'

He stared at Tim with mouth agape. 'You . . . you want to do . . . what?'

Tim took advantage of his confusion to push his way in. 'Thanks, son. I'll just be on my way. I'll start with the first floor.'

But the lad had more gumption than he had given him credit for. He chased after Tim before he could reach the stairs. 'Here now, you can't be disturbing the residents of this building.'

'It's all right, lad. I've done this plenty of times.'

The boy pulled on Tim's arm and yanked him back. 'Who do you think you are? Sherlock Holmes?'

He politely but sternly removed the boy's hand from his arm. 'It's funny you should mention Mister Holmes. He was my mentor. I was one of them Baker Street Irregulars when I was . . . well, just about your age, and now I'm doing a job for him. So if you will pardon me . . .'

'Oh.' The lad glanced across the street, perhaps hoping to catch a glimpse of Sherlock Holmes, and then looked back at Tim. 'I . . . I don't know . . .'

'Look, you could be helping out with this important investigation. Were you here minding the door last night, round quarter past nine?'

'Well . . .' The boy wore a sheepish expression. 'I was, but, er, to be perfectly honest, sir, if you won't tell anyone—'

'Mum's the word.'

'Well, I sometimes take a bit of a nap unless I hear the bell or a latchkey.'

'So you didn't see anything outside?'

'No, sir. What is the nature of—'

'It doesn't matter. Now, will you let me get on with it?' Tim turned halfway to the stairs until he considered and slid his arm across the boy's shoulders. 'What's your name, son?'

'Wilbur, sir. Wilbur Thompson.'

'Well, Wilbur, me lad, why don't you come with me? A smart lad like you. You never know, you might grow up and decide to be a detective yourself. Maybe for Scotland Yard.'

'Scotland Yard? Truly, sir?'

'Inspector Wilbur Thompson. That sounds good, don't it?'

But then the lad screwed up his mouth as if in pain. 'No, sir. I cannot leave my post.'

'Well, then, be a good lad and keep an eye out. If you see a black bloke with a bowler outside pacing before the building, that's me partner, Mister Watson. You can tell him I'm inside. I won't be too long. I hope.'

Before the boy could say another word, Tim trotted up the stairs to the first floor and knocked on the first door on his right that faced the street.

A pretty young maid answered. 'Yes, sir?'

He doffed his hat and held it to his chest. 'Good afternoon, miss. I am enquiring of the good people of this building whether they saw anything last night outside the window on Baker Street that might have struck them as peculiar.'

She shook her head. 'Peculiar? I didn't see anything.'

'May I enquire of your employer? Here is my card. I am Mister Badger of Badger and Watson Detecting Agency.' He popped his homburg back on his head.

She read the card, looked up at him, and couldn't help but smile at Tim's boyish grin and good looks, and said, 'One moment, if you please, sir.' She carefully closed the door and Tim waited. Maybe he'd get lucky at the first one. He didn't fancy spending the rest of the day asking the whole ruddy building if they saw anything.

As it turned out, the man and his wife had seen nothing, having retired at nine. Tim thanked them, stood in the corridor with hat tipped back off his forehead, and whistled as he looked at all the doors and up the turning staircase.

FOUR
Watson

Ben peered into the shops along Baker Street. He wanted to ask if they had seen anything late on Saturday, but it being Sunday now, they were all shut up tight.

He stood on the pavement and leaned back, looking up the large brick building directly across from Mister Holmes's flat, and whistled low. 'Blimey.'

'Are you Mister Watson?' came a young voice. Ben straightened and noticed a lad in livery and a drummer boy's cap with its heavy chin strap under his jaw. He stood at the top of the stairs to the residential building above the shops below.

He approached the stairs and began to climb. 'I *am* Mister Watson. Have you talked to a Mister Badger?'

'Yes, sir. He said to tell you he's here investigating, knocking on doors.'

'Blimey. That's a lot of doors.'

'Yes, sir. He went up not more than a few minutes ago. Went to the first floor, might be on the second by now.'

Ben tipped his bowler. 'Then, if you don't mind, I'll be joining him.' He made for the stairs till the boy spoke again.

'You're really detectives?' The boy's smile was genuine. 'Detectives for hire?'

Ben smiled back. 'We really are. Mentored by Mister Sherlock Holmes himself.'

'Cor!' said the little chap.

Ben gave him a friendly nod as he touched the rim of his hat, and climbed the stairs.

Badger could be anywhere. Might even be inside a flat. But he walked down the corridor anyway, peering around the corners. No Badger. He might be on the second floor by now, as the lad said, and with a grunt, he climbed to the floor above and just caught the movement of a potted palm. He leapt up the last steps two at a time and when he looked to his left, he just caught sight of

Badger being welcomed into a flat, and he trotted forward in pursuit before the door closed. He grabbed it, and the footman there said, 'Here now!'

'That's all right,' said Badger. 'That's me colleague, Mister Watson.'

Ben breathed hard, catching his breath, and nodded to the man, taking his bowler from his head.

'We're waiting to see Mister Blanchard,' said Badger. 'The footman said he might have seen something.'

They waited in the entry with its inlaid table in the centre, a crystal vase sitting on it with its spray of tall flowers. With a staircase to the left, it looked as if these flats had at least two storeys each, which cut down on the number of flats to ask. A small mercy, but a good one.

Presently, the footman returned. 'Come this way, gentlemen.'

They followed him to a drawing room where a man in his forties sat in a chair by the fire smoking a pipe and puffing a cloud of smoke around him. 'Oh, *two* of you? So you're detectives, are you?'

'Indeed, sir,' said Badger, his hat in the crook of his arm. 'Detectives for hire. I am Timothy Badger and this is my colleague, Benjamin Watson. Your footman mentioned that you might have seen something out of the window last night on the street concerning the terrace house across the way.'

'I see you leap right into it. Very well. Yes, I did. I was agitated last night and did not prepare for bed until much later, especially after what I saw.'

'And what was that, sir?' asked Ben.

He looked Ben over, slightly suspicious as most white men were. 'Well, I was standing in the window of my room, smoking and gazing out of the window as one might. And below, I noticed a carriage – a barouche coach with its lights extinguished, which was strange for the time of night – standing by the kerb in front of two hundred and twenty-one. Sherlock Holmes lives there, I hear tell. Only saw the man a few times. A rather restless individual. And so I was looking out and saw a man hustling another fellow down the steps. The man did not look pleased to be out of his home at so late an hour. Indeed, he was wearing a smoking jacket and only one shoe.'

'Just one man?' asked Ben. 'The one doing the "hustling".'

'Yes,' said Blanchard. 'Just one man, though later there appeared another chap.'

'Did the coachman at any time leave the carriage?'

'No, he did not.'

'And what did the other man in the smoking jacket look like?' asked Badger.

'Fortunately, the street lamp was nearby and I could see his face, and an awful aspect it was. He looked afraid. He had a moustache much like mine and he wore a smoking cap. His hair was brown.'

'And what of the gentleman "hustling" him out, as you say?' asked Ben.

'I could not see his face. He was facing away from the lamp light, you see. He had on a hat and gloves and an Ulster coat. He was quite covered.'

Badger almost edged Ben out of the way when he asked, 'What of the coach driver?'

'Bundled for the weather. Couldn't tell at all what he looked like. It was a decent carriage, two black horses. No arms or other indications on the sides.'

'And the other man,' said Watson, 'the one who came out last. What did he look like?'

'Taller than the other two. The coach waited for him, because he got into the back. He wore dark clothing, with his coat lapels folded up to his ears. Couldn't see his face as he wore his hat skewed lower. A bowler. Like this.' He mimed pulling a hat low over his face.

Badger asked, 'Could you see if the coachman's boots were muddied?'

'No, I am afraid not. Too far away and too dark. The coach lights weren't lit. Ruddy dangerous, if you ask me.'

Ben nodded. 'That was very thorough, sir. We thank you for your detailed observations.'

The man raised his chin in satisfaction. 'Thank you kindly. Rotten luck. I do hope the fellow is all right.'

'So do we, sir,' said Badger. 'In which direction did the carriage go?'

The man sat up with squinted eyes. 'The road runs the one way. South.'

'Forgive me, sir,' said Ben, 'but after witnessing this, why did you not call on the police?'

'In all truth, I was uncertain at first as to what exactly it was I saw. Could have been a prank by old school chums.'

Badger was at Ben's elbow again. 'But, sir, you yourself said that he looked afraid.'

'Yes, well. You see, the farther away the incident got, the more questions I began to form in my head. *Was* he afraid or just put out?'

'And your conclusion?' asked Ben.

The man ran his hand over his shaven chin. 'I began to feel he was afraid.'

'Thank you, sir,' they said in unison. They took some additional notes on the man's particulars, looked out of the window themselves – and, yes, there was a clear view of 221 down below – and then left him.

Standing in the corridor, Ben looked over his notebook before raising his head to the doors and floors above.

'Do you think there's any point in asking anyone else?' asked Badger. 'Someone in a flat higher than Blanchard's would not be able to see more of the men's faces.'

'Let's leave a note with the doorman for any other residents to contact us if they saw aught. This Mister Blanchard seemed to be quite thorough enough.'

They left their information for the doorman in the drummer hat, but before they left, Ben remained and asked, 'How long has this Blanchard fellow been in the building?'

'Oh, now, let me see. He's a fine, upstanding gentleman. No trouble. Hardly any visitors. Been here as long as me, and that's four years.'

'Brown hair with a moustache?'

'Yes, sir,' he replied, puzzled.

'Thanks.' He touched the rim of his hat again and motioned for Badger to follow him outside.

Badger was at his heels. 'Why'd you ask that?'

'Because I wanted to make certain that *he* wasn't the kidnapper planted here to throw us off the trail.'

'Ooh, you *are* suspicious, aren't you?'

'It don't pay not to be.'

'But where does this all leave us now, Ben? We don't know the carriage. We don't know the men involved. And I haven't the least idea how we find out.'

'Well, Tim, as I reckon it, we have to take a different tack. If we can't reckon *who* right now, maybe we'll have better luck figuring out *why*.'

'Yes. I see what you mean. Oi, Ben. The drawing room at Baker Street.'

'What of it?'

'Maybe the good doctor was leaving us some clues. Let's go back to Dean Street,' said Badger, 'and look at what we've got.'

Ben didn't even argue against Badger's insistence on a cab, and they quickly arrived at 49 Dean Street and hurried up to their flat.

Ben set the Gladstone with the scientific instruments on his table and opened it, pulling each item out carefully: the cigar ash in the phial, the casebook notes, the slipper, the folder with the footprint on the papers. They both stood over them, simply looking, perhaps even hoping that some secret bit of information would leap out at them.

Badger picked up the slipper and studied it, running his fingers over the surface of both the top and the bottom sole. It seemed like any ordinary man's indoor slipper, with an extended vamp, quilted lining, leather sole, and a subdued heel. He handed it to Ben who turned it over and checked the bottom of the sole. Yes, it had the appropriate wear, meaning that it was likely Doctor Watson's. The label sewed to the inside bottom of the shoe said *Scriven & Sons*.

'I reckon this merely fell off him,' said Badger.

'Right,' said Ben, handing it back to his colleague as he picked up the phial. 'I'm going to examine this ash to determine what brand it is.'

'Good. I'll look at Doctor Watson's casebook here.'

'Leave nothing to chance,' said Ben over his shoulder. 'I marked what pages it fell on.'

'Good thinking, Ben.'

Ben was busy with his chemicals, looking at his notes, and finally pulled down his collection of ash from fifty brands of cigars and concluded that it was a Partagas. He made a note in his book.

Badger spread the papers on the table to examine the footprint stamped on them.

A knock on the door brought in the petite figure of Katie Murphy. Ben immediately forgot all and set down his notebook to give her his full attention. He felt his shoulders tighten, wondering how she would treat him and how he was to treat her now that they were more familiar with one another.

She faced him in her usual businesslike manner. 'Mister Watson, Mister Badger. Mrs Kelly wishes to know if the two of you will be needing a light supper, after all, since your plans have changed? And I would just like to say, if it's in keeping with my situation, that I am sorry to hear about Doctor Watson. And Mrs Kelly and I would be pleased to help in any way we can.'

Ben felt a flush of relief loosen his shoulders. 'That is very much appreciated, Miss Murphy. I am sad to say that I have not yet met the good doctor, but certainly will make his acquaintance in due course.'

Badger gave her a brief smile. 'That's a grand thing, Murphy. I knew the man well. Truth to tell, I don't know if he knew me name, but with Ben and me on the case, we'll soon put it to rights. I do admit to being a bit peckish. If it ain't too much trouble, some sandwiches would do us good.'

She glanced back at Ben and he nodded his agreement.

'Beer or tea, gentlemen?'

'Let's keep a clear head,' said Badger. 'Tea it is, Murphy, and thank you.'

Ben jerked his head towards Badger. *Turning down beer? He must be out of sorts.* Of course, this was possibly the biggest and most important case of their brief careers. A clear head was necessary.

The maid soon departed, and Ben could not help watching her leave with her sure gait and erect shoulders.

Badger was at his side. 'Find out anything?'

'Yes. We are looking for a bloke who smokes a Partagas cigar. Likely he is a gentleman since they are fairly expensive. So not some ruffian from our late parts of town.'

'Right. Not the hobnail bloke. I can't imagine a man from the East End cutting out letters from the newspaper to write a note either. He'd dash it off on whatever paper was handy. That's good work you've done.'

'What about you? Any clues from the doctor's casebook?'

Badger fixed his hands in his trouser pockets. 'I tell you, Ben. They were all notes on old cases – some I don't recall at all. It could be that he made certain to set the case book down on that particular spread of pages to help us or the police. Or . . . it could just as easily have been random, if he dropped it when he was startled. Like them pages that got trod on.'

'We cannot leave the possibility that he *might* have been able to leave us a clue intentionally. What were the papers about that got stepped on by our hobnailed bloke?'

'Not much. A calendar page, an accounting sheet like a bill, other memoranda. But I did make note of what they were in case they might be relevant. I propose I go on to *The Strand Magazine* to look in their archives for the old stories mentioned on those casebook pages. And, er, to get the help of Miss Littleton.'

Ben narrowed his eyes. 'What do you need her for?'

'Well, I'm not used to such things, going into archives and all. She might be very helpful.'

The longer Ben stared at him, the more fidgety Badger became. 'Are you sure that's why?'

He straightened. 'Cor, Ben. I take this very seriously.'

'All right. You go on, then. I'll go on to see if I can discover the carriage that was used. It might well be one for hire. Even gentlemen of means may not be able to have carriages of their own.'

'Good. As soon as Murphy returns with the sandwiches, I'll be off.'

While Badger made more notes in his book, Ben got down the pamphlet of carriages for hire from the bookshelf and made his own notes. Presently, Murphy returned and set a plate of sandwiches on the table, along with the tea – careful to avoid the pages with the footprint on them – and left them to it.

Ben hadn't realized how hungry he was. He slathered his bread with the delicious mustard Mrs Kelly provided in the castor set, and dug in. Badger took two big bites, swallowed it down with the tea, then added mustard to another sandwich and popped it into his coat pocket.

'Gotta rush, Ben. I'll be back . . . well, don't know when.'

Ben lifted the pamphlet and slapped it into his other palm. 'There are a fair few liveries in the city. Let us hope I don't have to go through all of them. I'd best start writing some letters.'

'You know what would save more time?' Badger slurped one more bit of his tea as he stood at the table. 'Why don't you gather the Dean Street Irregulars? Maybe they could find out.'

Ben was struck silent by his friend's ingenuity. 'Blimey, Tim. That was a ruddy good idea of yours, after all.'

'I knew I'd be vindicated!' He saluted with his tea cup. 'Look, just call for Ned Wilkins. He's usually on the corner of Charing Cross and Northumberland Avenue. He's got dark hair that's never seen a comb and a dented bowler.'

'Where did you ever find him?'

'Same way Mister Holmes found us Baker Street Irregulars. Looked for us trying to fingersmith him.'

'He didn't! This Ned didn't pick your pocket?'

'He tried, and I was bloomin' impressed. *Almost* didn't feel a thing. We became fast friends . . . after I gave him a pointer or two.'

'Tim!'

'It's all right. He's making his way to the straight and narrow. But these things take time. I'm off. They get a shilling a day. Don't take no guff from them. Good luck!'

Ben watched him slap his homburg on his head and rush out of the door with the same admiration as the day he met him five years before, when Tim proposed this ridiculous scheme of the two of them becoming detectives when Badger was barely nineteen and Ben was on the cusp of twenty-one. Badger had been running from some coppers and fell through the roof of the blacksmith's stable where Ben had been working. He didn't know why he had done it, but Ben had hidden Badger from the police when they came round. And just as they were about to beat the information out of him as to where Tim was, they left. And then the brass of Badger to show off the shoes he had stolen that got the rozzers after him to begin with. And then proposing that they become detectives . . . Even after five years of plying their new trade – or trying to – Ben scarcely believed that Badger really had known Mister Holmes . . . until Ben met Holmes himself when the man stepped in to give them a helping hand with a new flat and new clothes: the means to get proper clients instead of relying on their tatty flat in the East End. It was all so absurd, really. Ben Watson from Camden being a detective for hire! It didn't take him long to realize that it was his surname – Watson – that had inspired Badger to ask him to be his colleague. But it didn't matter. He thanked his lucky stars that Badger had fallen through his roof. This job of his made his mother proud.

Proud that he was capturing criminals, that he was putting his mind to work instead of getting his hands dirty with the more menial jobs he'd had before.

'And blimey,' he whispered, 'Tim was right.'

FIVE
Badger

Tim took a cab to Miss Ellsie Moira Littleton's Mayfair townhouse and told the driver to wait. He trotted up the steps and rang the bell, humming a music hall tune to himself as he waited in anticipation of seeing her. It had been a while since they had been together. Perhaps it was a fortnight or more ago that he and Ben had both sat in her parlour relating the details of their latest case for inclusion in another of her stories for the *Daily Chronicle*, and making it more exciting at her urging. 'Now, gentlemen,' she'd say, 'surely there can be more of a chase here and there, and maybe a wound or two?' Watson didn't approve, of course, but that was because he was a strait-laced bloke and brooked no nonsense. But Miss Littleton knew how to make a story sing so that it was as exciting as a Sherlock Holmes tale. And then he sobered, because it was *Doctor* Watson who made those tales as exciting as they were through his own writing of the Holmes and Watson adventures for *The Strand Magazine*.

The responsibility for finding the good doctor suddenly bore down on Tim again.

But before he could fall into a morose state, the front door opened.

'Who are *you*?' asked Tim, looking the strange footman up and down.

'I am Rogers, the footman here. May I help you, sir?'

Tim touched the rim of his hat. 'I had no idea Miss Littleton had engaged a footman. Please let her know I'm here. Er . . . Mister Timothy Badger, that is.'

'Forgive me, sir, but are you certain you are at the correct house?'

'What d'you mean?'

'There is no Miss Littleton at this address.'

'Ah, now. You're having me on. Of course this is Miss Littleton's address. Late of Sir Reginald Arthur Littleton, Baronet of March?'

He reached out and tapped the footman in the chest with his knuckles. 'I know Miss Littleton likes a jest as well as the next man, er . . . woman, but I'm in a bit of a hurry.'

The footman looked down at his chest where Tim had tapped him and slowly looked up again. 'I do apologize if I led you to believe otherwise, sir, but I must say again that this is not the residence of any Miss Littleton. Sir John Brawly lives here and has done since one week ago. He purchased the house a fortnight before.'

'What!'

Tim stepped back off the entry and looked up at the house and its address number. It was the same as he recalled. But what was this business about her *selling* the house? Without telling them!

'I . . . I don't know what to say. Do you know where she might have moved to?'

'I regret to say that I do not.'

Tim's heart clutched tight in his chest. He knew her finances were in a bit of difficulty since her parents died, and that she had sold some of her furniture and things to maintain a certain propriety, and got herself the job as a reporter, of course, but he had no idea it had got to the point that she had to sell up.

He tossed his thanks to the footman before he flew down the steps and back into the hansom. 'Driver, take me to the *Daily Chronicle* just as fast as you can.' *Did* she work on Sundays? He hoped she did.

The driver was as good as his 'Right-O, guv'nor,' and in no time, he pulled up in front of the *Daily Chronicle* building on Fleet Street. Tim paid the cabby and ran inside. He didn't stop at the long front desk and, instead, wended his way quickly through the countless desks busy with men writing their stories, some with coats on, some off, some with their hats, some without, bent over their desks with pen and paper and the occasional typewriter, with a perpetual haze from cigar, pipe, and cigarette smoke that they seemed to create in constant furious puffs.

Her desk was in the back of the room near a stairwell corridor and heating pipes. And there she was, elegant profile concentrated on her page. Her hair always seemed to be the worse for working on her journalistic endeavours, with loose strands falling into her face and pencils stuck into the pouf of auburn hair crowning her head. Her bottom lip was twisted between her teeth as she tried to compose her prose and etched her lines on to the paper, paused, etched again, until what she read seemed to satisfy.

'Miss Littleton!'

She startled back, eyes wide, but as soon as she recognized Tim, she composed her face and smiled. 'Mister Badger.'

'What do you think you're playing at?'

'I beg your pardon?'

Frustrated, he grabbed her arm and yanked her from her chair. 'Where can we go to talk?'

'You must unhand me first, Mister Badger.' His fingers released and she adjusted that lacy sleeve. 'This way.' She led him to the corridor and past the stairwell to some doors. She tried the first door and peered in, then gestured for him to follow. It appeared to be some sort of private office with desk, chairs, and bookcases up to the ceiling. The window faced another brick wall outside.

She turned up the gas. 'My editor sometimes uses this office, but often he is out. It is a private place for an interview when a neutral location is indicated. Now.' She sat in one of the upholstered chairs and offered one opposite to Tim. She was in her working woman attire: a lacy white shirt bloused over her cummerbund with a no-nonsense tweed skirt. Her appearance was charming, as usual.

He sat and leaned forward. 'What the ruddy hellfire is going on?'

'I am afraid I do not know what you mean, sir.'

'What I mean is, I turn up to your Mayfair house and someone else is living there!'

'Oh.' She sat back and toyed with a long necklace that terminated with a small lady's watch. 'Pray, what business is it of yours?'

'What business?' He jumped to his feet and paced. 'It's very much my business. This is Tim Badger you're talking to.'

'And I repeat. What business is it of yours?'

'It's plenty of my business. We . . . we work together, don't we? And . . . it's only polite to let your business associates know when you've changed addresses.' He paused his pacing and looked down at her, just as she turned her blushing face away from him. He knelt at her chair instead of standing over her. 'And . . . we . . . you and me . . . we have a sort of . . . personal understanding. Don't we?'

She twirled and twirled the watch on its chain. 'I have not the least idea what you are talking about.'

'Yes, you do,' he said softly. 'We . . . kissed, not too long ago. Two cases ago.'

'As I explained at the time, Mister Badger, it was only an expedient gesture to fool our prey into why he found us where he found us. Er . . .'

'It wasn't *just* that . . . Ellsie.'

She stood and moved around the desk to grasp the back of the chair. 'I explained that to you . . .'

'And I don't believe you for one minute. But all that aside, why didn't you tell Ben and me that you had to sell your family home?'

'I do not know how much more I can explain that it was no one's business but my own.'

'Ellsie. I know you've been hard up, but we didn't know it was that bad. We . . . we could have helped.'

'I do not see how.' Her eyes roved everywhere but at him. *For God's sake, woman, look at me!*

'Ellsie . . . Miss Littleton. Surely you know by now that we care about your welfare. We're partners, just like Ben and me are partners. You write up our cases and it helps us all. Why wouldn't we care to discover that you were having such troubles that you would move from Mayfair?'

'Ah. My apologies, Mister Badger. I did not look at it that way.'

'Well . . . do so! Where . . . where are you now?' He cringed to think of it, that she might have been forced by circumstances to move to his and Ben's old neighbourhood. Or some women's boarding house! Just how hard up was she?

'If you must know, I'm near Soho Square. Thirteen Greek Street.' She sat wearily again in the leather chair behind the desk with a whoosh of breath. 'My father's debts proved too much, and I found that one person just did not need to live in such a big house. My solicitor found a buyer for a quick sale, I paid my father's debts, and I had enough left over to purchase the modest terrace house on Greek Street. So . . . I suppose, in a way, we are neighbours now.' She offered a shy smile, and his heart unclenched.

'You should have told us.'

'I . . . well, I realize that now. I suppose I was too proud to say anything.'

'Not to us. You know Ben and me have had, well, *humble* beginnings, I reckon you'd say. We understand.'

'Yes, I suppose you do.'

'Blimey.' He thought of her modest household and what it meant when an employer was in reduced circumstances. 'And what about Cynthia?'

'What *about* Cynthia?' She raised a brow and brought up that haughty chin to glare at him under lowered lids.

Ha. She's jealous. He cheered considerably. 'I mean your maid, Cynthia. Is she still in your employ?'

'Of course she is. What would I do without her?'

'A reporter with a maid,' he guffawed.

'And you are a detective with a maid. I don't see the difference. I did have to get a more inexpensive housekeeper and cook, and I made sure that my former employees were well seen to. Does that put your mind at ease, Mister Badger?'

'It does indeed. Faithful servants are worth more than gold. I'm sure you understand that.'

'Yes, I do. Now' – she looked at the watch hanging from its chain – 'was there anything else? I must get back to work.'

He put his palms on the desk and slanted towards her. 'No. We need your help.' He looked over his shoulder in case anyone might have crept through the door. 'Doctor Watson has been kidnapped,' he whispered.

'Great heavens!'

'Mister Holmes's landlady came to tell us. The doctor has been kidnapped and Mister Holmes is out of the country. It's up to us to find him and we need your help.'

She stood abruptly. 'Anything I can do, Mister Badger, I shall!'

All but the salute, he thought. *That's my bricky girl!* 'Right now, I need you to go with me to *The Strand Magazine* offices to look through their archives for old stories written about Mister Holmes's cases.'

She scrambled around the desk, eyes alight. 'Then what are we waiting for!'

Out of the door she went, and he hurried to follow her back to her desk. She shed the pencils from her hair, pushed her arms through the sleeves of her short jacket that barely fell to her waist, donned her boater and thrust a long hat pin through it. She grabbed her handbag and led the way, weaving through the desks and tables of busy male reporters.

Once they got outside, Tim hailed a cab and they got in.

'Where to, guv'nor?'

'*The Strand Magazine* offices.'

The cab surged forward at a good clip, the driver skilfully weaving in and through the traffic. Tim slyly glanced at his companion out of the corner of his eye. The game was afoot, and her face was alight with it. She was a stunner, with her petite nose, her blushed cheeks, the soft creaminess of her skin . . .

Pull yourself together, man. Think of Doctor Watson! he admonished himself. There was no time to fritter away his mind on non-essentials. And mooning over Ellsie Littleton was decidedly non-essential to their present problem. Mister Holmes would have said the same.

As they rode through town, she suddenly turned to him. 'Tell me everything you know.'

Tim balked. Ordinarily, they saved all the details until the case was solved so that she wouldn't interfere and get in the way of their investigating. But this was a different circumstance. Tim felt they needed all the help they could get. Her expectant face shimmered in the fluctuating shadow and light from the passing traffic and buildings.

What would Ben say? ran through his head. Miss Littleton was *not* Watson's favourite person. He considered her a nosy parker and interfering. But these were desperate times. 'All right. But no interfering and no writing a word until the investigation is done.' She nodded her agreement. 'Well, then. Last night, Doctor Watson was abducted from his drawing room at Baker Street. The man who took him smoked a Partagas cigar – which ain't a cheap brand, so he must be a gentleman of some kind, especially since he hired a barouche coach, no markings or arms on it. There was a muddy footprint left on some scattered papers on the floor from a hobnail boot, so likely not from the man with the Partagas. The good doctor lost a slipper in his encounter with his kidnapper and dropped his casebook under his desk. Ben and me weren't certain if he dropped it intentional-like or if it fell to a random page, but for the moment, we are taking the liberty of believing it *might* have been intentional. The pages referred to old cases through a list of story titles – and one might yield the clue we need, so we need to see those cases in full, and *The Strand Magazine*'s archive could be just what we need.'

'My, Mister Badger. That was all very thorough. But why my help?'

'Because . . . well. Blimey, I've never gone through archives before. And I know you have.'

'I'm quite flattered. And also intrigued. I know how important this is to you. We must keep a treasure like Doctor Watson from harm, but I must insist on working with you thoroughly and completely throughout this venture. I shall not be shuttled to the side this time. Is that understood?'

'Oh. I don't know how Ben will take that—'

'Take it or leave it, Mister Badger.'

'Miss Littleton!'

'I will not be waiting genially in the shadows. I must be there for the story as it happens. I insist.'

He frowned and sat back, arms folded tightly over his chest. 'That's devious, that.'

'Nevertheless.'

'Very well. You win. But I don't take kindly to your insistence in this particular case. You're using our own desperation against us.'

'It is only to write a better story, Mister Badger.'

'It had better not be at the expense of the good doctor,' he gritted out, and then he turned away from her to stare out of the window. Why did she have to be so stubborn all the time?

He brooded . . . until he felt her gentle touch on his arm. 'Forgive me, Mister Badger. You are certainly right. I took advantage of you. I apologize. I am used to doing so in order to get my way these days. You have no idea how difficult it is for a woman like me to be taken seriously. All the cards are stacked against her.'

Maybe for very good reason, he mused. But then he thought about it and slowly relented. 'I understand, Miss Littleton. I do. But let's focus on the mission here, shall we? It's to save the doctor's life.'

'I am quite chastened. And I will do my best. I promise.'

They rode on in silence. She faced the window, but he had the feeling she wasn't seeing anything. Finally, they arrived at Burleigh Street off the Strand and the cabby stopped before the magazine's offices. Tim paid and helped her out of the cab. 'Now, Miss Littleton. What shall we do?'

'We will go to their front desk and ask to see the archive. And a good thing it is that you are here, Mister Badger, or they might have discounted me entirely.'

'But surely with your credentials as a journalist . . .'

'That avails me nothing at times, Mister Badger. It is, after all, a man's world.'

'Cor,' he muttered. He was of a mind that women *didn't* belong in a lot of places, but if they had the job and proper credentials, there was no need to be bad-mannered about it.

He hoped they, too, would be opened on a Sunday, and as he walked through the door, he felt himself grow larger with authority and . . . a bit protective of Miss Littleton, ready to pounce on anyone who naysaid her. He was relieved to see lights on and a clerk working at a desk within the front door. 'My man,' he said, nose held a little higher than usual when he approached the clerk, 'we are looking for the archives of *The Strand Magazine* as concerns stories about Mister Sherlock Holmes.'

The clerk, a man of middle years with a balding head and a black pair of pince-nez perched on the bridge of his nose, looked Tim over. 'It's Sunday.'

Tim looked around at the empty desks and dark offices. 'What does that matter?'

'There are very few staff here today.'

'It is a matter of some importance.'

The man sighed. 'And you are . . .?'

Tim produced a calling card like a magic trick and presented it under the man's nose. 'I am Timothy Badger of Badger and Watson Detecting Agency. It's very important that we see them.'

The clerk glanced at Miss Littleton. 'She's not Watson, is she?'

'No, I am not,' she said, pushing Tim aside and presenting her own card. 'I am Ellsie Moira Littleton, reporter for the *Daily Chronicle*. I assist Badger and Watson whenever I can. In fact, I'm the person who writes their stories for the *Daily Chronicle*.'

His face shone with recognition, and at that, Tim warmed.

'Well, Miss Littleton,' said the clerk, coming round the desk with eyes only for her, 'I see no reason why you cannot see the archives. Come this way, please.'

He led them to a set of metal stairs, and down they went to a lower level – where he unlocked a door – and reached what looked to be a basement. The clerk paused to turn a switch that illuminated

the whole space with electric light. Shelves ran the gambit across and in rows, full of labelled boxes.
'The archivist isn't in today, but I can help. What month and year are you looking for?'
'Oh, erm . . . well, you see,' said Tim, 'I don't exactly know. Don't you have the Doctor John H. Watson penned stories organized by . . . by themselves?'
'Is there a journal or card files cross-referencing author to month and year?' asked Miss Littleton.
Tim stared at the woman with awe. *Blimey, I never would have known to ask for that. I ain't even certain what it is she said.*
'Yes,' said the clerk. 'Right over here.' He directed them to a large cabinet with at least fifty square drawers with brass frames and handles. On the labels inside the frames were letters in alphabetical order.
'Thank you very much,' said Miss Littleton dismissively. 'We can secure what we need from here.'
The clerk measured her, then Tim, then her again before he seemed to decide it wasn't worth the trouble and left them to it.
'What do we do with this?' asked Tim, gesturing towards the little files.
'Allow me to show you. If you ever use any other archives, they are usually prepared as this is. And there is usually an archivist to assist. But we shall take care of it ourselves, shall we? Let us first look for Doctor Watson's name.' She ran her finger down the rows of drawers and found the W's. Tim wasn't sure what to expect, but he didn't reckon on tightly packed cards once she pulled out the long drawer.
'W-A, W-A . . .' she muttered, pushing at the cards to flip through them. 'W-A-T . . . Ah! Here it is. Do you see the card? "Watson, John H., Doctor", last name first. And do you see these entries? These are all the stories listed that he wrote and published in *The Strand Magazine*.'
'Well, I'll be jiggered. Who'd have thought?'
'Yes, it is rather convenient. Now, see this here? If we choose the names of the stories, these numbers indicate in which issue they might be found on these many shelves. Which titles are you looking for?'
Tim retrieved his notebook from his inside coat pocket. He licked his thumb and turned the pages. 'All right, then. *The Case*

of Mrs Etherege's Husband, *The Case of the Darlington Substitution Scandal*, *The Dreadful Business of the Abernetty Family*, *The Arnsworth Castle Business*, and *The Case of Old Abrahams*.'

'Very well. Write these numbers down.'

Tim licked the end of his lead pencil and wrote the numbers next to the titles as instructed, reading them back to her to make sure he got it right.

'What's next?' This new form of information excited him, gave him hope that something could be done, and he vowed to use it again in different ways if it turned out to be helpful.

'We go to these other shelves with all the boxes and find those issues of the magazine.'

'What a wonder!' cried Tim, following her to the shelves marked on the ends with a set of numbers. 'The modern world, eh?'

She smiled at Tim, appearing excited by his excitement. 'Yes, it *is* marvellous, isn't it? I do so enjoy researching things.'

'You've got the mind for it, if you don't mind my saying. I mean, your other stories in the paper are deep with information. Not like some of them other reporters.'

She seemed taken aback and gazed at him, eyes glittering. 'Why . . . Mister Badger. How kind and how astute of you to say. I thought you never read the *Daily Chronicle*.'

'Oh, well, I–I like to keep abreast of the news. Might be a case in it. And . . . also, whenever I see your name, I naturally want to read it.' He gave a mischievous smile back.

'You are full of surprises, Mister Badger.'

They found the correct shelf for the first one and walked down the aisle, counting down to the correct series of numbers. 'There it is!' Tim cried, just a bit surprised that it actually worked. He took down the box and opened it. He rummaged through the many copies of the magazine until he found the one with the cover exclaiming, *New Sherlock Holmes Story! The Case of Old Abrahams.*

'We are quite lucky they had not yet the time to bind them together in a book. It is usually the case that a magazine binds all the issues of one year into a hardcovered book for archiving. They must not have got to these yet. Let us take that one out and set it on that table, then we can collect them all and see what there is to see.'

Tim removed it, put the closed box back on the shelf, and left the magazine on the library table in the middle of the room.

They repeated the process until all five titles were collected. He thumbed through the first one. 'It's going to take a while for us to go through all of these and take notes,' he said. He pulled his watch from his waistcoat pocket. 'Won't you have to get back to your paper? It's almost half past six.'

She gathered the magazines. 'We won't worry about it. It is a Sunday. It was luck that you found me there at all today, as I was doing some rewriting on my latest story.' She was suddenly standing in front of him, and before he could say or think anything, she grabbed his waistcoat, pulled it opened and stuffed the magazines down through it.

'Here now! What do you think you're doing? We can't take these.'

'Of course we can.' And she closed his coat and began buttoning it.

'But Miss Littleton! That's stealing.'

'It is *borrowing*, Mister Badger. We will return them when we are done.'

'But . . . but . . .'

'Hush, now. I hear the clerk returning.'

He turned in time to see the same clerk coming down the steps, clomping on each metal tread. 'Everything all right? Did you find what you were looking for?'

Tim tried to keep his eyes steady and his face stiff. *Do NOT touch your coat*, he admonished himself. He just *knew* the clerk could see the magazine-shaped rectangle under his clothing. 'Everything's tip-top, my man. We found what we needed. Er . . . thanks. Come along now, Miss Littleton.' He took her elbow and rushed her to the stairs, forcing the clerk to press himself back against the hand rail. They hurried up, and Tim felt the rush of blood pounding through his heart like the old days when he'd fingersmithed the pocket of some rich punter and was able to slip away without notice.

He held her elbow all the way out of the door and down the street, where he was finally able to relax and step off the kerb, looking for a cab to hail.

'That was fun, wasn't it?' she said close to his ear.

But he whirled on her and pointed a finger into her face. 'Don't do that again. The reputation of Badger and Watson Detecting Agency is on the line.'

'Don't vex yourself, Mister Badger. You will return them, as I said. It's just a little bit of larceny for an important cause. Now, if you will hail a cab and see me back to the *Daily Chronicle*, I will be much obliged.'

Tim waved his arm and whistled, and a cab pulled out of traffic and stopped for him. 'Where to, guv? Miss?' He raised his topper.

But Tim was thinking. 'Miss Littleton, since you don't have to return to the *Daily Chronicle*, why don't you come back to Dean Street with me instead and help Ben and me? I know you could be of great help, and you'll get your chance at last to work with us on an important endeavour as it happens.'

Her face seemed to glow; she was that pleased. After begging and cajoling to be part of their investigations for some months now, here it was being laid out on a platter. Even though she had already insisted earlier.

'I would be most happy to accommodate you, Mister Badger.'

He couldn't help the flutter in his heart, like a persistent moth whirling round a lamp.

'Forty-nine Dean Street, cabby!' he said cheerfully.

SIX
Watson

Ben made his way to Charing Cross and Northumberland Avenue, prowling for the lad Badger had told him about. He was searching so vigorously that he almost didn't feel the hand reaching into his pocket. He grabbed the wrist with an iron grip and swung around, staring down at a boy desperately trying to free himself, one who fit Badger's description: wild, dark hair and a dented bowler that had fallen to the pavement in their tussle.

'Ned Wilkins, I presume,' he said, glaring down at the lad.

The boy stopped struggling and looked up at Ben's face. 'And you wouldn't by chance be Mister Watson, would you?'

'I am. Now don't run, boy. I've got a job for you and the Dean Street Irregulars.'

'I can't run with that grip of yours.'

Ben side-eyed him as he slowly loosened his grip.

The boy remained, rubbing at his wrist before he bent to retrieve his hat. 'Wotcher, Mister Watson.'

'Here's the thing, Mister Wilkins. I need you to gather your gang just as quick as you can. I need you to go to all the livery stables in London and ask who might have hired a barouche coach with driver and two black horses last night or a day prior. Get me? That's a *barouche* coach, a four-wheeler.'

'Right-o, guv. Oh, and that's two shillings a day, ain't it?'

'No, my young chap. It's *one*. Don't be greedy. But the first fellow who finds the right place gets extra. And we need the information just as fast as you can get it.'

'Meet you at the Dean Street flat, then?'

'Right. Good luck!'

Ned said no more and rushed away, feet slapping the pavement, hand on his hat to keep it on. Ben hoped that the lads would do the job. Badger put a lot of trust in those boys, but Ben reckoned that he had trusted Badger too all those years ago, and look at them now.

He turned . . . and ran right into a gentleman on the street. He raised his bowler with an apology on his lips . . . when he recognized the man. 'Why, if it isn't Mister Miles Smith, of Tottenham Court Road.' He was that kind solicitor they'd met on their first successful case in Bloomsbury.

'Oh! Do I know you, sir? Why, yes I do! You're that private detective. One of a pair.'

'Yes, sir. I'm Benjamin Watson and my colleague is Timothy Badger.'

'That's right. I am very pleased to see you again, sir. I hope all is well?'

'Come to think of it, all is not well. It's this latest case of ours. I'm wondering, Mister Smith, if you don't have a moment to talk on a delicate matter of police business.'

'Of course. For Badger and Watson I do. Shall we go to my offices?'

'Where were you headed, sir? I wouldn't want to interrupt your day.'

'Not at all, not at all. I was just heading to my favourite public house for a spot of dinner. If you wish to attend me, I should be glad of the company.'

'I shall be delighted, sir.'

It was only a few blocks away at Charing Cross Road, and they found themselves seated in the dark wood and gaslight of The Porcupine.

The proprietor, a jolly fellow with red nose and cheeks and a receding hairline, greeted the solicitor, obviously being used to his custom. Smith ordered a shepherd's pie and wine, while Watson, having consumed Mrs Kelly's hearty sandwiches, only ordered a porter.

The landlord departed to get their order, and Ben hunkered down at the table between them to speak as quietly as he could amid the noise.

'Mister Smith, this is a delicate matter.'

'I am used to delicate matters, Mister Watson.'

'So in confidence, I tell you now. Doctor John H. Watson, confidant of Mister Sherlock Holmes . . . has been kidnapped.'

'No!' he gasped.

'And because Mister Holmes is out of the country on government business and unable to be reached, it is up to Badger and Watson to find him double quick.'

'This is horrific. How can I help?'

'We have received a ransom note for the sum of five hundred pounds.'

'Oh dear, oh dear. What do you intend to do?'

'At the moment, we do not intend to pay it. We hope to string out the culprit until we can secure the good doctor's release. And nab the villain.'

'And what is it I can do on the matter?'

The landlord returned with a tray bearing the pie and full glasses. He chatted amiably as he served, even as Smith replied absently. Finally, the man departed and Smith leaned in again. 'What can I do to help, Mister Watson?'

'Your advice would be most appreciated. I don't know whether or not you, in your capacity as a private solicitor, have ever encountered the like.'

'Sadly, I have. A mere few times, mind you. The kidnappers were almost certainly someone the victims knew. Family members, mostly.'

Ben recalled the state of the room at 221 Baker Street. The doctor had been serving his guest sherry and was interrupted, perhaps, as the culprit explained the purpose of his visit. He must have known the man in some way or another.

'I do not think it is family, but it seemed to be someone he knew.'

'When is the ransom due?'

'Noon tomorrow. But as of yet, we do not know where.'

'That doesn't leave much time, does it?'

'No.' Ben picked up his pint glass and drank a dose of the dark, rich beer. He licked his lips and wiped the foam from his moustache with a finger. 'How did *you* handle these situations?'

'I served as go-between, receiving messages and sending them to the kidnappers. The clients' family members were all returned in good health.'

'Were the culprits ever apprehended?'

'They were usually looking to get funds to leave the country. Most of them *were* apprehended before they could escape and are serving their time in prison.'

'That's good to hear.'

'But there was at least one where . . . well.' He stirred his fork into the pie but did not partake of it. 'In one instance, the person was abducted and subsequently killed.'

Ben set down his glass. His brow furrowed. 'Oh. Yes. That is always a possibility with the unknown. We have not yet reckoned who it might be or the reason for the kidnapping. The ransom does not seem to be adequate funds to escape and start a new life in another country.'

'Yes, I see. It does not. Then . . . there might be another reason why he was abducted.'

'I've been swirling that about in my mind.'

Ben fell silent. He could feel the scrutiny of Mister Smith as they both considered the next actions.

'In this particular case, Mister Watson, I agree that the ransom should not yet be paid. See what you can tease out of this kidnapper. He might reveal his motives.'

'That's what we hoped.'

'The devil of it is, there is no one way to deal with rogues like this. You have to feel them out, so to speak. Assume that they are reasonable before violence can occur. If the man is a gentleman, there is no reason to expect that he would use violence. On the other hand, that may be his plan of action. Merely *being* a gentleman does not necessarily preclude unreasonable and violent acts.'

'Very true, sir,' said Ben with a sigh, picking up his pint glass again and taking a drink. 'It is obvious we must glean more information before we can make any more moves. I can only hope my colleague Mister Badger will have more to share with me.' He took his pocket watch from his waistcoat and flipped it open. 'I must fly.' He laid out several coins for his beer, took a last drink, and rose. 'I thank you for this valuable information and for your kindness in sharing your own experiences.'

'Do not hesitate to contact me, Mister Watson. There might yet be something I can do. I will be glad to assist.'

Ben shook his hand and thanked him before leaving the pub for the dull, waning sunshine outside. He took an omnibus this time back to Dean Street and trudged up the steps to their flat. When he opened the door, he did not expect to see Badger and Miss Littleton sprawled on the floor, flipping through a scattered collection of *The Strand Magazine*, used teacups on the floor beside them and a likely now cold teapot sitting on the drawing-room dining table, with strewn sugar cubes and an empty milk jug nearby.

'What the devil is going on?'

They both looked up at him, but it was Badger who spoke first. 'We're reading through copies of *The Strand Magazine* to get a clue about the stories on those pages of Doctor Watson's casebook. So don't just stand there: start reading.'

SEVEN
Badger

Watson huffed a breath, grabbed a magazine, and, with a grunt, sat on his chair by the fire and opened the cover to start reading.

The room was quiet. This was a different experience for Tim. He had asked for tea from Mrs Kelly and she had brought the tray up just as quick as you please. There had been the clatter of cups, the clink of sugar cubes and milk dollops dropped into cups, of tea being poured, and then a brief bit of conversation before Tim spread the magazines out on the carpet. For some reason, Miss Littleton plopped on to the floor with her teacup to start reading, and it seemed a natural thing to do to join her. He rested his back against the settee and occasionally raised his eyes surreptitiously from the page to watch her read, eyes on her work, her skirts bunched around her. She never spilled a drop as she lifted her cup to drink, and even scooted across the floor to reach the teapot on the table – never rising to her feet to do so – to pour more into it, dumping out the sugar cubes from the sugar bowl on to the table in order to grab them. He hadn't realized how pleasurable it could be to investigate *with* her . . . even as he reminded himself this was serious business.

Tim was just finishing reading *The Dreadful Business of the Abernetty Family* when Watson arrived. Tim took slurping sips of his tea every now and then as he read. It was quite a scandal. As far as he could tell, the entire family had no redeeming qualities whatsoever. He assumed Doctor Watson used a fictitious name for the family as Miss Littleton sometimes did, but he wasn't certain if other details were also falsified.

'Miss Littleton,' he said, looking up from the magazine pages.

She raised her head and quirked a brow.

'When you write up our stories, how much fiction do you add? I know you change the names, but do you leave in all the rest of the facts?'

'As much as I can, Mister Badger. But I do take care of the innocents involved and try to use a fictitious name for them, as you say. But even so, I suppose if one already knew the particulars of the crime, one can make assumptions. Outright murderers get no relief from me. They deserve to be named, especially once hanged.'

Tim exchanged a look with Watson, who shrugged.

He set that magazine aside and picked up another, thumbed through it, and found the next story, *The Arnsworth Castle Business*. The silence continued, with only the ticking of the mantel clock and its occasional chime amid the soft breaths of Miss Littleton as she came across an interesting fact in the story she was reading, and then the scritch of her pencil on her writing pad, as well as the turning of the magazine pages by all three of them. Tim's story seemed to be about a man swindling the owner out of their property and selling it to a foreign concern. Miss Arnsworth was duped, but Mister Holmes got her property back in the end . . . even after Miss Arnsworth was tricked into revealing where her jewellery box was.

After a time, he turned to Miss Littleton and Watson. 'Well? Anything that looks suspicious or concerning to our case?'

'I read *The Case of Mrs Etherege's Husband* and *The Case of Old Abrahams*,' said Miss Littleton. 'There was nothing about a kidnapping and, as usual, there was the despicable nature of the criminal. In the first story, Mrs Etherege's husband had gone missing, but it turned out that he had been in hiding from disreputable creditors. And in the Old Abrahams case, the man was a safecracker and, though accused of the theft, in this instance wasn't guilty, with some disgusting anti-Jewish sentiment from the police involved. Now, true, the former involved a missing man, but we have a witness to the particulars of the doctor's abduction, so it cannot be compared to that one. What of your reading, Mister Watson?'

The man set the magazine down on his thigh and sighed. 'I just got done reading *The Case of the Darlington Substitution Scandal* – a case similar to *The Scandal in Bohemia*, being solved in the same way, with a woman who was protecting her no-good husband when he substituted a forged document for one that his employers had entrusted him with. He was keeping the original for blackmailing, but the woman revealed the hiding place when she had to snatch up her baby to protect it. I don't see how this one might signify with our case. Well, it was a good try, Tim.'

'Yes, I see that now. It was just a coincidence, after all, that the doctor's casebook landed on those particular pages.'

'A shame,' said Miss Littleton, taking the discarded magazines and stacking them neatly on a side table. She rose and dusted off her skirts. 'My goodness, look at the time. I must be going home.'

'To Greek Street,' said Tim, rousing a look from Watson.

'Greek Street?' he said, not missing a beat.

She stared into the coat-stand mirror to fasten her hat to her hair with a long hat pin, and then shrugged into her coat before Tim could jump up and help her. 'Yes, Mister Watson. I have already been chastised by Mister Badger for not informing you earlier that I have moved to a different address. Thirteen Greek Street, right here in Soho. As I explained to Mister Badger, I found that I had too many of my father's debts to pay and it was more expedient to sell the family home. Sentiment doesn't pay the bills, I am afraid, and, surprisingly, I am quite happy at my smaller accommodations. They suit me well and I am more at ease without the burden of so many debts. I don't mind telling you that with what was left over, I don't truly have to work, but as you know, I enjoy it.'

'Well, I am sorry to hear about your troubles. There would have been little we could do but add our sympathy to the situation, but I am pleased to hear all is well with you now.'

'That is very gracious of you to say, Mister Watson. I appreciate the sentiment.'

'Then I will walk you home, Miss Littleton,' said Tim, already donning his coat and hat.

He noted that Watson seemed on the brink of saying something . . . but didn't. 'Good evening, Miss Littleton,' he said instead.

'I will see you tomorrow, Mister Watson.'

'Tomorrow?'

'Gotta run, Ben. Seeing Miss Littleton home.' Tim snapped the door closed, but not before catching a glimpse of Watson's frown.

'You are devious, Mister Badger,' she said with a smile as they set out on the pavement. 'Why didn't you just tell him I will be part of your investigation as it happens? You will have to do so eventually.'

'I know. But I'd rather do it later than now.' They walked only a few steps before Tim offered her his arm.

'That's really not necessary, Mister Badger.'

'But it's safer, you on my arm.'

She chuckled softly, seeing quite clearly through his ploy, but soon slipped her hand under his elbow and on to his sleeve where she lightly held it. 'Is this how you treat all your detective associates?'

'Only the pretty ones.'

'Oh, indeed. And do you consider Mister Watson pretty?'

'Here now. You are the only female that we associate with.'

'Besides Miss Murphy.'

'That's Ben.'

'He does attend to her, doesn't he?'

'Our Ben is in love, I'm afraid.'

'Dear me.'

'It's not as bad as all that. We aren't much better than servants in the scheme of things. Why shouldn't he call on a house maid?' But then his words sank in and he paused and shot a glance at her.

She was calmly looking at the street ahead of them, but he noted how her jaw clenched. *Stupid to admit we were like servants when I've got me arm out to a baronet's daughter.* 'That is . . . I mean to say that—'

'Mister Badger, I have told you before, class means nothing to me anymore. I am no longer part of the aristocracy. Who I choose to associate with makes no matter. And a detective is a respected profession. Especially one linked to Sherlock Holmes.'

He wanted to say more. He wanted to ask her to dine, to tea, to the music hall again. But he reckoned that this was not the proper time. Not in the middle of such an important case. It was enough that he would be seeing her more often now that they were investigating together.

They continued south down Dean Street and took a left at Bateman Street. The darkness that enshrouded the roads was only broken by the glow of the street lamps and the quiet step of the occasional copper patrolling. Tim had to damp down the urge to run in the opposite direction when he spied the rozzer. Old habits and all. But he politely touched the brim of his hat instead to the bobby who saluted back.

They reached the end of the road that became Greek Street and there was her house, a pale stone entry at street level with a black-painted door. 'Here we are,' she said airily. But he did note a strain to it. 'What time shall I meet you tomorrow?'

'Well, the ransom was called for noon, but we have yet to hear from the kidnapper as to where to go. So as soon as possible in the morning, I reckon. We will be going to Baker Street early. Shall we say eight?'

'That will suit, Mister Badger. A pleasure.' She stepped back from him and extended her hand. He took it and shook it gently.

'May I . . . may I have your latch key?'

'Oh, certainly.' She reached into her handbag and grabbed the key, handing it over.

He stepped up to the door and unlocked it. The gas lamp hanging in the entry was lit but dimmed. It seemed just as nice as her family home, with marble floors and a decorative table with a vase of flowers. He handed her back the key and stepped aside for her to enter.

'Thank you, Mister Badger.' She took his hand again and kept it. 'This is going to be most interesting working with you. And Mister Watson, of course.'

'I'm looking forward to it too.'

'Good night,' she said, still hesitating, still holding his hand. He didn't mind one bit. 'Oh.' She let his hand go as if she had forgotten it, and stepped into the house. She watched him as she slowly closed the door.

Tim couldn't help smiling. Even as he admonished himself, he just couldn't help it. He had hopes of a kiss on the cheek, either received or given by him, but the moment passed and it seemed inappropriate anyway.

A hansom cab trotted by and he flagged it down to wipe the smile off his face. He thought he'd take another look at Baker Street again. Concentrate on that. Not that he would awaken Mrs Hudson. If he wanted to look in on the flat . . . well. He had ways to get in without a key.

'Two hundred and twenty-one Baker Street, my man.'

He sat back in the darkness of the cab, watching the quiet streets go by his window as they rode on, the horse's hooves the only sound as it clopped in rhythm over the cobbled stones. Only a few hansoms were still out; most had gone back to their livery stables

The Misplaced Physician 59

and the cabbies gone home for the night. It made Tim wonder how Ben had got on with the Dean Street Irregulars. He had forgotten to ask. He hoped he had found Ned Wilkins. Ned was quite a lad. Reminded him a lot of himself when he was a child, with all the brass and grit of an older boy. Yes, Ned could get the job done. He was sure of it.

As they approached the guv's house on Baker Street, Tim pushed up the trap door and spoke to the driver. 'You can stop here. No need to make a noise before his house.'

'All right, guv.'

It was several doors down from 221. Mrs Hudson must be having a bad time of it and he didn't want to disturb her. He paid the cabby and surveyed the street. All was quiet, as it should be. The street lamps were all lit. The windows were dark.

He glanced across the way to the window of Mister Blanchard and saw a small light in the window behind the lace curtains. The gentleman was still awake, suffering from sleeplessness. Tim admitted that he was glad not to suffer from that. Out like a snuffed candle he was, every night.

Though that made it difficult to break in by the front door with the watchful Blanchard overlooking all.

What was he thinking? It wasn't as if he was taking a crowbar to it. He'd use his lockpicks and would look as if he was just having a bit of trouble with his key. He took out the picks and approached the steps, climbing them and readying his instruments. He didn't crouch, since that would be a dead giveaway, but stood up straight and set them both in the keyhole, shook them a bit, and bob's your uncle! He opened the door as quietly as possible, damping down the urge to turn to Blanchard's window to give him a wave.

He closed the door as quietly and carefully as he'd opened it, and made his way up the stairs, skipping over the step that he knew Mister Holmes had made squeak so that he would be alerted to intruders. He cracked open the door to the flat and stepped inside. It was quiet and still. And cold. Mrs Hudson had not laid the fire. She probably agonized over whether she should or shouldn't. He reckoned she might change her mind on that tomorrow, wailing that Doctor Watson shouldn't come home to a cold flat.

The light from the street lamp below offered a mere glow in

the room through the lace curtains. The heavier curtains had not been shut. Seldom were they.

He closed his eyes to see what he could discern that way, as Mister Holmes sometimes did when investigating. He detected the vague smell of cigarettes, Doctor Watson's cigars, and Mister Holmes's dreadful shag pipe tobacco permeating the wallpaper, curtains, and carpets. There was also the lingering aroma of coffee and pastries which had probably wafted up through the stairwell. There had been the warmth of habitation . . . but now there was a hole where it was meant to be.

He opened his eyes and, in the gloom, surveyed what he had seen before. There had been the scattered papers over there by the doctor's desk with the imprint of the hobnail boot. The casebook of now apparently random stories lying face down on the floor *under* the desk. He still couldn't help but feel that it had been placed on purpose, but as to the code, he did not understand it. Yet. But if code there was, he was certain he and Ben . . . and maybe even Miss Littleton could crack it.

And there was Mister Holmes's chair. Worn, the stuffing pushed around and flattened from use, and the slightly darkened back between the wings where his head usually lay. Tim looked below it to the carpet, the place where he had frequently sat when he was one of the Irregulars and used to look up at the man as he spoke on this matter or that. The voice rang in Tim's head and he heard those cultured tones say, 'It is my belief, Watson, founded upon my experience, that the lowest and vilest alleys in London do not present a more dreadful record of sin than does the smiling and beautiful countryside.'

The doctor would sit in his chair by the fire with his paper and a cigarette, or perhaps at his desk, writing and absently listening to his strange companion. If he replied at all, it was to say, 'Excellent, Holmes' or 'How extraordinary, my dear fellow.'

Tim didn't understand half the time what the men were saying, but they sounded beautiful, like some of those music hall gents. He had to admit that at times he forgot he belonged to the group of unsophisticated and ragtag boys from the slums of his old neighbourhood in Shadwell. He felt, rather, that he was part of a trio, of Mister Holmes and Doctor Watson and himself, sitting in on an amiable conversation, and he, too, would nod his head sagely and think to himself, *That's a fair assessment, Holmes.*

Invariably, though, he'd awaken and the other boys would urge him to go, follow Jimmy Wiggins back to their various hidey holes, sometimes together, sometimes separately. Was it then, in his youngest of days listening at the feet of Mister Holmes, that Tim conjured the notion of his being a detective one day? He couldn't quite remember, but he did remember when it came to full flower, and that it was a year before he knew he'd be too old for the Irregulars, that he would be too big and obvious as a suspicious young man loitering about in the streets. And maybe he could be the detective himself, using the method and getting himself a Watson. And damned if he didn't do just that, with a man whose name was made to order. Ben Watson knew it was foolish when Tim met him five years ago, still wet behind the ears and telling Watson his scheme. Watson only half believed him in those days. He certainly knew now.

The soft silence was only stirred by the ticking of the mantel clock, the settling of the house itself, a truss relaxing, a doorway arch sighing.

Then there was a creak on the stair.

Tim's eyes flew wide open and he crept to the closed door and listened. Definitely someone coming up the stairs.

He curled his hand around the doorknob, and before he remembered he didn't have a weapon of any kind, he yanked the door open and faced a shadowy figure on the landing. They both froze for mere seconds, neither doing anything but bleating out harsh breaths . . . before the man turned and flew down the stairs.

In an instant, Tim was after him. The man held to the baluster as he whirled around the tight corner at the bottom of the stairs at the tile floor of the entry and speared out of the front door. Tim was at his heels, ready to leap on to the man, but the man was sincere in his desire to evade capture.

He turned down an alley, and Tim was hot on his tail. Their footsteps echoed between the brick walls of the taller buildings. Tim kept his eye on him. It was a trick of the light and shadows that made Tim think the man might have eluded him, but there he was, pulling himself over a fence and down the other side.

Not on my watch, my lad, he swore. It put a fire in his belly, and he ran, hit the fence, and was over in one smooth cartwheel. He caught sight of the man just turning the corner, and off he went after him.

But once on Northumberland Street, Tim's strength was giving out. *No!* he chided his legs. He was finding that it was a lot harder to pursue than it was *being* pursued. And maybe it was eating regular and rich food which slowed him. Whatever it was, even as he did his best to follow down the quiet streets of London, he couldn't quite catch up.

Tim slowed, lungs screaming, heart shattering his chest. He threw his body forward to rest his hands on his knees and inhaled great gobs of air.

Couldn't catch him. Could barely see him – certainly not his face. But he had noticed one thing.

The man wore hobnailed boots.

EIGHT
Watson

'Returning to the scene of the crime,' said Ben, shaking his head. 'I thought that was only in penny dreadfuls.'

'I reckon not,' said Badger, who still seemed to be kicking himself for not catching the bloke.

'Don't beat yourself up, Tim. He was just faster.'

'Maybe I should have had a gun.'

'Maybe you shouldn't. What if it had been Mrs Hudson on the stairs and you shot first, asked questions later?'

'I reckon you're right,' he said woefully.

'I know I am. Look. It's late. It's been a hard day. Let's both get some sleep, get up early tomorrow.'

'Yeah.' Badger rose and paused. 'Oh. I might have forgot to mention that, er, Miss Littleton will be here tomorrow morning.'

Ben folded his arms over his chest. 'And why is that?'

'Because she's . . . she's going to investigate. *With* us.'

'No, she ain't.'

'Yes, she is. Ben, I promised her.'

'And once again, Tim Badger thinks this agency is run by one man. It's a partnership. I should have been consulted.'

'It's just that she wouldn't agree to help me at *The Strand Magazine*'s archives if she didn't get to investigate along with us. I didn't think it would hurt. We need all the help we can get.'

'You couldn't ask me?'

'How was I to contact you in a timely manner? It was a quick decision that needed to be made.'

'I don't like it, Tim. She's insinuating herself into our business more and more, and I don't like it.'

'She does good work for us, Ben. You know that. She gets us clients.'

'I still like to be consulted.'

'I know. And I'm sorry. I made what you might call an executive decision. It had to be done, as far as I was concerned.'

'You're not thinking with your brain.'

Badger drew himself up. 'I resent that, Ben Watson. True, I like the lass. Very much. But she was most helpful. I learned a lot about researching in archives that I will use in the future. And you know she'll write a smart story that will be read by thousands.'

'As long as we get the doctor back safe and sound.'

'Yeah. We . . . we do need to do that.'

In the morning, Ben was still a bit put out that Miss Littleton would be joining them, taking notes on all they said and did. It was unnerving. But Badger was Badger. He couldn't fault the man too much. Ben knew there was something smouldering between the two of them, and Badger never did tell him the full story about something that had changed between him and the woman a few cases back. Which, of course, put him in mind of his own infatuation with Miss Katie Murphy. It was hard to blame Tim *too* much.

Ben washed and trimmed his beard, dressed, and once he was presentable, emerged from his room the same moment Badger did.

'Good morning, Ben. Blimey, but I'm feeling all a-rumble in me tummy.'

'It's nerves. Waiting for that ransom note.'

'And what about that, Ben? Five hundred pounds is a good sum. I'd like to have it too. But it ain't enough to run away with once you release your victim. I would have reckoned he'd have asked for a couple of thousand.'

'Yes. It is strange. I hope it doesn't mean . . .'

'Don't even *think* it, Ben Watson. Gawd Almighty, don't even breathe it.'

'No, no, of course not.' He was not going to think that Doctor Watson was no longer alive. That *would* be unthinkable. How would they ever face Mister Holmes again? 'But there's got to be a reason a gentleman asks for so small a sum.'

'Maybe it's a wager,' said Badger. 'Gentlemen are always making wagers with each other on the most ridiculous things.'

'That's logical, that. It's a possibility.'

'I wonder, Ben,' said Badger, pouring his coffee from the pot on the sideboard and placing his cup on the table beside his table setting. He grabbed his plate and looked under the lids of the warm chafing dishes. 'I wonder if this ain't a case, after all, of some school chum playing a prank. It might be that his school chum is holding him for ransom as a big joke to all and sundry and won't let the doctor go in order to play it out. Maybe Doctor Watson didn't know the fella had sent notes to Mrs Hudson *and* us.'

'That's another good thought, Tim. After all, there was no blood, no harm had come to the room.'

'But there was that hobnail bloke that I ran into last night what left his foot mark on them papers.'

'There is that. I wonder if he wasn't sent to Baker Street to retrieve something the kidnapper wanted. What reason could there be for him to come sniffing around?'

'It's a puzzle,' said Badger, scooping kippers on to his plate. He sat down and added sugar and milk to his coffee. Stirring it, he looked up. 'Something we missed, maybe?'

'We didn't find anything from the kidnapper,' said Ben, crunching on a piece of toast. 'Just the ash from the cigar.'

'No, we didn't. He couldn't have meant to *leave* something last night, could he?'

'Crikey,' Ben muttered. 'I hope that wasn't the ransom information he meant to leave.'

Badger clinked his cup loudly back on its saucer. 'And I scuppered it by being there.'

'Don't worry, Tim. I'm sure they will find a way to make certain we get that information. The man wants his five hundred pounds, doesn't he?'

But *did* he? Ben began to wonder. It seemed so straightforward at first, but it was becoming more complicated as they went on. 'No use speculating until we have the material in hand.'

They finished their breakfast in silence and froze on the spot, cup nearly to lips, fork in hand, when they heard a knock on the door.

Ben tugged the serviette from his collar and wiped his mouth and beard. 'Come in!'

And there was Ned Wilkins, bowler askew, followed by three young boys, including the young black child Badger told him about. They trotted in, ripped trousers, ragged shirts, and floppy shoes too big for them, and all.

'We're here, guv, to tell you what we found out and to collect our brass.'

The four boys moved forward and gathered around their table, eyes scanning the food. Badger grabbed the rest of the toast and the plate of kippers and sausages and handed it over. They used their grubby fingers to swipe the fish and sausages from the plate and dispatch the toast double quick.

'Well?' said Ben.

The young boys licked their fingers and wiped them down their dirty and ragged shirts.

'That there is Bert,' said Ned gesturing towards the black child. 'Tell 'em, Bert.'

The boy looked up at Ben with widened eyes. Ned nudged him. 'I told you, Bert,' said Ned under his breath. 'The man's black as soot, just like you.'

Bert looked up at Ben worshipfully and never even glanced at Badger once. 'I went to the livery stables at Saint Pancras, and they said a bloke hired the coach you was looking for.'

'And what was the bloke's name?'

'Called himself a Mister Matthews of Southwark.'

'"*Called* himself"?'

'That's what the man said, because he didn't believe that was his name. Said he was suspicious.'

'Had he returned the rig and coachman yet?'

The boy shook his head.

'That was right good detecting, that,' said Ben. 'But what are these other boys here for?'

'They found other carriages at other livery stables fitting your description, guv, but I reckoned the suspicious one was the right bloke.'

'Good job, Ned!' said Badger.

'Cheers!' said Ned with a bright smile and a dirty raised chin.

'But best give us them other names too,' said Badger. 'Just to be safe.'

Ben shook the hands of all the boys and made sure to give them the money they earned. 'And Ned,' said Badger, pulling the boy aside, 'here's the brass for the rest of the boys. Tell 'em "good work"!'

Ned tipped his hat. 'Thanks, guv. Anytime at all. The Dean Street Irregulars are ready for action!'

'Post a boy by each of the stables, Ned,' said Ben. 'And see if the rig returns. And when it does, find out from the driver what happened to his riders.'

'Right. Cheers!'

They burst through the door like a herd of water buffaloes just as two shrieks let out. Badger leapt towards the door, and there was Mrs Kelly and Miss Littleton pinned against the wall as the boys rumbled by. Miss Littleton's shocked face found Badger's. He let out a guffaw.

'You have now been introduced to the Dean Street Irregulars, miss.'

'Great heavens,' she huffed and adjusted her hat. 'Well! That was certainly something. So you were just like one of those boys, Mister Badger? When you were one of Mister Holmes's Irregulars?'

'Just like it, Miss Littleton. Just as wild and ragamuffin as they are. With brass in me pocket from Mister Holmes himself. Why, I'd be surprised if none of them boys want to be detectives too after they've been at it a while.'

'What an excellent mentorship programme, gentlemen. I applaud you. And what did they discover?'

Ben nudged a besotted Badger out of the way. 'They discovered that the coach, driver, and horses were hired by the Saint Pancras livery stable, and the man that hired it was a Mister Matthews of Southwark, but the owner at the stable doubted that was the man's real name as he seemed "suspicious".'

'Oh, very good, Mister Watson.' She opened her notebook and pencilled in the information. 'Has the coach been returned?'

'Not yet, but Tim and I instructed the Irregulars to keep an eye on that stable for its return to question the coachman as to what happened to his fare.'

'How efficient you are,' she said, writing and shaking her head in surprise. 'Now.' She slapped her notebook closed and lifted it like a salute. 'Are we ready for this venture?'

'Just remember,' said Ben, spearing her with his glare, 'that this is serious business. We don't yet even have proof of Doctor Watson's continued health.'

'Oh, that's dreadful.' Her hand was at her heart over an eyelet blouse. 'I . . . I did not think about that. It is *un*thinkable!'

'I'm ready,' said Badger, losing his ever-present smile. 'Let's go to Baker Street and see if anything's waiting for us.'

They took a hansom cab, the three of them tight together in the carriage, and got to Baker Street at quarter past eight. Mrs Hudson seemed to be waiting for them at the door and opened it upon the second chime of the bell. She narrowed her eyes at Miss Littleton.

Miss Littleton offered her hand. 'I am so pleased to meet you, Mrs Hudson. I have read so much about you. I am Ellsie Moira Littleton, reporter for the *Daily Chronicle*.'

'Badger!' she cried accusingly. 'You brought a reporter?'

'No, Mrs H, this is *our* Doctor Watson, so to speak. She writes our cases and they get into the papers.' They all climbed the stairwell together and opened the door to Holmes and Watson's flat. 'But she won't publish nothing till the entire case is solved and the doctor is back home safe and sound. Right, Miss Littleton?'

'Of course. I give you all my word.'

Ben heard Mrs Hudson mumble something about nosy parkers, and he couldn't help but agree. Mrs Hudson seemed to have a great deal of experience with reporters, mused Ben, and didn't stop squinting doubtfully at her. *Cheers, Mrs Hudson.*

'Has the post arrived yet, Mrs H?' asked Badger.

'Not yet. And I am getting worried.'

Ben walked to the middle of the drawing room and gestured towards the chairs and settee. 'Let's all just sit down and get comfortable until it does.'

Slowly, the three of them moved to different seats and waited, studiously avoiding looking at one another. Though Miss Littleton scoured the room as if trying to memorize everything she saw.

'Can I bring you tea?' asked Mrs Hudson.

'That would be very nice,' said Miss Littleton, beating Badger and Ben to it. Once Mrs Hudson left, the reporter turned to the men. 'I thought that it would help to keep her busy, take her mind off it all.'

They said nothing in reply. Badger settled back in his seat, tapping his foot as if he were playing a drum.

Ben lit up a cheroot, after first gesturing to Miss Littleton to ask if he could. She was accommodating. He glanced at her once the cigar was lit, and she didn't move a muscle. Just sat stiffly with her handbag clutched firmly in both hands, eyes still darting around the room.

The mantel clock became their companion, ticking and ticking and chiming on the quarter hour. *Where is the bloomin' post?*

The bell.

Everyone jerked at the sound. They listened to the steps of Mrs

Hudson as she strode briskly across the main entry to the basket at the door that caught the letters through the letter box, scooped them up, and trod up the stairs, one step at a time in a sedate manner. She knocked on the flat's door and entered without waiting for permission. She sorted through the letters and froze at the look of one. She handed it to Badger with all solemnity.

Ben expected Badger to tear it open, but he knew his business, and carefully tipped his jack knife through the envelope's lip and then tore it gently down the fold. He gingerly retrieved the note from the envelope while three other heads peered over his shoulder. The kidnapper didn't bother with cutting out letters this time. Instead, he wrote out the detailed instructions with a pen.

'J-pen, I'd say,' said Badger absently. 'On the same fine paper.'

Ben read the instructions aloud: *'Bring the money to the post office on Tottenham Court Road and St Pancras Street. Wrap it in hessian, place it in the wire rubbish bin, and then leave. No police.'*

'What about Doctor Watson?' said Mrs Hudson's strident voice.

Badger turned over the page, but there was nothing there. 'It don't say. I don't like this, Ben.'

'What other option do we have?'

'We can pay half,' said Badger, 'and leave a note saying that we demand to have proof of life.'

Mrs Hudson wailed at that, bringing her apron up to her nose.

'And more than that,' said Miss Littleton, startling him. He'd forgotten she was there. 'We can place ourselves in and around the post office. The kidnapper likely wouldn't know what I look like. And one of you could disguise yourself.'

Ben stared at an equally staring Badger. 'I could put on a false beard and moustache. Maybe look like an old codger,' said Badger.

'And where would you find that?'

'I know of a place. I'll go now.'

'Tim , . .'

'We've got just under four hours to go. I'll be back in plenty of time.'

With that, he glanced once at Miss Littleton before he tore out of the door and bounded down the stairs.

'When he gets an idea,' said Miss Littleton, 'he certainly must act upon it at once.'

'He surely does,' said Ben. 'We'll need the Dean Street Irregulars for this too. You stay here, Miss Littleton, while I go fetch them.'

'But . . .'

'Miss Littleton. See what help you can render to Mrs Hudson.'

She was ready to fly as much as Badger, but he saw her expression change as she took on the role of a solicitous Great Lady. There was something about the nobility in charge that calmed servants, he observed. Though Mrs Hudson was no common servant.

With her reassurance, he hurried out of the door to Charing Cross.

NINE
Badger

Tim walked briskly to Wardour Street, it being only a few streets away, and pushed open the shop door that promised *All The World's A Stage: Theatrical Costumes and Enhancements. Nigel Dawber, Proprietor.* The bell jangled over the door as he glanced around. The place was crowded with all sorts of things for any theatrical production. From the ceiling hung the more lavish costumes, things to be found in operettas – silk dresses with wide skirts and glass jewels sewn to them. Shelves were loaded with men's and women's hats, both current styles and fanciful. And there were wigs and fake beards in glass-fronted display cases. He headed there and leaned down close to look.

'May I help you, sir? Oh, blimey, it's Tim Badger.'

'Wotcher, Nige.' He looked up and found that the bald, small-moustachioed man that he knew from previous encounters suddenly had a head of luxurious red hair, a wildly combed moustache that formed into wide side whiskers, and a bulbous nose with glasses perched upon it. 'Ooooh. Now that, my man, is just the sort of thing I'm looking for. I need to change my appearance.'

'You've come to the right shop, mate. You'll need wig, beard, moustache, and stage make-up.'

'I was thinking of looking like an old man.'

'But can you *act* like an old man? You see, for those of us in the profession' – and here Nigel straightened and thrust his thumb under his lapel – 'it's not merely the outer look of make-up and costume, but the inner performance.' He gestured over his whole body. 'We'll fix you up and then we'll try it out, shall we?'

He directed Tim to a seat before a mirror that already had spirit gum in a bottle, various brushes and powder puffs, sponges, cardboard sticks of make-up, pencils, scissors, and combs on the vanity table before it. The proprietor waved his arm dramatically. 'Let the transformation begin!'

Tim marvelled at all the steps the man performed, explaining carefully how to apply the make-up and what not to do as he glued, painted, patted, and slowly altered Tim's familiar features into that of an older gentleman. A little putty on his nose made it a bit longer and droopier. The grey wig, bushier eyebrows, long beard and moustache, and carefully blended wrinkles on his forehead and the corner of his eyes made a shocking difference.

'Cor,' he muttered before he was muffled by Nigel shoving false teeth over Tim's own to make them toothier and more rabbit-like.

Nigel took him to a wardrobe with different suits of clothes. He chose something a bit shabbier, older in style, and fit Tim up with it, and with a cane now in his hand, and getting old-man lessons from the proprietor, Tim tried it out by walking outside. He stood before the shop looking in the window, and when he saw a lovely woman walking by, he fell into a fit of coughing. The woman rushed to him, rested a hand on his shoulders, and bent to look into his face. 'Are you quite all right, sir? Here. Sit down. I'll ask this shopkeeper if he has water.'

Tim sat on a wooden bench outside the shop as if all his bones ached and looked up at the solicitous woman. 'No, no,' he said, scratching his voice a bit and speaking slowly. 'Just the look of your pretty face is a balm to me.'

She smiled with pinkening cheeks and patted his shoulder. 'Are you sure? I'll sit with you until you are better.'

She sat beside him, this nice young woman with apple cheeks, kind eyes, and curls in her brown hair. He patted her hand. 'Oh, I feel much better now. So much better!' He leapt from the bench and did a little jig before he kicked up his heels. The woman jerked back, aghast. 'All it takes is a pretty lass!' he chortled, grabbing her hand and kissing it.

The woman jumped from her seat with a shriek and ran away down the pavement.

Tim laughed and caught the look from the proprietor leaning against the doorway. 'I'd call that a good result,' said the man with a grin.

'Brilliant. What do I owe you?'

'Let's see. Beard, moustache, side whiskers, wig – with two more of the set in brown – false chompers, sticks of grease paint, sponges, putty, costume . . . Three shillings will do.'

Tim dug his coin purse out of his pocket and paid. Then Nigel handed over a package wrapped with brown paper and string. 'There now, your own clothes and some extra make-up. Good luck with your venture, Tim. Come by any time.'

'Thanks, Nige. I need to stand you a pint.'

'I'll take that.'

He waved his goodbyes and proceeded to walk slowly with his newly acquired cane and new face back to Dean Street to try it out on Mrs Kelly and Miss Littleton.

He rang the bell on 49 Dean Street, and when Mrs Kelly answered, she looked at him suspiciously. He had decided that when she opened the door, he would use a slightly deeper voice along with his old-man scratchiness, and she didn't seem to twig. Up the stairs she led him, and when she knocked, it was only Miss Littleton there. 'Shall I bring you a cup of tea while you wait, sir?' Mrs Kelly asked.

'That would do very nicely,' he replied. He tipped his hat to Miss Littleton and took a seat by the fire, being careful *not* to take his regular chair.

'Do forgive me for sitting before a lady,' said Tim, trying to enunciate carefully over the false teeth and to rid himself of his Cockney accent. 'But these old bones . . .'

'Of course, don't think anything of it. Are you here to engage Badger and Watson? I can assure you they are the best in their field. Why, they've never failed to get their man.'

'That is extraordinarily good to hear, young lady. I have a problem of great importance. Are you, by chance, their assistant?'

She smiled in a most indulgent way. 'Well, I suppose I flatter myself into thinking I am. You see, I am a reporter and I have the pleasure of writing up their fascinating cases for the *Daily Chronicle*.'

'You don't say! Why, that's extraordinary. A young lady like you, a reporter! What next, I wonder.'

'Women have been writing stories for a very long time, I dare say. Jane Austen, Emily and Charlotte Brontë, George Eliot, Mrs Gaskell. Some great writers of literature.'

'Popular nonsense. Does anyone read those anymore? Those were books written so long ago and just for women.'

He could tell she was affronted and held in his giggle. 'Well,

I don't think they can be dismissed as mere popular literature because they are still read, I assure you.'

'Yes, yes, of course. Ah, here's the tea.'

Mrs Kelly brought in a tray with the tea things and Miss Littleton offered to pour. Tim felt his moustache slipping and pressed a hand to it. When she had fixed his cup and handed it to him, he quickly took a sip . . . but then the moustache stayed on the lip of the cup.

'Ruddy hellfire,' he hissed.

Miss Littleton looked on aghast, but as soon as she recognized him, she leapt to her feet. 'Mister Badger!'

He tipped his rabbity teeth into his palm. 'Ha! I had you going until my bloomin' moustache made its escape.'

Her ire turned quickly to admiration. She sat slowly again. She leaned in to scrutinize his face. 'What an amazing transformation! I applaud you. But I *will* get you back for it.'

'Please do,' he muttered with a smile.

'A good disguise, though. I do hope Mister Watson is successful in garnering the help of your Dean Street Irregulars.'

'He will be. Those boys need the brass.'

Just as he spoke, there was a commotion at the entryway and a rumble of running feet on the stairs. He popped his moustache back on and stood by the tea, leaning heavily on his cane.

The boys burst in and surrounded the furniture in the drawing room. Some drew off their hats when they spied Miss Littleton . . . and glared suspiciously at Tim.

Watson came up at the rear, taking off his bowler. 'I apologize, Miss Littleton, for this outburst. Less of a regiment, more of a stampeding herd.'

'I have already met some of them. Gentlemen,' she said with a nod. The older ones elbowed the younger ones to take off their hats. 'I do hope you can help in this endeavour. I am Miss Ellsie Moira Littleton with the *Daily Chronicle*, and I write and publish the stories of Mister Watson and Mister Badger's cases.'

There was a lot of 'Hello, miss' and a little bowing, before they all seemed to direct their attention towards Tim.

Tim doffed his hat. 'Boys. A pleasure to make your acquaintance.'

'Who's this old duffer?' asked one of them.

'Oi!' said Tim, tearing off his beard with a yelp. The spirit gum was far more adhesive to his chin and jaw than his upper lip.

Even Watson's mouth dropped open. 'Tim . . .'

'Mister Badger!' the boys chortled, and pushed at him like old mates.

'Good disguise, eh?' he said to them all.

'Too good,' said Miss Littleton.

'Did Mister Watson tell you boys what we wanted?'

Ned Wilkins pushed forward. 'We're to sprinkle ourselves in and around the post office on Tottenham Court Road and St Pancras Street. Watch for the bloke who takes a hessian sack from the rubbish bin inside. Can we bring him down, sir?'

'Not unless me or Mister Watson gives the signal.'

'All right. When do you want us there, sir?'

Tim looked to Watson.

'Quarter past eleven,' said Watson. 'And don't look suspicious and *don't* fingersmith. We don't want no rozzers coming at us.'

'Right, guv,' said Ned, tipping his hat.

But before they could leave, Watson asked, 'Did the coach and driver arrive back at the livery stables?'

'Nah,' said Ned. 'Me boys are still staking them out.'

'Make sure they do. I am finding you Irregulars to be quite effective.'

'Why, thank you, guv,' he said to Watson with a bow.

'All right, boys,' said Tim. 'Away with you. We'll see you later right here for your payment.'

Out of the door they went, just as a-jumble as they had entered.

Miss Littleton sat and poured herself tea. 'Well! Such industrious employees. And so eager.' She dropped a sugar cube into her cup and sat straight-backed with it, the saucer carefully clutched between her fingers. 'I suppose all we need do now . . . is wait.'

As far as Tim was concerned, the waiting was terrible. He kept rubbing his forehead, and then he had to reapply his 'wrinkles'. Miss Littleton looked on with interest. Tim had put his package on the table and brought out his shaving mirror. 'You see here, Miss Littleton,' he said, proudly showing off his newly acquired wares, 'this is spirit gum. Made with resin so it sticks like a bast— Er, like it'll never let go. And in this bottle is the elixir to remove it. These are sticks of grease paint to even out the look of the skin and create delicate shadows, like wrinkles.'

'When did you learn all that?' asked Watson.

'Oh, I watched Mister Holmes transform. And I know a fella who was once an actor and now sells the stuff in his own shop.'

'Remarkable,' muttered Miss Littleton, avidly watching the process while taking notes.

'You just do a little blending. Mind you, very close up in bright light would give the game away, but if you are careful and keep to some shadows, it will all go well. And there you have it! Old Man Tim again.' He swivelled in his chair and showed off his handiwork.

'That's something, that,' said Watson. 'Maybe next time, you'll be an old woman.'

'I'll wager I can be. And you'd never notice.'

'I think I'll take that wager,' he said with a chuckle.

Tim glanced at the mantel clock. 'Say, Ben. What are we going to use for ransom money?'

'Like I said, we aren't going to pay that. It will be a bundle of newspapers in the shape of pound notes. And a letter explaining that we want proof of Doctor Watson's health.'

Miss Littleton paused with her teacup poised near her mouth. She returned it to the saucer. 'Isn't that rather taking a chance? Shouldn't we at least have some good faith money in there. Say, one hundred pounds?'

'The thing of it is, miss,' said Watson, 'we haven't got a hundred pounds.'

'But I can get it.'

Both Watson and Tim froze. 'You?' said Tim.

'Of course.' She pushed her teacup and saucer away from the edge of the low table in the drawing room. 'I am still a woman of *some* means . . . even though I now live more frugally.'

'But . . .' Tim somehow didn't translate in his mind her being well-off enough to live on her own with having the means to get her hands on one hundred pounds so easily. 'We can't possibly take your funds.'

'Why not? I offer it freely. And anyway, even if it is taken, I trust you two to get it back.' She glanced at both of them in turn. 'Don't you trust yourselves?'

'Well, it's like this, miss,' said Watson. 'Just what if it *is* taken?

The whole exercise here is to follow the bloke and track down where Doctor Watson is being kept. But if he gets away from us with *your* money, where will that leave us?'

'But Ben,' said Tim, 'you said yourself: the culprit wants his ransom, and he won't be happy with one hundred pounds if he asked for five.'

'I dread to think what he might do to Doctor Watson if he thinks he's been tricked out of his ransom,' she said, finger gently tapping her lip in thought. Tim was unable to tear his eyes away from the sight.

Watson frowned and slowly began to pace the room. 'Are you saying that we should somehow get the five hundred pounds and leave it at the ransom drop?'

'I know where to get it,' said Tim, popping up from his chair.

'Now, Tim,' said Ben, 'we cannot resort to illegal means.'

'Whose resorting? I'm not going to steal it, man. I'm going to ask a very important personage to loan it to us.'

'And what makes you think he will?'

'Trust me. I think he very much will. Let's go.'

'Go?' Miss Littleton stood. 'Go where?'

'Whitehall,' said Tim. 'That's where he can be found this time of day. Mycroft Holmes, that is.'

TEN
Watson

'You all right, Tim?'
   He watched as his friend squirmed in the seat between Miss Littleton and himself.
   'I just feel funny going to Whitehall in disguise. I hope it ain't illegal.'
   'It was your idea,' said Miss Littleton.
   'I know. But I forgot I didn't look like m'self.'
   She shared a look with Ben.
   'It'll be all right, Tim,' he said and settled back. Would Sherlock Holmes's brother, Mycroft Holmes, have the ready cash? Would he give it to them for this venture? Would they lose it? Now he wasn't so sure it *would* be all right.
   Their cab arrived before what used to be a palace. Whitehall's gate was more daunting than Ben thought it might be. He'd never been near the place himself, and the two gatehouses and the large square walls that embraced the courtyard like open arms behind the high, metal fence, with an imposing clocktower watching over all, was more intimidating than he reckoned. How would they ever be let in?
   Badger climbed out of the cab and did his performance of an old man, using the stick to balance himself while putting out a hand for Miss Littleton. Ben got out after her and adjusted his waistcoat.
   'Well . . . now what?'
   Badger looked over the gatehouses and the horse guards, conspicuous both inside the courtyard and outside the metal bars of the tall fence, and turned back to Ben. 'We just ask politely.'
   'Nonsense,' said Miss Littleton, marching forward before either Ben or Badger could stop her.
   They hurried to catch up, for it was plain she was heading straight for one of the red-coated and helmeted guards at the far-right gatehouse.

'Soldier,' she said in her firm, no-nonsense tone to the horse guardsman. 'May I speak to someone in charge? I am Ellsie Moira Littleton, daughter of the late Sir Reginald Arthur Littleton, Baronet of March. And I should like to speak to Mister Mycroft Holmes.'

Ben gave a terrified stare to Badger, and Badger returned it, one that seemed to say, *We are out of our depth.*

The guard nodded stiffly to her. 'I shall enquire, my lady.' He turned on his heel, stomping his booted foot once, and marched forward to talk to another guard. That guard nodded to the first and made his way in a quick march to yet another guard nearer to an arch in the main building, who in turn seemed to convey his orders to *another* guard who disappeared into the shadows, presumably to carry the message still further into the halls of the government.

They waited. Badger seemed to use his nervousness to look even more feeble. So much so that a guard ventured forward to offer him a seat in the guardhouse. With a sly smile directed to his friends, Badger allowed the man to take his arm and help him forth until he was seated on a wooden bench. Miss Littleton soon followed, and Ben took up the rearguard.

They waited some time – fifteen minutes by Ben's watch – before a guard made his way across the courtyard to speak to the guard in the gatehouse. That guard – the first they encountered – returned to the three, stood to attention, and addressed only the woman. 'I regret to say, Miss Littleton, that Mister Holmes is not currently in his offices. But it is believed he can be found at his club.'

'I know it,' said Badger, rising too fast, forgetting his old man posturing, but he quickly recovered by rubbing his lower back and using his cane to walk back to the kerb.

Ben hailed a cab and they all got in as before, except that Badger was pressed against Ben this time.

'The Diogenes Club, driver,' said Badger, and they fell back into their seats as the cab jerked away from the pavement and moved through traffic along Whitehall.

'How should we approach this, Ben?' Even as ridiculous as Badger currently looked, there was no mistaking the concern on his face.

'My evaluation of the Holmes men is that it is best to use the direct method.'

'Just ask him?'

'He must be a reasonable man,' said Miss Littleton. 'Else he wouldn't be working at Whitehall. Well . . .' she considered. 'I don't suppose that is an entirely valid recommendation.'

'All them lords and elected ministers?' asked Badger. 'They're supposed to be the cream of the crop.'

'They are ridiculously hidebound when it comes to rights for women,' she said with a sniff.

'Oh,' he said. *'That.'*

'You needn't say it in so disparaging a manner, Mister Badger.'

'Here we go,' muttered Ben under his breath.

'Be reasonable, Miss Littleton,' said Badger. 'You can't have the same rights as men, simply because you aren't a man. I mean, would you have a female prime minister up there in Parliament when she was . . . you know . . . in the family way?'

'And what's wrong with that? A woman has given birth to every prime minister ever elected. The queen herself is a woman in one of the longest and most successful reigns in history. And now you're quibbling over the rights of half the population?'

Badger shook his head indulgently. 'It's just not the same. Men are stronger, wiser, and have a deeper understanding of politics and what's what. We come from warriors, knights of old. You cannot expect to be equal in *every* way. Now really.'

'Mister Badger.' She moved in the seat to face him as directly as possible. 'I would implore you to lay newspaper articles written by men side by side with mine and you would be hard pressed to tell the difference . . . except that mine are better researched with an underlying empathy for the poor souls who find themselves in reduced and desperate circumstances.'

'Miss Littleton . . .'

'Tim,' said Ben from the side of his mouth. 'You're already in the hole. Stop digging.'

Badger glanced at Ben and suddenly seemed to see the wisdom in his words. He closed his mouth and relied on a shrug to appease her. But clearly, she was not appeased as she went on with her argument while the cab rattled on through to Waterloo Place.

The hansom stopped before the Diogenes Club, a Georgian structure with tall windows and a grand front entrance with a portico and architrave borne by double columns. A golden figure of Diogenes the Cynic holding up a lantern with a dog sitting beside him stood guard in the middle of the architrave, while a union flag fluttered on the roof from a flagpole above it.

Ben climbed out first and Badger next, but as Miss Littleton tried to exit, Ben forestalled her. 'I'm afraid this is as far as you go, miss. You can stay in the cab. This is a gentlemen's club. No women allowed.'

'We'll see about that!' She pushed past him and stepped lightly on to the mounting block and then to the pavement.

Ben stood his ground. 'Now, really, Miss Littleton. You must yield to the proper order of things. Please stay with the cab until we return.'

'I shall do no such thing.' Just as at Whitehall, she marched forward and the two men were helpless to stop her. They caught up quickly.

Ben finally grabbed her arm once they'd reached the door. 'Miss Littleton, I must insist. *We* are in charge of this investigation, and there is no need to cast unnecessary fuss over it. Please remember why we are here in the first place. It is to save the life of Doctor Watson. It isn't about women's rights.'

She seemed to finally hear him and wore a chastened look about her. Without another word, she stepped back and allowed Ben to ring the bell.

An old footman with long, grey side whiskers answered immediately, looking them over. His eyes especially seemed to glaciate when they roved over the woman.

'Badger and Watson Detecting Agency to see Mister Mycroft Holmes,' said Ben. 'I am Benjamin Watson and this is my' – he paused while measuring Badger in his costume and make-up – 'er, friend. Mister Holmes is acquainted with me. And the matter is most urgent.'

The footman stared openly at Miss Littleton. 'Women are not allowed in the club, gentlemen.'

'She won't be going in with us,' said Badger in a stern voice.

'Very well. Please come with me.'

Miss Littleton stepped down from the portico with a glum aspect as they went inside and the door closed on her.

'She's got gumption,' said Ben quietly.

'That she does,' Badger replied.

As Ben suspected, they were taken down a side corridor to what a shiny brass plate designated as the *Stranger's Room*, where guests were usually left to await the member they wished to meet. They were greeted by walnut panelling on the walls, long library tables, and cushioned wingback chairs. There was a small fire in the grate bounded by a polished brass fender, and large crystal vases with subdued flowers springing from them that sat on side tables. The room smelled of furniture polish and pipe tobacco.

Once they were well inside, the footman left them there and closed the door.

'I'll do the talking,' said Ben.

'But I'm the one that was acquainted with him.'

'And do you presently *look* like Tim Badger?'

'Oh. Yeah. Too hard to explain. You do the talking.' Badger moved to a chair and sat, looking for all the world like an old man. Perhaps he might present as a club member just sitting by the fire, his back to the door. Ben straightened, hands behind his back, and stood elegantly (he rather thought) while facing the entry.

The heavy oaken door opened after a few minutes, and the portly figure of Mycroft Holmes bustled into the room. He was more imposing than his brother in many ways. No one knew exactly what he did at Whitehall, but Badger made him think it was more important than the prime minister, performing secret doings for queen and country of which most people probably didn't want to know the details. Excepting, of course, Miss Littleton.

'Benajmin Watson,' he drawled and seated himself in a wingback chair. He flicked a glance at the old man in the other seat facing away from him and said, 'And Timothy Badger.'

Badger snapped around and stared. 'How did you know?'

'It is *Badger* and Watson, is it not? I knew immediately you were not a member for I know every one of them . . . and I can detect the merest whiff of grease paint and spirit gum. Did you assume you would fool me?'

'No, sir. No, indeed.' He scrambled to his feet and stood beside Ben. 'But we do come here for urgent business, sir. And to, well . . .'

But he couldn't complete his thought. There was an enormous noise outside the door. Shouting, feet scuttling across the marbled floors, a tray crashing to the ground, more shouting, and finally the door was cast open and a dishevelled Miss Littleton stood in the doorway. 'I am coming to this meeting, gentlemen!' she announced.

Two footmen were on the verge of grabbing her when Mycroft waved his hand.

'This is highly irregular,' said one of the footmen. 'Mister Holmes, it is strictly not allowed. This young lady crept in by the tradesmen's entrance and . . .'

'I do not believe you can restrain this particular young woman. She is the daughter of a baronet and a celebrated journalist, after all, and will brook no nonsense. Miss Ellsie Moira Littleton, do come in, even as highly irregular as this incident is. You may go, gentlemen, but do bring tea. The Ceylon and Assam, if you will.'

Miss Littleton swept her hands up over her puff of hair and assembled all the loose strands into order once more.

'I do not believe the members of the Diogenes Club will be amused by your presence here, Miss Littleton, but since I am a governor on the board, I do not think it will affect *my* membership unduly.' A smile flashed across his face but quickly dispersed. He pulled a tortoiseshell snuff box from his waistcoat pocket and paused with it in his hand. 'But one never knows. Pray, explain your presence here.'

He proceeded to indulge in the snuff, giving a horn blow of a sneeze before he wiped his nose with a red kerchief.

Ben gave her a death glare, and she shut her mouth. 'We are here to tell you of grievous tidings and to ask for your help,' he said.

'You mean about the kidnapping of Doctor Watson?'

'How the ruddy hellfire did you know that? Oh. Begging your pardon, miss,' said Badger.

The door opened to admit the footman with a tray of tea things, which he set down on the side table next to Mycroft. He proceeded to pour, and instead of milk and sugar, he dropped slices of lemon into each cup. He handed the first to Mycroft, the next to Badger, then to Ben, and finally, and reluctantly, to Miss Littleton.

Mycroft sipped and set the cup back into his saucer as the footman left again. 'You are both here coming to ask me an important boon. Miss Littleton's presence would imply a sensational story; Badger is in a disguise, which tells me of its secrecy; my brother Sherlock is presently out of the country and unreachable; my spies told me yesterday of some unusual doings at Baker Street, and I can think of no other event of greater importance that would bring the three of you here all at once to talk to me. It is very simple.'

'Your spies, sir?' asked Badger witheringly.

'Of course. It is in the interest of the country to keep an eye on my brother and his cohort.'

Badger pointed a finger at him. 'Then why didn't they tell you that the doctor was kidnapped and for you to do something about it?'

'My brother was not involved. They didn't deem it of too much importance.'

Badger went spare with a hanging jaw. 'Not important!'

'Steady, Tim,' said Ben, trying to use appeasing tones even as he squelched his own outrage. 'Mister Holmes, *we* do deem it of the greatest importance. And we are investigating the matter. We have received a ransom note and another with instructions.' He took them from his waistcoat, unfolded them and handed them over to Mycroft.

Mycroft read it quickly and handed it back. 'Five hundred pounds seems more like a gratuity than a true ransom.'

'Yes, sir. We noted that as well, and so we are working on the motive, because the culprit – a gentleman, we've determined – certainly cannot be moved by financial gain.'

'And so you have come to me for the ransom.'

They fell silent in their discomfort. Until Miss Littleton, in her impatience, spoke. 'I offered them a loan of one hundred pounds.'

'Very generous for a person in your declining financial situation.' He didn't acknowledge her huff of protest. 'But it is advised in these sorts of situations not to pay. They want so little in recompense, and so, as you say, they are not motivated by the money. I would say they wanted something from Doctor Watson himself, and that the ransom is only a diversion. What avenue have you pursued in order to find the men responsible?'

Badger moved to speak, but Ben gave him 'the look', and he sat back with a frown.

'We have deployed the new Dean Street Irregulars to obtain from what livery stable the coach and driver were hired, as the coach had no insignia and we deduced that it *was* hired. They found the livery stable involved but the coach and driver have not yet returned their hire. We have our own spies watching in order to obtain from the driver where he took his fare when he is back.'

'All very admirable. Slow, but possibly efficient in other ways. Is the doctor still in London?'

'That information, sir, we have yet to obtain.'

'Have you deduced this?'

'Well . . . there is a likelihood he *is* here in London, but to me it seems he must be more easily kept outside the city in the country.'

'Because?'

'It is more logical to keep a man hidden far away from any prying eyes or ears of strangers.'

'Excellent. My brother has chosen you two well enough. Not perfect, certainly. But adequate. And so the answer to your query must be that no, I will not give you the five hundred pounds. It seems to me – as it must surely seem to Mister Watson here – that it is a fool's errand you are being sent on. But, by all means, stake out the drop and see what transpires.'

Badger did move forward this time. 'But, sir, we were afraid for Doctor Watson's continued safety.'

'If the ransom was so little, as I said, then Doctor Watson himself was the reason for keeping him captive. And for whatever reason they want the good doctor, his continued health will be foremost. I shouldn't worry over it.'

Badger exhaled a relieved breath. 'Well, then . . .'

'You seem awfully opinionated for someone not acquainted with all the facts,' said Miss Littleton.

'Not acquainted with the facts? I dare say, it is you three who are delinquent in obtaining many facts at all. I have as many facts as you, and this is my determination. You are free, of course, to get the opinion of the men of Scotland Yard. I am sure Inspector Lestrade would have an opinion. The wrong one, to be sure. Now.' He stuffed his kerchief back into his coat pocket. 'Is there anything else, gentlemen? And Miss Littleton?'

Badger and Ben exchanged subdued glances. There seemed to be very little left to say. Except that Ben offered, 'Mister Holmes, we appreciate your seeing us. If your . . . your spies happen to find out anything further, we would be most grateful if they should relay that to us.'

'Of course,' he said absently, but Ben wasn't convinced he would.

'Thank you for your time, Mister Holmes,' he said with a bow. 'Come along, Tim. Miss Littleton.'

'Before I go,' she said, and Ben heaved a great sigh, 'I should just like to say to Mister Holmes here that I am personally appalled at his lack of empathy.'

'Empathy, young lady? What is the limit of one's empathy? For one individual caught up in something very likely of his own making? Or should I rather be concerned with the issues of an entire country? What is greater?'

'It is all the same, sir. One cannot divorce oneself from empathy of the individual or the entire country that the individual resides in. It is quite impossible not to see that an entire nation or even one street is not more important than the other.'

'Well, I cannot waste my time on the one person when an empire must needs be considered. The bigger picture, Miss Littleton, must always be utmost in one's thinking. At least at Whitehall.'

'Well, then I must remind you, sir, that the rest of us live down in the fog well below the grand halls of Westminster. *We* must deal with the individual's plight day in and day out. And I further say that I am personally glad I am in the gutter with the rest of humanity, and not on a pedestal as you seem to be, short-sighted to the crimes perpetrated on the everyman and woman.'

Mycroft clapped slowly, only piquing Miss Littleton further. 'A speech worthy of Parliament, Miss Littleton, and of as much use. Good day.'

Ben and Badger could both see she was winding herself up for more when Badger grabbed her arm. 'Come along, Miss Littleton. I think we are done here. Thank you, Mister Holmes, for your, er, suggestions.'

He bustled her out of the door and down the corridor, much to the chagrin of the footmen standing by, some still cleaning up the detritus from the spilled tray of broken tea things. Once out of the door to the fresh air, she wrenched her arm from him and fumed on the pavement.

'What a useless individual,' she swore.

'He has his uses,' said Badger. 'He told us not to worry about the ransom, and that keeping Doctor Watson was the real goal of the thing.'

Ben nodded. 'Yes. That is strange. Maybe we should go over them stories in *The Strand Magazine* once more.'

'But not before we deal with this ransom drop. I'm anxious to see who comes for it,' said Badger. 'My money's on Mister Hobnail.'

ELEVEN
Badger

Tim sat on a bench inside the post office, leaning on his cane with both hands, looking for all the world as though he were a simple old man, dozing over his walking stick.

Ben Watson, Tim noted, had had the foresight to bring with him several envelopes he was addressing on one of the high tables in the centre of the marble-floored space. Tim himself had seldom been in a post office and wasn't quite certain what the wall of brass drawers was all about, but he allowed his head to nod to his chest while surreptitiously eyeing the room under his false bushy brows.

Miss Littleton was doing much the same as Watson, writing out cards and then waiting in the queue to purchase a pre-stamped envelope.

Every now and then, Tim spotted an Irregular doing a spot of begging. Some were successful, some were pushed unceremoniously out of the way. It reminded him of his own childhood, right enough. And that's when the begging turned to fingersmithing. He always reckoned the uncharitable ones deserved it. It was the poorer blokes who seemed to be the most charitable and offered coins, and he made it his philosophy not to steal from them.

All were in place, and he eyed the clock over the workers' grille as the time ticked down to noon. The big hand clicked to the twelve and chimed out the numbers. Tim watched the bin where the hessian sack had been deposited. No one drew near it.

Just then, at the door, there was a commotion. A group of young gentlemen trundled in, talking and laughing. They blocked the view of the bin as they made their noisy way through. A porter quickly approached them to beg for quiet, as all the patrons had turned to look at them and their hubbub. They only laughed at being scolded, made their way in a circuit around the centre tables, and left again as quickly as they had entered.

Tim's skin rumbled with goose flesh. He cast a glance towards the rubbish bin and saw that it was empty.

'Ruddy hellfire!' he cried. 'Ben!'

Watson looked at the bin and cursed under his breath. He ran outside to catch one of the gentlemen, with Tim at his heels.

'Pardon me, sir,' said Watson to one of the young men, still laughing and smiling. 'How did you come to be in the post office with your chums at this time?'

'Oh, I don't know any of those gentlemen. A man came up to me and offered a pound note to walk a circle in this post office with other like-minded men. Easy earnings, eh, for such a silly prank?'

Tim was on his other side. 'What did the man look like? The one who paid you.'

'Well, he was a plain gentleman. Brown hair, brown moustache, well-made suit. A little older than me, possibly thirty-five, forty. Medium height and build. Nothing special. But his money was welcomed.'

'What colour was the suit?' asked Miss Littleton, coming up from behind.

The man looked her up and down in a way that made Tim want to plant his fist to his jaw. 'Well, now. All this interest in that man when *I* am available.' He smiled in a most unpleasant manner. Tim was gratified when Miss Littleton offered him nothing but a sneer of distaste.

'Your information is all I crave, I can assure you. What was his suit like?'

He seemed only slightly affronted but continued his vacuous smile. 'Brown tweed. Norfolk jacket, with knickerbockers and boots. Sort of a funny chap.'

'Which way did he go?' asked Watson.

'He came in with us, then left before us. That's all I know.'

They let the man go and commiserated. 'We've been tricked,' said Tim.

'He was clever,' said Miss Littleton.

'Too clever,' said Watson.

Miss Littleton looked back through the doors. 'Is there anything that can be gleaned from the site?'

Watson said nothing but pulled open the doors again and walked in. He was careful as he walked a wide circle around the wire rubbish bin. Tim looked too. No muddy footprints.

'Could it be Mister Hobnail?' asked Tim.

Ben shook his head. 'The man we questioned called him a gentleman, and by his suit and ready cash, this wasn't the hobnail accomplice.'

'Then we're back to nothing.' Tim kicked at the pavement.

'Not precisely,' said Miss Littleton. 'He will soon find that he has been tricked as well. He paid out at least ten pounds to these men as a distraction. We will receive another letter from him today.'

Tim brightened. 'She's right!'

A crowd of ragged boys suddenly surrounded them. 'Too bad, guv,' said Ned.

Tim bent down to him. 'Did any of the boys catch a glimpse of the bloke?'

'Oh, aye. Seb and Bert's got him on the run.'

'Why didn't you say so! Where'd they go?'

All the boys pointed down Tottenham Court Road.

'What are we waiting for?' cried Tim and took to his heels.

He pricked his ears, listening for running feet. It wasn't easy with the traffic noises of horse hooves, clattering wagons and hansom cabs, the rattling of the omnibuses, and the press of people walking along the pavement to and from their afternoon luncheons and teas. But he *thought* he heard them amid the shouts of what sounded like small boys.

He shouldered past people, who gave him odd stares, forgetting again that he was made up like an old man. No matter. He turned a corner and saw the tail end of flapping coats and shirttails from two boys who looked as if they could run no more.

'Where's he got to?' Tim yelled.

They turned and he saw how red their faces were, how ragged their breathing. They were all in, but they pointed into what looked like a derelict brick warehouse. Tim saluted them and tore open the door to rush inside. And there he froze, keeping his breathing under control and listening hard.

It was, indeed, a warehouse long out of use, with broken glass on the floor from empty window mullions, discarded papers and bits of plaster lying about, and some wooden chairs tipped over, a leg busted here, a back snapped off there. Light shone down in long rays of grey light with a city's population worth of dust motes suspended within it.

He listened . . . until he heard a floorboard above his head creak. He searched and saw a rickety wooden stair and took it as carefully as he could while still making haste upward. The footfalls moved, treading faster, and he quickly gained the floor above, standing still and listening more.

There! To the right, and off he went round square, metal columns, minding the holes in the floor, the dark shadows in the corners, and thought he could just make out a figure hiding in the gloom. He stomped forward, raising his cane. 'I've got you, my man. No need to struggle about it.'

But even as he approached, he noticed too late the footfalls coming up rapidly behind him. He turned only to be greeted with something hard coming down on his temple, and down he went into blackness.

He slowly awoke to the soft feel of someone bathing his face. The subtle scent of roses reached his nose and the foggy image of a beautiful woman was bending over him. 'This must be Heaven,' he croaked.

Then the unmistakable face of his colleague came into view. 'Not Heaven, my lad. Are you all there, Tim?'

'Ben? Ellsie? I mean . . . Miss Littleton.' He tried to sit up, but it was a mistake. His head rang like a gong. He put his hand to it. And then he noticed his bushy eyebrows, moustache, and beard were gone and the face make-up had been removed. Miss Littleton smiled indulgently over him. When he looked around, it was clearly their drawing room on Dean Street. 'Hoo! Me head.'

'Yes, you have quite a goose egg, Mister Badger.'

His fingers lightly touched the swollen part of the side of his head and he let it be. 'I almost got him, Ben. Didn't quite see him . . . but his hobnail friend did me in.'

'It's a good thing your head is so hard,' said Watson, but Tim easily caught the shadow of concern in his eyes.

'It's hard to kill me,' he said in a bragging tone. But he lay back and closed his eyes. 'It's the trying that is vexing.'

Miss Littleton laid a cold cloth over the bump on his head and he relaxed. She sat beside him, and he wondered if she realized she was absently combing her fingers through his hair. It helped to soothe.

'What now, Ben?' he asked, eyes still closed.

He felt Watson's footsteps walk slowly across the room. 'I don't know. Mister Holmes's method doesn't seem to be yielding results for us.'

'But it is. As Miss Littleton said, he spent ten pounds on that distraction. And he only wanted five hundred in ransom. What is it about Doctor Watson that he wants, because it can't be money. He wants to use him in some way.'

'Yes, yes. We must concentrate on the why. The magazines.' His footfalls tromped to the table where they left them in a pile, and Tim heard him slide the first one off the pile and flip through the pages. 'The question is, did Doctor Watson have the time with his kidnapper to use his casebook to leave us a clue? And what *was* that clue?'

The settee dipped as Miss Littleton rose. 'Where is his casebook?'

Watson moved across the room again and retrieved it from his chemistry table. 'Here. I've marked the page where it landed face down.'

She must have taken it, because she settled down on the settee again, and he could hear the swish of her skirts and the fragrance of roses returning to his sphere. 'Story titles, as you said before, Mister Badger. Notes on changing some little fact here and there, publication deadlines scrawled at the margins . . .'

'About the bloke,' said Tim, eyes still closed. It seemed to hurt less that way without the light from the lamp in his eyes. 'The young man said that he was dressed in a Norfolk jacket.'

'Yes,' said Watson. 'Would a man living in London walk about in a hunting jacket? Did that mean he's from the country?'

'As you conjectured,' said Miss Littleton. 'Then perhaps Doctor Watson isn't in London, despite the letters being posted here.'

'So as not to give away the location by the postmark,' said Watson.

'Then we *must* look over the stories again,' said Miss Littleton. 'Have you pen and paper? I suppose I could take notes in my notebook . . .'

'Here, Miss Littleton,' said Watson, striding towards the desk he used that was part of a bookcase.

She rose again and Tim felt bereft of her scent and presence. He settled back into the pillow at his head. 'I should be helping.'

'You're convalescing,' said Ben. 'We'll let you know when we need help.'

'I'll be the brains, eh?' He offered a smile.

'You'll be lucky if there's any left after the bashing you took.'

'Oi! Ben.'

A male hand pressed his shoulder. That took the barb out of the man's words. He was consoling Tim the only way he knew how. All Tim could think was *Poor Miss Murphy. I suppose he'd shake hands with her instead of stealing a kiss or two.*

Tim heard the inkpot lid being opened, a pen dipped in it, before Miss Littleton said, 'Tell me again, Mister Watson, about the stories *you* read. In greater detail, if you will.'

Watson paced. Tim longed to do so as well. It seemed to help them think. But the ache in his head wouldn't allow it. Instead, he concentrated on the stories he'd read, trying to break them down into little pieces.

'I read *The Case of the Darlington Substitution Scandal,*' said Watson. 'It was familiar in the sense that the solving of it was similar to *The Scandal in Bohemia.* In it, a woman was protecting her no-good husband when he substituted a forged document for one that his employers had entrusted him with. And then he kept the original for blackmailing. The man was a scoundrel, unfeeling, single-minded. He didn't care that his wife was vexed, and even used his own infant child's crib as a hiding place.'

'He sounds cold enough to perpetrate a kidnapping,' said Miss Littleton. 'What was the name of the man?'

'Charles Darlington. In prison, I suspect.'

'But if it happened so long ago, he might be out by now.'

'True. Make a note to investigate that man. If . . . if it *is* his true name.'

'Dash it!' she swore. 'I do not suppose we know whether Doctor Watson used true names or not.'

'He did,' said Tim. 'But . . . not all the time. Like you, Miss Littleton, he tried to spare the innocent from scandal. But he had no patience with true criminals.'

'And so he *might* have used his real name,' said Miss Littleton, 'despite the wife and child left behind. Although it seems likely that she would have used a pseudonym for herself and the child once he went to prison. The newspapers would have reported his

true name. I will look in the *Daily Chronicle*'s archives to find the original article.'
'That's good thinking, Miss Littleton,' said Tim.
'Thank you. Next?'
'That was the only story I read. Tim? Are you able to talk about the stories you looked at?'
'I can but try. Let me see. *The Arnsworth Castle Business*. Concerning a Miss Arnsworth. She was duped by unscrupulous property investors and nearly done out of her home. She was tricked into revealing where her jewellery box was and the criminals got hold of her deeds. But Mister Holmes saved the day.'
Miss Littleton's fidgeting showed her concern. 'Was she kidnapped or otherwise held hostage?'
'Well, she was intimidated and a prisoner in her own home. I reckon that's as bad as being kidnapped.'
Tim couldn't help but open his eyes and turn his head just a little to look at her. She was poised with her pen over the paper, the other end of the pen touching her lips. 'And the name of the culprits?'
'Two men. Ralph Barrington and Sidney Gough. They, too, are in prison. Again. It is unknown as to whether these names are true, but I have no reason to suspect they are not.'
'And the other story?' asked Watson.
'That would be *The Dreadful Business of the Abernetty Family*. It seems the whole family were schemers but they had fallen on hard times. So they invited some of the aristocracy to a gala and planned to steal their jewels. They succeeded in some of it, but were foiled when one of the older ladies confronted them and then hired Mister Holmes. Now, the youngest man in the family swore his innocence, but the whole family was packed off to Fleet. Any one of them could be out by now.'
'And I took on *The Case of Mrs Etherege's Husband* and *The Case of Old Abrahams*,' said Miss Littleton. 'In the first, Mrs Etherege's husband had gone missing, but it turned out that he had been in hiding from disreputable creditors. He hadn't been kidnapped as the wife supposed when she hired Mister Holmes. Now, the creditors had not been sketched out with much detail, let alone names, and so I believe we can exclude this story from consideration. Then the second story. In the Old Abrahams case, the man was an accomplished and well-known safecracker, and

though he was accused of the theft, in this case, he hadn't done it, and, in fact, helped Mister Holmes and Doctor Watson to solve the crime. It was a most interesting case.'

'I see a pattern here,' said Watson. 'None of these crimes involve a murder. And so any one of the perpetrators could be out of gaol and back to a criminal enterprise.'

'Well done, Mister Watson,' said Miss Littleton. 'And it must be that the good doctor recognized the culprit when accosted by him.'

Watson nodded. 'If it is indeed one of the people in these five stories – or let us rather say, *four* stories, as Miss Littleton suggests – then the doctor must have had enough time to flip through his casebook and carefully place it. How do you suppose he accomplished that?'

Tim lay back and closed his eyes again. 'Doctor Watson was an accomplished actor as well, and he must have twigged who the fella was without letting on that he had, and pretended that he still didn't know him. He's a cool one, is Doctor Watson.'

He heard Miss Littleton scratching on her paper. 'You both certainly know your jobs. You have no idea how I am enjoying watching you come to your insights. I know you didn't want me here, Mister Watson, but it certainly fleshes out the story for me. Well.' She made a particularly hard jab at the paper, dotting a full stop.

'*Can* we eliminate one of Miss Littleton's stories,' said Tim. 'I mean, this man hiding from his creditors when all the world – even his wife – thinks he's been kidnapped. Did the good doctor go along with it and then get away? Perhaps that's why the punter only wanted five hundred pounds in ransom. Because he ain't got him no more.'

'An interesting idea, Mister Badger, but if Doctor Watson *did* get away, why hasn't he reappeared, even to Scotland Yard, if he felt Baker Street was unsafe?'

'Doctor Watson would never stay away from Baker Street,' Tim muttered. 'He'd have found a way to secure it. All right, then. Let's eliminate that story, as you said.'

'So we are agreed. We shall call on your expertise, Miss Littleton, to look in the archives of your newspaper for all these criminal stories. I don't know whether you can find them based on their publication dates because as Tim has told me before, sometimes Doctor Watson took some time or even years before he penned them.'

'I shall get the help of the archivist who might have insights about that.'

'Then, if you please, Miss Littleton, you will investigate Ralph Barrington and Sidney Gough from *The Arnsworth Castle Business*, the safecracker Abrahams from *The Case of Old Abrahams*, the youngest Abernetty from *The Dreadful Business of the Abernetty Family* . . . Oh, and what was the fellow's Christian name?'

'Kenneth,' said Tim, turning the cloth to the cooler side to press it gently to the bump on his head. 'Kenneth Abernetty.'

'Very good. In the meantime, Miss Littleton, I'll see to this bloke here with the broken head.'

'I'm all right, Ben,' said Tim, eyes still closed in case opening them split his head wide open.

'I don't think a cup of Bovril will help in this instance. I'm having Mrs Kelly call for a doctor.' He must have walked to the fireplace because Tim heard him yank on the bell rope.

He listened as Miss Littleton gathered her things, stuffing the papers into her little handbag, he assumed. 'Then I shall be off. Do not run away while I am doing my research.'

'We wouldn't dream of it,' said Watson.

Her skirts moved past Tim and the door opened. 'Please take care of yourself, Mister Badger. We need you healthy to proceed with this adventure.'

'I shall do me best, Miss Littleton. I extend my thanks to you for ministering to me.'

'It was the least I can do. Gentlemen.' The door closed after her, but it soon opened again. Had she returned? But no, it was the gentle Irish lilt of Mrs Kelly that he heard.

'What can I do, Mister Watson?'

'Mrs Kelly, I would be obliged if you could engage a physician to tend to Mister Badger. He seems to be in a bad way with his head injury.'

'Oh my! Of course, Mister Watson. We do have a gentleman who attends to us now and again. I shall send word to him to come at once.'

And with that, Mrs Kelly swept out of the room.

Tim wondered if he'd ever be able to open his eyes again without the room spinning.

TWELVE
Watson

A bespectacled, grey-haired, but surprisingly spry old gentleman by the name of Doctor Alfred Fenwick arrived. Ben stuck to his side, seeing if he could discern good news from bad from the doctor's inscrutable face.

'Your friend must rest for the next twelve hours at least. He's taken a nasty blow, but he should do better by morning. He will have a rather harsh headache for a few days. Give him some of this morphia powder in a glass of water' – he handed Ben several packets – 'and he'll be right as rain. I must say, I am gratified to be able to assist the protégés of Sherlock Holmes. You must continue with your good work, gentlemen. In the meantime, let us move Mister Badger to his bed.'

They lifted Badger by his arms and allowed him to walk between them. 'I'll help him from here, Doctor Fenwick.'

'Very good. Now you rest, young fellow. Doctor's orders.'

'Yes, sir. Thank you, sir.'

The doctor bustled out of the bedroom and then down the stairs to the street again.

'How are you feeling, Tim?'

'Like me head was used to scoop out the Metropolitan Railway.'

'You'll get better. You have to. We have to find Doctor Watson.'

'I haven't forgotten. I'll just take a nap. I'm sure that'll help.'

'You must follow the doctor's advice. I'll give you some of this powder, eh?' Ben poured a bit into a glass of water, stirred it, and gave it to Badger, who drank it down with barely a wince and burrowed into the bedcovers. Looking his friend over before he drew the curtains, Ben walked quietly out of the room. 'Get well, Tim,' he muttered and sat in his chair by the fire, thinking of the four cases and how they could possibly relate to Doctor Watson's abduction.

* * *

After a time, Ben looked up from his newspaper since his mind couldn't concentrate on it. He had to *do* something! He rose and moved to his chemistry table. He picked up the letters and examined them with his big magnifying glass. A blurry watermark with a crown and something below it that he couldn't quite make out. There were fine lines running through the paper from the wire mesh the paper acquired from its manufacture. 'I must make myself a collection of writing paper,' he mused. Just like his ash, soil, and iron nail collections, it could be useful for comparison. 'But is this writing paper important as a clue?' Of course it was, he admonished himself. Wouldn't Mister Holmes inspect everything? It said so in the stories. So what did this paper tell him about the kidnapper?

He rubbed it between his fingers, feeling the tooth of the paper, the stiffness. It was good writing paper. He took his wooden rule and unfolded it to measure it. Five inches by eight inches, something typical for male letter writers. This one was cream-coloured and the envelope . . .

He thumbed through the papers before him. Ah! The first envelope. Gummed. No sealing wax. The handwriting on the front of the envelope was a good clerk's hand. Done with – as Badger had aptly supplied – a J-pen nib: narrow nib to almost a point, but flattened just at the end for a skilled wide or narrow penned line. Done by a gentleman, not someone like Badger, or even himself, though Ben had worked on improving his hand when he sent out invoices for their detecting work.

It was not *un*common paper, but still better than most. This *was* significant, then. The Norfolk jacket. The special paper. These all indicated a gentleman. It couldn't be faked. For even though Ben was intimate with these details, Badger wasn't the sort of bloke who would have known what to use and how. 'That leaves out the safecracker, then,' he muttered. It wasn't likely a safecracker would wear a Norfolk jacket or have decent writing paper. That left three stories now from Doctor Watson's casebook clue.

He picked up the letters again and held them up to the light. He wondered if this *was* rare paper, after all. Wondered if it could be got only in London. Or . . . only where the kidnapper lived.

He jumped from his chair and strode quickly to the bell rope by the hearth.

Mrs Kelly arrived and Miss Murphy soon after. They both stood before Ben with expectant expressions. 'Mrs Kelly, Miss Murphy. You indicated a willingness to help any way you could.'

'Why, yes, Mister Watson,' said Mrs Kelly. 'Anything you wish, sir.'

'Then, Mrs Kelly, Miss Murphy, I am going to ask an extraordinary favour from you two. That is, if you will, for the both of you to venture into the city and scour the stationery shops. All you can find, and ask the proprietors about this letter paper.'

He rushed back to the chemistry table, put his rule against each letter, and tore off a strip, one for each of them. He handed them over. 'Further, tell the proprietor that the paper is five by eight inches with a watermark that has a crown. I can't quite make out the rest of it. Ask if it's expensive and common to London. Or where else it could be obtained.'

'But Mister Watson,' said Miss Murphy, 'what of the evening meal? Who will prepare it? We don't know how long we'll be out.'

'We'll be pleased with cold meats, Miss Murphy. This is far more important.'

'I'm not certain I know of many stationery shops,' she replied. Her nose crinkled in an adorable way. He shook himself loose of the thought.

'There may be a fair few.' He walked to the 'magic box' in the heart of the drawing room and withdrew a handful of coins. This was the box that was mysteriously refilled by Mister Holmes, conceivably in person, but they had yet to catch him at it. 'Here,' he said, awaiting their open palms to drop a considerable sum into each hand. 'Take the omnibus where you can, but don't be afraid to ask the cabbies when you must hire them. They would know. Go to as many as you can find. Each of you must travel in opposite directions so that you won't repeat. Hurry, now.'

'What of Mister Badger?' said Miss Murphy. 'Who will care for him?'

'Don't you worry. I'll stay here. There's more work I can do.'

Mrs Kelly began untying her apron from behind her back. 'Mind the bell. They'll be no one here to answer it but you.'

'I'll be listening out for it.'

Miss Murphy began to untie her apron as well, and as she exited to get her hat and coat downstairs, she turned to Ben. 'Don't worry, Mister Watson. We're on the trail!' He saw excitement glitter in her eyes. What was in the air that sparked such adventure in the eyes of two strong women – one a maid and one a former socialite? He supposed he saw a bit of what Badger liked about Miss Littleton in the bright face of the Irish maid he'd come to adore.

'Thank you both.'

He listened as they thumped down the stairs.

With the newspaper still not enticing him, he returned to his chemistry table and read over the letters. Nothing could be discerned from the little amount of information to be found in them.

The front doorbell chimed.

Ben hurried out of the flat and down the steps. The post! He reached the little wire basket attached to the post flap just as a handful of letters dropped into it. He shuffled through them as he climbed the stairs back to their flat. Mostly bills from the butcher, the greengrocer, and assorted other vendors. A remittance from their last client, and . . . an envelope with nothing but the address to *Badger & Watson Detecting Agency.*

Hurrying his steps, he made it back inside the flat and settled by the fire. Taking the letter opener lying on the side table, he carefully sliced through the top and shook out not one paper, but two.

There was no cutting out of letters anymore. Just the careful and skilled hand of the writer. With a J-nib.

> *Not nice, gents. A trick like that could make me very cross. But I suppose it is merely tit for tat. You want proof that Doctor Watson is alive and unharmed. See the second note. But I warn you, this is the last time. You two are as hard to take as a bacon badger! I will send a new letter with new instructions. Do not fail to make this drop, gentlemen – with the real money this time.*

He quickly snatched up the other note. He wasn't familiar with Doctor Watson's hand, but after rising again to fetch the doctor's casebook, he settled in and compared the look of them. Then he read it.

> *This business is most distressing, but I am assured by my captor that I will remain in good health and released upon*

receipt of the ransom. I trust that Badger and Watson know their business.
Dr John H. Watson

Ben read it over once more, and again compared it with Doctor Watson's casebook. It did look to be the doctor's hand. Oh, how he wished that Badger was awake and feeling better! He needed to consult with him. He may not look it, but his partner was a sharp bloke when it came down to it. Just because he wasn't educated didn't make him stupid. He was clever, quick. Like Mister Holmes, he focused on trifles, and that made all the difference in their investigations.

And like a conjuring trick, there he was suddenly, leaning in his bedroom doorway. 'What's going on?' he asked sleepily. His hair was ruffled and he didn't look to be in too much pain, but . . .

'What are you doing out of bed? Let's get you back in there. You know what the doctor said.'

'I know,' he said, complying when Ben grabbed his arm and gently led him back to his bed. He sat. 'But I heard doors close and people talking and—'

'You don't have to worry yourself, Tim.'

'Is that the post?'

Ben hadn't realized he was still clutching the papers in his hand.

'Is that a new ransom note?'

Serendipity. Badger was awake, Ben needed Badger, and the man was already plumping the pillows behind him to sit up.

'You're supposed to be resting.'

'I've rested. And that tonic did the trick for the pain. So hand it over.' He snatched it from Ben's hand before he could further protest.

'Blimey,' he muttered. 'He's being a gent about it. Let's see the other note.'

Without comment, Ben handed it to him. Badger whistled. 'Ruddy hellfire. That's Doctor Watson, that is. Cor.' His gaze rose to Ben's. 'What do we do now?'

Ben grabbed the chair in a corner of the room and dragged it forward to sit by the bed. 'I've got Mrs Kelly and Miss Murphy out investigating stationery shops to find that paper the kidnapper used.'

'Blimey! You've got your own downstairs Dean Street Irregulars. Well done, Ben!' He slapped his friend's knee.

'Well . . .' He didn't know why he felt embarrassed by his partner's admiration. Badger often said complimentary things about Ben's insight and judgement.

'Say,' said Badger thoughtfully. 'We've got all these women investigating for us, haven't we? It ain't dangerous . . . is it?'

'I shouldn't think so. Stationery shops are ordinary enough.'

But Badger was already absorbed by Doctor Watson's note. He cocked his head and seemed to be reading it over and over again, if the slight movement of his lips was any indication. 'Ben, look at his wording. It ain't up to the usual prose of our Doctor Watson, is it?'

'It is a grave situation. I'm certain he was distracted.'

'I reckon that's true, but . . . Look here. He says "business" twice. Now why do you suppose he chose them words?'

'He was nervous. Fed up, even.'

'I think it's more than that. He knew we were going to see his note. So he had to make it count while, at the same time, not throw suspicion on it. Ben, my man, I submit to you, that this is a clue.'

'From the repeated word "business"?'

'Yes!' He suddenly grabbed his head. 'Moved a little too quick just then.'

'You all right, Tim?'

He slid down a little against the pillows. 'I reckon that powder's worn off. But I got me an idea. Which of the titles in Doctor Watson's casebook had the word "business" in them?'

He stared at Badger. What had Ben said? The man was good with trifles while Ben had completely missed it. He owed it to his worry over Tim. But he got up and grabbed the doctor's casebook from the outer room. Opening the notebook to the marked page, he read aloud, '*The Arnsworth Castle Business* and *The Dreadful Business of the Abernetty Family.*'

'It's one of them, Ben. I'm sure of it. Doctor Watson laid down a clue for us. All we have to do is take them stories apart to find out which is the one.'

'This is what *you* are going to do. Lie down and rest, will you? I can't be partnerless in this agency. I need you, lad. Now lie back and get back to sleep.'

'All right. But just because me head hurts.'

Ben tucked Badger in, and the man looked up at him gratefully before he closed his eyes again.

Now Ben had to get working to study both stories carefully. Spread them out, dissect them line by line if necessary, just as a surgeon would do.

THIRTEEN
Badger

In his dream, Tim thought he was a circus performer, walking across a tightrope far up in the air under a striped tent. He was doing fine until his foot slipped, and when he fell, his head felt a sharp pain and he was suddenly awake on the floor of his room.

He rubbed the side of his head, and though it was sore and his head still throbbing, it didn't feel as bad as when he'd started. He carefully picked himself up from the floor and sat on the edge of the bed.

His bedroom door slammed open. Watson was standing in his doorway in his union suit. 'You all right?'

Tim chuckled. 'Fell off me tight rope.'

'What? Are you delirious?' He rushed forward and placed his large palm on Tim's forehead.

'No, it was just a dream. I fell out of bed.'

Watson sighed heavily. 'How are you feeling?'

'Much better. I'm ready for toast and coffee.'

'That does sound better. I was worried about you and your thick head.'

'Right as rain now. If rain were hard balls hitting the side of me head, that is.'

'Get yourself cleaned up and dressed, and I'll tell you what I found from the rest of our Irregulars.'

Tim liked the sound of that. Everyone had been busy while he was out cold. He took himself gingerly to his washstand and poured the cold water from the ewer into the large ceramic bowl and scrubbed his face with soap. He stropped his razor and gently shaved his chin, all the while examining his face in the small mirror above the basin for any signs of injuries. No black eye. That was good. Nose and lips were where they were supposed to be. He wiped his face with a cloth and took care of the rest of his toilet before he dressed. Clean chemise and pants, crisp shirt laundered and ironed under the tender hands of Katie Murphy, and his favourite pair of tan tweed trousers with the pattern of lines running down the legs. He snapped his collar to the back of his shirt and tied his tie. With braces in place, he donned his waistcoat and suit jacket and preened before the tiny mirror.

'Good as new, Tim me lad.' Though he had had to go easy when combing his hair.

He emerged to the delightfully rich aroma of brewed coffee. Watson was already at the table in the drawing room and looked up. 'Welcome back to the land of the living.'

'Grateful to be here.' Watson poured him a cup and he sat, inhaling the scent of the hot beverage prepared the way he liked it. 'Thanks, Ben. So what marvels have the Dean Street Irregulars – both downstairs and our street boys – come up with?'

The doorbell.

'That would be Miss Littleton,' said Watson, calmly pouring himself a second cup. It was then that Tim noticed place settings at the other two chairs . . . and a fifth and sixth chair added to that.

He didn't ask. He simply allowed it all to unfold. And when Mrs Kelly knocked on the door to allow Miss Littleton to enter, Tim stood to greet her . . . and noticed Mrs Kelly enter along with Murphy.

'Good morning, everyone,' he said congenially.

'Are you better, Mister Badger?' asked Mrs Kelly.

'So much better, thank you, missus. And Miss Littleton, a pleasure.'

She seated herself and smiled. 'I am glad to see you upright, Mister Badger.'

'Me too.'

Watson gestured to the other two places and the women took their seats. Murphy looked a bit uncomfortable, sitting with her employers and a guest of high estate, but Tim noted that when she glanced at Watson, she seemed to ease herself and even allowed Mrs Kelly to pour *her* a cup.

Tim smiled wide at this assembly and rubbed his hands together. 'Blimey! Ain't we a fine band of detectives!'

Watson cleared his throat to cue Tim to calm himself. It didn't matter. He suddenly loved this. Loved that the whole household was now involved in their enterprise. He saw it as an expansion of their work and felt surprise that Watson had resorted to it.

'We've still got an empty chair,' he said. 'Don't tell me Mycroft Holmes is on his way.'

Watson snorted. 'I don't think Mister Holmes is in the habit of making house calls. No, we're waiting for . . .'

They all heard the front door slam and a quick thumping up the stairs before their door opened unceremoniously.

'The little blighter!' muttered Mrs Kelly. 'Coming through just as you please.'

'Cheer-o, all,' said Ned Wilkins, doffing his hat. He didn't wait to be asked. He pulled out the chair and grabbed a bun from the basket on the table. 'A cup of that coffee, if you please,' he ordered.

Tim couldn't help but chuckle. Ned was the spitting image of himself at that age, all brass and confidence. Come to think of it, he mused, that was him now.

Mrs Kelly took up Ned's cup and poured it full of milk before setting it before him.

Watson squinted at the boy but resumed addressing the assembly. 'While Mister Badger was indisposed, I garnered the help of the staff to do some investigating.'

'And bless me,' said Mrs Kelly, 'it was quite an adventure, I don't mind saying.' She exchanged a glance with Murphy, who eagerly nodded her agreement.

Ned ignored the rest and continued scarfing down any food within his reach. He raised his nose to the chafing dishes on the sideboard and licked his lips, but he finally seemed to sense by glancing at the stern-faced Watson that he wasn't allowed to do quite as he pleased and remained sitting, slurping his cup of milk and tearing at another bun.

Miss Littleton pushed the butter towards him. 'It would have been better if Mister Watson had sent me a letter in a timely fashion to tell me to abandon research on the other stories, but I was able to put them aside in a reasonable time to focus on the two he suggested.'

'It might be a good thing to know all the particulars,' said Murphy, unburdened by talking to her betters as equals. She was certainly growing in Tim's esteem. 'We only knew our part in it.'

'Well, as you know,' Watson began, 'Doctor Watson was kidnapped three days ago now from his Baker Street flat. From the scene of the crime, he seemed at first to know his kidnapper or assumed he was a new client, for he invited him in at a late hour. But things quickly turned when he realized the situation. He had enough time to leave us a clue.' He dug in his inside coat pocket and placed the casebook on the table. 'He had the presence of mind, once he realized who the culprit was, to leave this casebook open to reveal the titles of several cases that he and Mister Holmes solved a few years ago which included one involving this kidnapper. He'd left the casebook on the floor below his desk, face down, and, I must assume, unseen by this nefarious person. We had only the physical evidence of cigar ash from a brand Doctor Watson did *not* smoke, a hobnail boot's muddy footprint left on some random papers on the floor, a decanter of sherry and two glasses, and an eyewitness from the flats across the street who saw a dark coach with its lanterns unlit outside, waiting for the hapless doctor to be conveyed to it and to parts unknown. The last was so hastily done that the good doctor lost his slipper in the taking. The landlady of two hundred and twenty-one Baker Street received a kidnapper's note the next day with the letters and words cut from several newspapers, and we ourselves received one with a single word – "Don't" – warning us off helping. Of course,' he said, drawing himself up, 'we ignored the warning and proceeded to investigate. We drew the conclusions from the evidence that the man was a gentleman working with an accomplice – the hobnailed fellow – and was displeased when, at the ransom drop, we had not given him the very small ransom he had demanded. He was spotted by Ned's Dean Street Irregulars at the drop and pursued by those enterprising boys. We discovered that both the gentleman – who wears a Norfolk jacket and knickerbockers – and his hobnailed companion had been there, but their activities were covered by the clever method of hiring random young gentlemen to serve as a blind, a crowd to shield the men while they grabbed the drop. Some of our Dean Street Irregulars pursued, and Tim gave chase to an abandoned warehouse. And that's how our Tim here got coshed in the head by one of them.'

'My money's on Hobnail,' said Tim.

'The kidnappers sent us a handwritten letter admonishing us for trickery—'

'The nerve,' said Tim.

'And,' Watson continued with a warning look at Tim, 'with a note written by Doctor Watson himself, proving he was still alive and in good health. Miss Littleton here, a reporter for the *Daily*

Chronicle, and the chronicler of our own adventures, researched in her newspaper archives details of those cases penned by the good doctor that he and Mister Holmes investigated. Since Doctor Watson left us the clue of this casebook, we researched the stories mentioned, but it was only after the doctor's carefully penned note and the use of the word "business" twice that Tim twigged that this was an important clue as to the stories to follow. Two had the word "business" in their titles: *The Arnsworth Castle Business* and *The Dreadful Business of the Abernetty Family.* We could now focus our research – or, in this case, Miss Littleton could – on these two tales. And since we had the physical evidence of the notes, I asked Mrs Kelly and Miss Murphy to enquire in as many stationery shops as they could about this particular letter paper. And now we await everyone's report with keen interest.'

Tim clapped his hands. 'Very good work, Ben. Let's see that last note from the kidnapper.'

Watson took the note from his pocket and handed it to Tim, who read it aloud.

'Not nice, gents. A trick like that could make me very cross. But I suppose it is merely tit for tat. You want proof that Doctor Watson is alive and unharmed. See the second note. But I warn you, this is the last time. You two are as hard to take as a bacon badger! I will send a new letter with new instructions. Do not fail to make this drop, gentlemen – with the real money this time.'

Tim cocked his head at it, but then refrained since it gave his temple a throbbing ache. 'What's this crack here about me? Why is he calling me a "bacon badger"?'

Watson seemed perplexed, but it was Miss Littleton who chuckled at Tim. 'He isn't calling *you* a "bacon badger". It's a sort of pastie. Exclusive to Buckinghamshire.'

'Buckinghamshire? Maybe the bloke is from there!'

'That would certainly seem to be a logical conclusion.'

'Well, then.' Tim was all smiles again. 'Let's have it, ladies. Let's have the news from the "Downstairs Irregulars".'

Mrs Kelly blinked up at him, until she seemed to realize Tim was talking about her and Murphy. 'Well, I'll begin then, shall I?'

Watson renewed her cup with more coffee and she nodded to him.

'Thank you very much, Mister Watson. Well, as instructed, we both went in different directions to cover more ground. I went north and west, and Murphy went south and east. I must say, London has a fair few stationery shops of which I was not acquainted before this. With this sample' – she opened the handbag that was in her lap and took out the torn bit of paper – 'I enquired of each proprietor. I didn't have much success for some time, until I found a little shop on Bayswater Road. The very solicitous owner – a Mister Charles Rawlins – was pleased to see it and told me it was very fine paper and could be ordered through his shop but it was more easily found in Buckinghamshire, as the factory was situated in that county.'

'And that was precisely what *I* found,' said Murphy, looking only at Watson, Tim noted. 'A shop on Old Kent Road said the same thing. And so I call that a confirmation.'

'I would too,' said Tim. 'Wouldn't you, Ben?'

'I do. Well, that was excellent work, ladies. And Miss Littleton? What have you to add?'

'This has all been illuminating, ladies and gentlemen. I researched the specifics in both stories, and I must say, the evidence of the true events I found through the newspaper reporting of the time pointed me to one case in particular. And with the mention of Buckinghamshire, I've come to the inevitable conclusion that the story we are looking for is *The Dreadful Business of the Abernetty Family*. The titular family had estates in Milton Keynes – that's in Buckinghamshire,' she said with a directed look at Tim, 'though those estates were forfeited to the Crown after the family had been incarcerated. I have since discovered that the family involved had all died, either in prison or very soon once released. All but one son, the one who had vociferously claimed his innocence – Kenneth Abernetty. His current whereabouts are unknown.'

'Blimey,' said Tim. 'Did you find a reason for him to want to kidnap Doctor Watson?'

'Only in the specific sense that he and Mister Holmes were responsible for his ruin. I should think that was enough. Mister Holmes not being in the country, he took what – and whom – he could get.'

'Yet still,' said Watson, 'if he was completely ruined, then why such a small ransom?'

'And spending ten pounds just as a distraction,' she went on.

'And hiring a coach. He obviously had some funds set aside or hidden from the authorities.'

'Buckinghamshire,' mused Tim. 'In the country. That accounts for his Norfolk jacket. And for the complete disappearance of Doctor Watson.' He turned suddenly to Ned who was still slurping up milk and slathering heaps of butter on to his bun, much to Mrs Kelly's consternation. 'Ned, what of the coach and driver?'

He froze, wide-eyed, swallowed the lump bulging his cheek, and set down his cup back in its saucer. Wiping his hands down his disreputable coat, he settled himself. Tim noted proudly that he wasn't concerned at all by the company round him. 'I done what you told me, Mister Badger. I had me boys watch those two livery stables, and finally a coach and driver returned to the first one, at Saint Pancras. The man was questioned. Got all chippy with me boys, in fact, but when they told him there was a bob in it for him, he was all *How d'ya do*.'

He mimed touching the brim of an invisible hat as Tim imagined the coach driver did. 'Go on,' he urged.

'Well,' said Ned, sitting back in his chair and seeming to enjoy having a fascinated audience, 'he said he didn't know the man who hired him, didn't know what the bloke was up to, and when he pulled up to Baker Street, the man told him to douse his lanterns and sit and wait for him and another bloke. Presently, he said a confused fellow came down out of the building missing a shoe, but they both got in and the driver was told to take them both to the railway station.'

'Which one?' asked Watson.

'Euston Station. They both got out and went inside, and that was the last he saw of them.'

'What time was this?' asked Tim.

'Round about half past nine.'

Tim looked hard at the boy. 'Wait a mo. Where did *you* get a bob to give to the driver?'

Ned smiled and rocked his chair back . . . before the fiery eyes of Mrs Kelly forced him to set the chair back on all four legs again. 'Got it from his own pocket, didn't I?'

Oh yes, *just* like Tim was at that age. He smiled back, but when he caught the look Watson was giving him, he thought he should take a more parental tone. 'Now, Ned, that was, er, very wrong.

You can't be a Dean Street Irregular and fingersmith at the same time. It ain't done. It reflects badly on Mister Watson and me.'

'I'm sorry, guv. I just had to think quick.'

'That's all right, lad. Just don't let it happen again.' And then he winked at him from the side that Watson couldn't see.

Appeased, Ned set to on a third bun.

'It sounds to me,' said Tim, 'that a trip to Buckinghamshire is in order. But where in that whole county do we go?'

'May I suggest the small village of Milton Keynes?' said Miss Littleton.

FOURTEEN
Watson

Ned Wilkins ran off so quickly that Ben felt he should count the silver. Mrs Kelly and Miss Murphy didn't seem concerned, however, and thanked him and Badger for their little adventure, 'But it's time for us to return to the business at hand,' said Mrs Kelly. 'That of caring for this house. The floors won't sweep themselves.' She left their flat at a good businesslike clip, but Miss Murphy lingered.

'Bless me,' she said to him, 'does that mean I'm a detective now?'

She was all smiles. He reckoned he couldn't blame her. He found it stimulating as well. 'Certainly, miss. And a right good job you did your first time out.'

'Well, to be sure, it is a bit like shopping and keeping a house. There's more to it than cleaning and cooking. There are problems to solve. Not exactly life-or-death mysteries, you understand. But if something in the house breaks, there's the question as to whether we fix it ourselves – and learn mighty quick how – or we find an honest man to hire, which is not as easy as one might think.'

'Solving problems. Yes, I suppose that is the crux of any job, isn't it?'

'It is indeed. But now, I am afraid, I must be getting back to my work.' She sighed. 'The glamourous life of a detective must be set aside for now.'

'Glamourous, is it? I hardly think so. Sometimes it's chasing a vile criminal down some slimy alleyway. More like scrubbing the dirt out of London.'

'And I'd best get back to my own scrubbing. Good luck on your venture, Mister Watson.'

He gave a little bow. 'Miss Murphy.'

She hesitated at the door and turned back to him. 'Do call upon us at any time you need help. Since we are adequate to the task.'

'I surely will.'

She left in her little bouncing step and he stood in the doorway and watched her go all the way downstairs. When he closed the door at last and turned back to the room, Badger was grinning at him like a fool.

'It's a treat to see love bloom,' said Badger.

'Go on with you,' he said, feeling his cheeks heat.

'Well, gentlemen,' said Miss Littleton. 'It seems it is time to get ourselves to Euston Station.'

'No, Miss Littleton,' said Ben. 'It's time for Tim and *me* to set out. Thank you for your help, but now it's men's business. Danger lies ahead.'

The expression she wore could probably melt a lesser man with its piercing disapproval. But he stood his ground. Just barely.

Until Badger sidled up to him. 'Look, Ben. I promised her she'd go all the way through this case.'

Badger wanted her with them. It was clear on his besotted face, no matter the peril.

'It's dangerous, Tim. We've got no right dragging her through it. We're going right into the lion's den.'

'Pardon me,' she intervened, 'but isn't that rather up to *me* to decide? I did make a bargain with Mister Badger.'

'And it was a fool's bargain,' said Ben.

'Oi!' came the sharp retort from his partner.

'Tim, may I remind you that you made this bargain without consulting me? And as a full partner in this agency, I declare that bargain now null and void.'

'Oh, I see,' said Miss Littleton bristling and poised to pounce. 'I've done half the work for you and now you feel you can cast me aside? No, gentlemen. I am holding you to your agreement.'

'Now, Miss Littleton. Let's not be difficult . . .'

'Very well,' she said, adjusting the layers on her cambric eyelet blouse. 'But tell me, have you ever travelled by rail?'

Badger stopped in the doorway, his hat barely pressed to his head. Ben had no choice but to stop behind him, trapped in the room. Badger turned to him with desperation in his eyes. 'I haven't ever been on a train before. What about you, Ben?'

Ben sighed deeply. He hadn't. Not in the passenger side, anyway. He worked as a fireman in a locomotive for a brief time, but didn't have to navigate the ticketing and schedule side of it. He could study the schedule and make it out, he was certain. Probably. He frowned and pivoted towards the insufferable woman.

She had donned her coat and was buttoning it up. 'Well? What are you waiting for? The intrepid detectives should be flying from this flat to their adventure at the railway station. Don't mind me, a mere woman, who has travelled innumerable times on England's railways, who knows the schedules extensively, who knows the ins and outs of rail travel. But, of course, you don't need me, do you?'

Badger grabbed his arm and he knew what the man was going to say. He forestalled it by addressing her. 'Very well, Miss Littleton. For expediency's sake, we shall allow you to go along.'

'*Allow* me?'

'Please, Miss Littleton,' said Badger. 'We're now truly asking for your help. Again.'

She raised her chin imperiously and gave a curt nod. 'Come, gentlemen, and I will school you on the fine art of railway travel.'

Before he or Badger could hail a cab, she had stepped to the kerb and did so herself. The three of them crammed themselves inside as she told the cabby, 'Euston Station, please, driver.'

Off it went, the horse manoeuvring them into traffic and deftly winding in and out of wagons, omnibuses, and other hansoms, clattering over the cobblestones. The morning air was thick with fog and smoke, not nearly as bad as pea-soupers, but bad enough. It smelled of coal dust and reminded Ben of his time working as a chimney sweep. It wasn't a good job for a man with a girth like his, and he soon moved on to what he considered its opposite: that of a milkman. That was clean, but the early hours drove him down. It was soon apparent that it had not suited either. Driven to these various jobs to support his mother, nothing seemed to keep him there long . . . until he found his place at last as a detective, and if he hadn't met Badger with his unfaltering encouragement, it would never have even occurred to him to attempt it. Of course, once Sherlock Holmes stepped in as a benefactor, it certainly uplifted them to what they had today.

He cast a quick glance at Badger, who was pretending to look out of the window, but Ben knew he was looking at Miss Littleton instead. Speaking of love blooming, was it love for Badger? He'd been quite the ladies' man, but there hadn't been any since Miss

Littleton came into their lives. He certainly seemed besotted. But Ben well knew the outcome. Just because she wasn't part of the aristocracy anymore, it didn't mean that an uneducated and unlanded fellow from Shadwell had a chance with her. Oh, she enjoyed toying with him, he suspected. But he truly wished Badger would give it up, for that way only led to heartbreak, and Ben didn't fancy picking up the pieces.

Badger's gazing at Miss Littleton only made Ben wish Miss Murphy was sitting beside *him*.

Was he being smug about it since his own romantic interest seemed to be blossoming into . . . well, something? His mind drifted to the pert cheeks and charming smiles of Miss Katie Murphy. How she drank her tea or munched politely on her sandwiches and biscuits. Yet, just as quickly as he thought of her, he put those thoughts aside, admonishing himself for such indulgence. They had to concentrate on the business at hand – that of finding Doctor Watson and wresting him from his kidnapper's hands.

'You see, gentlemen,' Miss Littleton said, withdrawing a ragged booklet from her handbag, 'it is absolutely essential to familiarize yourself with your *Bradshaw*. It is a listing of schedules for rail travel anywhere you wish to go throughout Britain and Ireland.'

'Let me see that,' said Badger, and she handed it to him. 'Cor,' he breathed. 'Ben, this is a miracle book.'

Ben had heard of it but never paid it any heed, not seeing the need to travel outside of London. But now Ben did consider it. Yes, just as soon as he could, he would get his own copy.

The traffic seemed to slow once they reached Tottenham Court Road, and it reminded Ben to call upon the solicitor Miles Smith since his offices were along this street. He had been direct and honest with Ben, just as he had with their first successful case. He decided to contact him only once Doctor Watson was back home safe and sound.

'How about that Ned?' asked Badger, handing back the booklet to Miss Littleton. 'Enterprising fellow.'

'I somehow picture your face on that lad,' said Ben.

'That's the truth, that is. I *was* that scrapy gent once upon a time.' He smiled at Miss Littleton. 'You just don't know where the next Sherlock Holmes is going to come from, do you? Sometimes it's from the streets of Shadwell.'

'I must admit, Mister Badger,' she said, 'my opinion of street people has changed considerably upon meeting you. I blame my upbringing. We are taught as a class of people to care for the poor and sick, but putting it into practice has been challenging. Those of the upper classes think that a simple donation or two to one of many Christian charities absolves us. But I have learned through personal experience in my reporting duties that those donations are far from helpful, even though they might still be necessary. It will take a good amount of reporting to create real change in Britain. Consider the work of Nellie Bly.'

Badger cocked his head in that way that seemed to make people – particularly women – respond to him. 'I'm afraid that name isn't familiar to me, Miss Littleton.'

'She is an American journalist who changed the way her government responds to the insane. She and her editor got her temporarily committed to an insane asylum to expose the cruel and inhumane practices of such institutions. It takes courage and hard work to be a good journalist, gentlemen. That's why I insisted on going with you this time.'

Badger absorbed her words, but a devasted look washed over his suddenly pale face. 'Don't you ever think of doing such a dangerous thing as that other reporter, Miss Littleton. Why it's . . . it's . . . it's deadly dangerous, is what it is.'

'I am under no illusion that the British Empire is any better at treating these poor unfortunates.' She turned to face Badger squarely, her skirts and petticoats making a swishing sound. 'Did you know that a husband can institutionalize his wife for any reason at all? And she has no right to protest against it? That, gentlemen, is truly the insane aspect of all that.'

Ben entertained the fantasy of stuffing *her* into an asylum . . . but only for a moment. The desperate expression to Badger's face was enough to halt that train of thought.

'Tim's right, miss. There must be other ways to invoke society to change the way it does things.'

'Giving women the right to vote for their representatives would go a long way. Even electing a woman to the House of Commons would move more to empathy for their fellow man. No child should be exposed to the elements and live on the streets. Oh, I know how proud you were of your cleverness and nimbleness as a street urchin, Mister Badger, but I weep for that lonely boy who stole and lived like a wild animal in order to survive.'

Badger's fear for her appeared to change quite suddenly to one of indignity. 'I wasn't no wild animal, I assure you. And I had the good sense to get in with other boys in the same predicament. Together, we survived right well. And believe me, Miss Littleton, none of us wanted the life in an orphanage, getting hired out to the factories where our salaries wouldn't end up in *our* hands but in those of the people who ran them institutions.'

She pressed her lips tightly together. 'I understand your point, of course, but surely you wouldn't wish the same for your own offspring. If you had a child, you wouldn't wish that life on them, now would you?'

He sighed and admitted that he wouldn't. 'But I don't see no alternatives. There has to be something in between a corrupt orphanage and being a waif on the street.'

'That's precisely what we must make those in power aware of. That there must be alternatives. It's the government's responsibility. If only I could get an audience with the queen . . .'

Ben couldn't help releasing an explosive guffaw. They both stopped talking to stare at him. 'You, talking to the queen? I don't think so.'

She sat back into her seat, arms crossed over her chest, a low-lidded stare directed at him. 'You seem to think that making dreams come true is only for you and Mister Badger. Wasn't it only a fanciful notion the two of you becoming detectives?'

She had a point. But he didn't want to acknowledge that to her.

'It was *my* fanciful notion,' said Badger. 'But once I get something in me head, well . . . it's hard to get rid of it.'

'Then why is it so unnatural to imagine women getting the vote in order to captain their own lives? Or speaking to the queen in my capacity as a journalist? Or transforming poverty in London by reporting on it?'

'I concede it,' said Ben, looking down at his wide fingernails and suddenly pleased that they had no dirt under them when so many other professions he had practised in the past made them filthy.

To his surprise, that seemed to shut her up. She sat back, chin raised, with a self-satisfied expression on her lips. Though Badger was still staring at her with some puzzlement.

Don't try too hard to figure her out, Tim, he thought to himself.

She's a headstrong woman. I suppose, in the end, that's what you truly like about her.

The cabby pulled over into the queue of cabs at the railway station and announced, 'Euston Station!'

They tumbled out, Ben paying the cabby before joining his companions.

'Now, *I'll* get the tickets,' said Miss Littleton. 'For a first-class compartment, they should be about fourteen and eight.'

'*Each?*' gasped Badger.

'That includes return, of course,' she added.

'Fourteen shillings and eight pence,' said Ben, stunned at the cost. 'What if we don't go first-class?'

'Nonsense,' she said, fiddling with her handbag and digging out the fare. 'We'll need our own compartment so we can talk privately about the case and what our next move will be. It is the cost of doing business, of course. I'm off to the booking clerk!'

Before either he or Badger could say, the insufferable woman had already marched away towards the ticket counter.

Badger turned desperate eyes on him. 'Ben, is that right? Is it really that much money?'

'I . . . I don't have any experience buying railway tickets. And she seems to know all about it. We have to bow to her expertise in this.'

'Crikey,' he whispered. He clutched only once at his head, still in pain, no doubt.

She soon returned and handed over the printed tickets. They were more like cards, only the name of the railway was printed across the top, with the amount along with *First Class*, and each had their own printed number. What had they got themselves into? It was certainly one thing to pay for a hansom cab for chasing down culprits or information on London's streets, but quite another to buy first-class railway fares.

Ben reached into his coat and took out his coin purse. 'I can't let you pay for this, Miss Littleton. Let me give you some relief.'

'Don't be silly, Mister Watson. I consider it a privilege to be able to work with you two.'

Ben shook his head. 'I can't allow you to spend your own hard-earned money. This is our case.'

'And no one is paying your own fee.'

'We have a personal obligation. We wouldn't dream of taking a fee for such a situation as this.'

'Mister Watson, please don't be aggrieved. I am in a much better financial situation upon selling my house. Please. Let me do this for you two. And . . . for my imposing myself on your adventure.'

Ben still clutched his open purse, but Badger laid his hand on his arm. 'Ben, it's all right. If she says she can afford it, we must – as you say – bow to her expertise. But if you ever need anything at all, Miss Littleton, I'm your man. Er . . . that is, we're your men. I mean . . .'

'I understand you well, Mister Badger,' she said with a delicate blush to her cheek. 'And I very much appreciate the sentiments from you both.' Before he could stop her, she reached up and kissed Ben's cheek. And then she leaned into Badger and kissed his. Both of them were at a loss for words.

Maybe she wasn't so bad, after all, Ben mused, rubbing his bearded cheek, but at the same time, he thought, he still preferred the company and sparkling interest of Miss Katie Murphy.

She showed them on the ticket where they could find the coach number and the compartment, and as they walked along the train and appraised the shiny wood and polished brass, Ben decided that this might be the best way of all to travel. At least for long distances.

Ben hadn't liked spending the money on a cab at first either when they were more used to going by 'bus for distances farther than they could walk, but he understood its expediency. And now their sphere was widening to other parts of England, just like Mister Holmes and Doctor—

He pulled up short. He mustn't be thinking about such mundane things. He had the doctor's good health to consider, not the comfort of a first-class compartment. Even as they stood directly before it on the bustling platform.

'Here we are, gentlemen,' she said in a cheery tone. The compartment door was already open, and she stepped up smartly into it. She sat on the seat closest to the window and looked down at them expectantly, still standing on the platform.

Badger naturally moved in first and sat opposite her. Ben sidled in after and sat next to his partner. A conductor, with a tip of his hat to her, closed the outer door.

'Now we're ready, gentlemen. Soon we will be rattling along on one of England's greatest industrial achievements. After we are underway, the ticket inspector will come through and ask to see our tickets. We will present them, and he will punch a hole in them with an instrument for such. He will remember us and bother us no more. Simple.'

'Simple,' echoed Badger with an unmanly squeak.

FIFTEEN
Badger

He couldn't believe it. Not only were they shooting through the English countryside like a bullet through a gun – passing town after town, and even stopping for the occasional small railway stations in some of them – but he was sitting opposite the loveliest woman he had ever had the pleasure to meet.

The countryside flashed by, casting a favourable light on her face, though he couldn't imagine that face being unfavourable in *any* light.

He leaned forward towards her. 'So, Miss Littleton, you said you have done a lot of rail travel . . .'

'Oh, a fair bit. My family used to journey to our country estates quite often. And we did take the occasional trip to Scotland for the hunting season. My father was an avid fisherman and hunter.'

'Oh.' This was quite beyond his scope, and try as he might, he couldn't think of anything worthy to comment about that, except, 'So you had country estates, then?'

'Yes. Long gone too, I am afraid. It is a very expensive enterprise running an estate, what with a full complement of servants both indoors and outdoors. Father had to give it up to creditors years ago. But one does get invited occasionally to the country by friends and others often enough to make rail travel still important.'

'Must be nice getting invited to parties and to stay without any encumbrances.'

'There are many ways to pay, Mister Badger.' She turned towards the window.

He scooted to the edge of his seat and tried to capture her gaze again. 'I get the feeling that you don't do no travelling to these other people's estates much these days.'

Her body swayed with the train's motion and she eventually brought her gaze back to his. 'You are very astute. Of course, I expected that you would be.' She sighed. 'At first, well, I couldn't afford it. And I had my job as a reporter, so it was impossible to get away. And then, after a while, they simply didn't invite me anymore. I think they felt that now that I was part of the working class, we had nothing more in common. Silly, really. I am the same person I always was. My parents were the same people. I possessed the same likes and dislikes I always had done. The very same opinions. What possible difference did my financial situation make? But it did. First in subtle ways, and then more . . . overt. Being on this end of it, though, has been more than enlightening. It makes me want to delve journalistically into the differences between the classes even more and to fight the injustices. I am ashamed to say that it took my being in this unfortunate situation to see that. And in the end, who better to report on it?'

Tim thought about Edwina Lewis's scandalous offer and realized how little she seemed to know about her supposed friends. Perhaps she thought Miss Littleton was as shallow as she was. Maybe she *had* been . . . at one time.

Then he glanced at Watson to see if *he* understood what she was talking about, but Ben was looking at her, his brows furrowed. 'You mean your friends have disowned you?'

'Well, I suppose it can be characterized in that sense, yes. But in the end, what sort of friends were they, then? I know my class prides itself on its social mores and unwritten rules of society, and I lived by those rules as well, not really knowing any other way. And so, though it has hurt my feelings, I can stand back and look at it critically as an observer, as, indeed, I am with my profession as a journalist. I see how inadequate my class is in sympathy, and this is also why the poor in this country aren't treated better. When the generally held view of lower classes is that the poor are in their lot by their own fault, then there cannot be any reasonable social change.'

'Well,' said Watson, thoughtfully rubbing his knuckles into his bearded chin, 'it is a healthy way to look at it. I suppose action can diminish the hurt.'

'Indeed it does. Social stigmas aren't healthy for a society, and this long-learned behaviour must change.'

'And you think that women having the vote will do that.'

She slanted towards Watson now. Tim saw the light spring to her eyes as it always did when she was on a mission. 'It is imperative. Wives, mothers, daughters. We live every day with social stigmas, and we know it isn't *our* fault. *The fault is in our stars*, apparently, as Mister Shakespeare so aptly put it. We cannot have decent change in this country if we don't allow half the population, the population that makes England tick, their right to vote and hold office.'

Tim sat back. He didn't know if her undertakings were healthy or not, but they did give her something else to think about, he reckoned, so she could forget, for a time, that her friends were two-faced ninnies.

'Well, I say you don't need them friends,' said Tim. 'I think they're just jealous that you are becoming famous and they can never be.'

She smiled, and by that, he knew she wasn't feeling so melancholy. 'I don't know about that . . .'

'Oh, it's true. I can assure you. People know your name as well as ours. Ain't that the truth, Ben?'

Watson acknowledged that it was.

'You do have a way of looking at things, Mister Badger.'

Watson rose. 'I feel like a little walk. I'd like to explore the train.'

'Don't do anything to get yourself thrown off it,' said Tim, leaving Watson to shake his head at his unusual partner.

But as he sat back, Miss Littleton seemed to be staring at him through her lashes. 'And now we are alone,' she said enigmatically.

His collar was suddenly tight. He swallowed hard. 'Oh. Would you rather I get someone to . . .'

'Don't be absurd, Mister Badger. I have something to tell you.'

'Oh?' She couldn't be . . . she wouldn't be saying . . .

'Very soon I might be writing less frequently for the *Daily Chronicle*.'

'Oh no! But your livelihood—'

'Has been significantly improved. After I went to *The Strand Magazine* to research their archives for our case – *your* case, that is – they contacted me later to talk to their editor. It seems our stories in the *Daily Chronicle* have caught their attention, and they want to give *me* a monthly spot to publish my Badger and Watson pieces. I'll be making as much on these articles as I am receiving in salary for my work at the *Daily Chronicle*, doubling my income. And I have the both of you to thank for that.'

'Crikey! I had no idea. Congratulations, miss.'

She sat for a moment simply measuring his face. 'Whatever happened to you calling me Ellsie . . . Timothy?' she said softly.

His throat was immediately struck dry. 'Blimey,' he muttered. 'Well, I . . . I didn't know you liked it—'

'As it happens . . . I do.'

'And you . . . you just called me Timothy.'

'Indeed I did.' Her wide, smug smile infused her self-satisfaction. She rose and, with a little wobble with the train's motion, sat next to him. 'I hope you don't mind.'

'Mind?' he squeaked. 'N–not at all.'

She sidled closer. But suddenly, her cheeks blossomed with pink and she wouldn't look him in the eye. 'You know, I keep thinking about the time we kissed.'

'I do too,' he said huskily. *Blimey!* He never had trouble talking to girls before, but this woman always seemed to leave him on his back foot.

'And yet you haven't attempted to call upon me. Were you afraid I would say no?'

'Miss Littleton!'

'Ellsie.'

'You shouldn't be so bold. A woman ought not to—'

'Fiddlesticks! A woman is just as intelligent as a man. And therefore should have the same instincts, the same prerogatives. The same . . . interests.'

She got even closer.

'Ellsie . . .'

'I know I've been standoffish before, but I do like it when you call me Ellsie.'

Despite his discomfort, he couldn't help but grin. 'And . . . I'm not just a little charmed when you call me . . . Timothy.'

'Well, then . . .'

'Ellsie.' He slid back as far as he could against the window. 'I was under the impression that you . . . well, you seemed to have said before that you weren't looking for . . . for marriage.'

She paused. 'That is perfectly true. I don't need a man to fulfil my needs. I am becoming more financially sound by the day.'

'And that's . . . that's a good thing, surely. But a marriage ain't *only* for financial gain, now is it? It's about that certain bloke you're fond of, after all.'

That winning smile again. 'Of course . . . Timothy.'

'And, well, I was hoping that someday, that certain someone might be someone like . . . like maybe . . . me.'

She was suddenly leaning in even more, her folded hands now lying on his chest, her face near his. How did she get so close? He inhaled the scent of the rose water she used in her hair and swallowed hard. 'You *are* sweet, Mister Badger. I mean Timothy. Of course, I'm very fond of you. But marriage is out of the question.'

His cheeks heated and he felt a sharp twinge in his belly. He squirmed under her weight. 'Oh. I see. I reckon it's because of where I come from. But didn't you just say that your . . . your social class should be more open to all the classes?'

'Oh, Timothy, no. I *am* sorry. I am not making myself clear. I am simply not interested in marrying *anyone*. I have stated this many times before. I do not need a man to succeed. And I certainly wouldn't want one sending me to an asylum on a whim. I want to prove this to myself and all and sundry. A woman doesn't have to marry to be a credit to her sex or the community at large. She merely has to be useful in a meaningful way. I have nothing against your past.'

He ran his hand up his burning face. 'Then I'm confused. You don't have anything against me, but you don't want anything to do with me.'

She finally pulled back, her featherweight frame and her fragrant scent gone with it. 'But I didn't say that, Timothy. I have the greatest respect for you. In fact, I enjoy our time together, whether sleuthing or finding some other entertainment. And I am certainly open to the latter again. That's why I wondered why you haven't asked to call on me since that one time.'

'Oh. I see.' He felt stupid saying those words over and over, but he was just beginning to grasp that she wasn't interested in him as a permanent partner. 'But if you don't want to commit to me, are you going to see other blokes?'

'I haven't really thought about it. My time has been taken up with the work for you and Mister Watson.'

'So I'm convenient – is what you mean?'

'Timothy, you are taking this the wrong way.'

He jumped to his feet and paced, before the jostling of the train made him fall into the seat across from her. 'I don't see that I'm taking it the wrong way. You want a playmate, but not a husband. And here I was, thinking that I mattered to you. *"Timothy"* indeed!' He felt his face redden. 'I suppose Miss Edwina Lewis was right. She said you only wanted to dabble in the lower classes, is how she put it. And further, she said when you were done with me, she would be happy to take your place.'

'She said *what*?' Now it was her turn for a flushed face. 'Why, that harpy! What an incredibly rude thing to say. To you and *about* me!'

He tossed his head, crossed his arms over his chest, and turned away, watching the hills and farmland outside rush by the compartment window.

She muttered angrily for a brief time, before she quietened, seeming to change her tone after a while. 'Oh dear. Somehow, Mister Badger, I've hurt your feelings. And nothing could be furthest from my mind. Edwina Lewis notwithstanding – and I will have words for her at another time – I wanted to tell you that I was as interested in you as you are in me.'

'That ain't no reassurance. Because I had every intention of asking you to marry me. Someday. In the distant future. And here you are, throwing it in me face.'

She said nothing more, and he wondered what she was thinking. He flicked his eyes towards her. She was biting her lip. 'I apologize, Mister Badger. I had no idea of your intention. I am terribly flattered.'

'Flattery don't do much.'

'I *have* hurt you. I never wanted to do that. Instead, I wanted to assure you that I consider myself already – for want of a better expression – "your girl".'

His brows took turns flying upward and digging deeply into his eyes. The words rattled round in his brain until he finally understood what she was getting at in her longwinded way. '*My* girl?'

'Well . . . yes,' she said, suddenly shy.

He rose and stood before her for a long moment, merely gazing at her – at her gloved fingers fidgeting on her handbag, her cheeks blooming with the blush of the palest of pink roses – before he reached down, grabbed her by her arms, and lifted her to her feet. She didn't resist as he pulled her in, pressing her against him, and then he leaned down and kissed her.

It was very much like that other time when she had surprised *him*, but this time it was *him* leading the way, sensing her against him, his mouth on hers in so tender an embrace. He felt her hands against his chest, crushing the material of his waistcoat in her fingers, and her lips kissing him back, not shy anymore. Perhaps it would have gone on longer if someone had not slammed open the compartment door.

They broke apart so far that they both fell into opposing seats.

Watson stood in the doorway, mouth open. When he finally closed his jaw, his brows drew down into a dark burl. 'I leave you two alone for only a few minutes . . .'

'Sorry, mate, but you're the one who barged in.'

'I'm only going to say this once,' Watson growled.

'Once plus all them other times?' Tim muttered.

'Just once,' reiterated Watson. 'We are all working together. Mixing this kind of entanglement is fatal to this partnership.'

'Like calling on your own parlour maid?'

Watson scowled.

'How so, Mister Watson?' she asked.

'You write up our cases, Miss Littleton. What happens when you abandon our Tim after you're done with him?'

'Ben! Blimey!'

He glared at Tim. 'It's bound to happen. Or *you* will tire of *her*. What happens to our working relationship then?'

Why does everyone think she'll tire of me? he wondered angrily. Tim glanced at Miss Littleton. 'I *won't* tire of *you*, Ellsie. I swear.'

She looked at him, chin raised. 'And I shall not abandon you, Timothy. I'm your girl, after all.'

'Ruddy hell. So it's "Timothy" and "Ellsie" now, is it?'

She rose and laid a hand on Watson's arm. 'Mister Watson . . . Benjamin. I hope I can call you so since we are all friends. You must understand. Mister Badger and I . . . We have a unique relationship. Not only are we partners with you, but he and I are partners as well. Of a sort. There *is* undeniable mutual attraction.'

'Mutual attraction,' Tim echoed dazedly.

'We seem to understand each other. Oh, I know he doesn't agree with my stance as a modern woman.'

'Ellsie, how can you say that?'

She cocked her head and gave him a look. 'Mister Badger, you well know it's true. I accept that about you. Just as you accept that I will continue my endeavour to gain my full rights.'

'I'll be doing that?'

'Yes,' she said, looking at him steadily. 'You will.'

'Ruddy hell,' growled Watson again, flopping into his seat.

They were all silent for a time . . . until Watson, of all people, began a chuckle that bloomed into a full-throated laugh. The two stared at him.

'Miss Littleton,' he said, wiping the mirth tears from his eyes. 'Even you couldn't have penned this scenario in a penny dreadful. Well, now! Me and Miss Murphy, and you and Miss Littleton. It's mad.'

Tim's grin was back. 'Mad as can be, Ben.' He reached over and grasped Miss Littleton's hand and gazed at her. 'Mad in the best ever way.'

The ticket inspector slid the door open and Tim snatched his hand back. The man seemed to sense that Miss Littleton was likely a lady with her two servants, and he addressed his attention to her. 'Tickets?'

They each presented theirs and he punched a hole in them all. 'We'll be getting into Aylesbury Vale in a few minutes.'

Watson looked at his watch hanging from his waistcoat. 'It's on time.'

'I thought we was going to Milton Keynes,' said Tim.

'We are,' she said when the ticket inspector closed the door behind him. 'But this is the closest station. From there, we shall have to hire a coach of some kind to get to Milton Keynes.'

More money, thought Tim morosely. He couldn't help but think Watson would blame him for it.

But as they drew into the station, he began to feel a certain excitement. They were finally *doing* something, perhaps getting the upper hand on this kidnapper. They knew his name now – Kenneth Abernetty – and knew his location.

Tim smacked his fist into his palm without noticing he was doing it. *It's time to lay some hands on this culprit.*

SIXTEEN
Watson

Ben led the way across the platform and through the station to the road outside, where he expected to see cabs waiting. But there were none.

He turned to Miss Littleton – hating that he was on the backfoot with her and had to rely on her in this instance.

She seemed unconcerned and had that determined look about her, aware and scrutinizing their surroundings. 'I suppose we should probably ask the ticket clerk where the nearest livery stable is. This isn't London, after all.'

Of course. He knew that. Why was he so confused? He reckoned it was because of her and Badger's now blatant relationship flowering right in his face. Though she didn't take his arm, they did exchange some adoring glances at one another. He didn't like it. Couldn't help but think she would break Badger's heart. They were so unalike in all their experiences. How could anything like this *not* end in tears?

Miss Littleton marched to the ticket clerk, asked about the livery stable, and the clerk seemed to give his answer.

When she returned to Badger and Watson, Ben asked, 'So what do we know of Kenneth Abernetty?'

'He served in prison for some ten years,' said Miss Littleton. 'But there must have been family funds that were hidden from the police, for it was all confiscated after the trial.'

'What happened to the estate?' asked Badger.

'As I understand it, it went on the auction block. It was never purchased because of the perceived curse on the land and property. It certainly wouldn't be a very happy place to live, knowing all the swindles that went on there. And that the previous owners all went to prison and most died there.'

'That would be a woeful place to live,' remarked Badger.

'We shall have to hire a coach to take us to the estates,' said Miss Littleton.

'But we can't do that out in the open,' said Ben. 'Where is the element of surprise?'

Badger frowned. 'That's very true. We'll have to creep upon it. Perhaps near day's end.'

'And waste a whole day?' said the woman.

'Tim's right,' said Ben. 'We must be stealthy. He may or may not have reckoned we'd be able to find him. So let us get to the livery and consider our options.'

There wasn't even a horse trolley rattling down the high street of Aylesbury Vale – a small village of stone cottages and shops. They began to walk and soon saw the livery up ahead and hurried to the stable with its sign above the wide doorway that said, *M. Plover Livery for Hire*.

The three marched in and looked about for the proprietor.

'Now that I think on what you said,' she said to Ben, 'I suggest a trap instead of a coach. And we can operate it ourselves.'

'Eh?' said Badger, eyes wide.

'We won't need to hire a driver, Mister Badger. We can manage it ourselves.'

'You mean . . . *we'd* hold the bloomin' reins?' he squeaked. 'I've never so much as talked to a horse before, let alone driven one.'

'I can do it,' she said. 'I have many times—'

'*I'll* do it,' said Ben.

Badger pressed his hands to his hips. '*You* can drive a horse?'

'Course I can. All kinds of jobs required my taking the reins.'

'Bless you and your catalogue of jobs, me lad.'

While they discussed it, Ben noticed that Miss Littleton had pressed on ahead and engaged the liveryman in conversation. Ben jerked his head at Badger and the two of them quickly joined her.

The liveryman turned out to be Mister Plover himself and he did indeed have a trap and pony for hire for fifteen shillings a day. Before Ben and Badger could discuss it, Miss Littleton was agreeing and shaking the man's hand.

'Fifteen ruddy shillings?' whispered Badger. 'How are we to pay that *and* lodgings?'

'Er . . .' Ben looked in his coin purse. 'We'll have enough if we're thrifty.'

'I have a bit too.'

'Well!' said Miss Littleton, approaching. 'That's settled. He's preparing it for us and we can be on our way to stealthily examine the estates without calling undue attention to ourselves.'

'Next time, miss,' said Ben sternly, 'please consult us and speak of a price *before* you agree.'

'Oh, but I've paid it.'

'You what?' he said, scandalized.

'It was the most expeditious thing. Besides, I do have an expense account from the *Daily Chronicle* now. And since this is strictly business, it is certainly warranted.'

'Well . . . don't do that again. This is *our* investigation. And you must follow a certain . . . protocol.'

She seemed amused, with just the merest curl of a smile curving the side of her mouth. 'Yes, Mister Watson. In future, I shall consult ahead of time with you and your partner.'

'See that you do,' he muttered and turned away, looking for the trap and pony to be pulled round.

It was a sweet little two-wheeler, with seats atop facing inward on both sides. Ben would, of course, be in the driver's seat, while Miss Littleton and Badger would be in the back on either side. None of them had had time to prepare luggage, and it was just as well.

Badger climbed in hesitantly, but once solidly standing in it, he put out a hand for Miss Littleton. She grabbed her skirts, stepped on the little step, and pulled herself in. Ben hopped on to the driver's seat and lightly grasped the reins and the little whip.

'Where to? Do you have that handy bit of information, Miss Littleton?'

'I did tell the proprietor that we were looking for a cottage to let near the old Abernetty place, and he gave me excellent directions.'

Ben had hoped to trip her up, but she seemed to know her business, and without another word, he clicked his tongue and tapped the pony with the whip to get it going.

It wasn't long until they were on an unpaved country road, with houses and farmsteads dwindling, while flat plains and rolling hills of green greeted them. He took a glance over his shoulder at Badger, wide-eyed and looking all around him. He'd never been in such open country, having lived in the city all his life. The train was one thing, but to be in an open trap with a wide, clear sky above and nothing but green around him must have given him quite a turn.

'All right there, Tim?'

'Yeah. Just . . .'

'I take it you have never been out of the city before, Mister Badger.'

'I have not, Miss Littleton. It's . . .'

'*And did those feet in ancient time, / Walk upon England's mountains green: / And was the holy Lamb of God, / On England's pleasant pastures seen!*' She smiled. 'England's green and pleasant land indeed.'

'William Blake,' said Ben over his shoulder, just to show her she wasn't the only one who had read a book.

'Why, Mister Watson! You are full of surprises.'

'Not a bit of it.' He rolled his shoulders and snapped the reins impatiently again.

They found themselves between walls of green where the view was blocked by trees and the foliage in the verges, but then the road curved and opened before them again, with columns of trees on either side of the road. In the distance, a manor house, clad in honey-coloured stone, emerged from the pastures and stone walls that delineated each field one from another.

Ben felt her hand on his shoulder, and when he turned his head, Miss Littleton was right beside him. 'There it is. A lonely habitation.'

Perched on a hill, with woods, dark and tangled, beside it, the house seemed to look down sternly with its dark windows like eyes. Sheep grazed on the pasture before it, but there was no sign of humans moving about. All the windows were simply black rectangles. But, of course, it was midday and lamps in windows were not likely lit. He pulled the trap over to the side of the road, where the pony nibbled on the long sweep of grasses bending over the verge.

'It does look lonely up there,' said Badger. 'How the deuce are we going to be able to creep upon them unawares?'

'I wonder about them woods,' said Ben. 'Maybe there's a road or track through.'

Miss Littleton leaned forward almost over the side of the trap. 'It's possible. But how will we discover it?'

'When the guv talked about his adventures,' said Badger, 'he always said that the first order of business when you were in a strange place was to go to the nearest public house. All the locals would be there, you see, and at first you'd listen and then ask little questions that would lead to bigger questions.'

'That's excellent advice,' she chirped, writing it down in her notebook.

'All right. We'll find a public house,' said Ben, snapping the reins once more. 'And perhaps get ourselves a couple of rooms there for the night.'

He couldn't help but notice the blush that came to both faces in the back of the trap.

The Ploughman was a public house and inn at the end of a stretch of cottages, a butcher's shop, and a grocer's shop that also served as a post office at the outer reaches of Milton Keynes.

Badger waltzed in first, with a stride that said he was sure of himself in familiar surroundings, but as soon as Miss Littleton made an appearance, it was obvious to all and sundry that she was not the typical visitor. And when Ben walked in, no one bothered with subtle observation. He doubted that the inhabitants of this village had ever seen a black man other than in paintings or tavern signs.

They settled into a quiet corner table, and when the publican came round the bar and stood before them, it seemed he didn't know what to expect any more than their trio did.

Badger smiled up at him. 'A pint of bitter each for me and my friend here, and the lady will have a ginger beer. And if you could bring us some cold meats and cheese, we would be much obliged.'

The publican, with a walrus-like moustache that covered his lips and hid his expression, looked them over. His eyes particularly raked over Ben, and Ben was about to jump up and ask him just what the trouble was when the man pivoted and went to do his job.

'In fact,' Badger said loudly, 'I'll stake a pint for every man here! Just so's you all know we're friends.'

Ben glared at Tim, counting in his head the money they had.

But as usual, Badger seemed unconcerned. Out of the side of his mouth, he said, 'Relax, Ben. Everyone is suspicious of strangers. But they ain't that suspicious when he buys them a beer.'

He had to concede. Everyone suddenly looked more cheerful, the conversation restarted, and the room had a distinctly more relaxed tone.

'Well done, Mister Badger,' Miss Littleton whispered.

Presently, the publican brought a tray of two mugs of beer, a glass of ginger beer, and a plate of sliced beef, a wedge of cheese, pickles, and a fresh loaf of bread, along with a jar of mustard.

Badger rubbed his hands together, popped a serviette into his shirt collar, and offered the beef first to Miss Littleton, and then dug in with knife and fork on his own slices with a dollop of mustard.

'What would strangers be doing round here?' asked an old man on a wooden stool at the bar. He wore a long collarless workman's coat, stained and wrinkled, and a threadbare flat cap on his grizzled grey hair.

'Oh, a bit of rambling, a bit of riding in our trap,' said Badger cheerfully, cheeks pink. 'It's fine country here.'

That appeased the locals, though the old man still narrowed his eyes at them.

'Oh, aye,' said a man in rough woollens and wide braces. Ben decided he must have come from a farm. 'It's good country for sheep. You must be from the city.'

'London town, my lad,' Badger chortled. 'Time to breathe a little fresh air. Don't realize how sooty it all is till you get out here where a man can take a deep breath.'

'That's the truth,' said the man.

Miss Littleton took a sip of her ginger beer and wiped her lips with her fingers. 'We were wondering what that big house was on the hill.'

Another man in a patched work shirt and tatty bowler approached their table with his newly acquired mug of beer paid for by Badger. 'That's the old Abernetty place. It's a ghost house, just like its former owners. They was all hauled off to prison. Thieves, the lot of them.'

'Oh, so it's abandoned,' she said. 'How extraordinary.'

'Has been nigh on ten years. Was confiscated by the coppers and went to auction, but no one would take it. Cursed, they say.'

'It did look lonely up there,' said Badger with just the right touch of pathos, Ben thought.

'It's cursed right enough,' said a woman's shrill voice from a far corner. A drunken voice.

The men in the pub dismissed her with a wave of their hands, but Miss Littleton's eye seemed to spark, and she twisted round in her seat. 'Why do you say that?'

The woman got shakily to her feet. She wore a grey dress, black shawl, and black straw boater that had seen better days. Her brown hair was pulled back in a bun with strands of it flying free. She seemed to be young, perhaps in her twenties, but the gin made them hard years, and she already had the makings of wrinkles at the side of her eyes and mouth.

'If you're thinking about going up there,' she said to them, 'I wouldn't. He's right.' She motioned loosely towards one of the men who spoke. 'It's a ghost house. No one at all up there.'

She hovered over Badger and he shied back. Ben could smell the gin from where he sat. 'Did you know the Abernettys?' asked Badger.

'Everyone knew them,' she slurred. 'That was ten years ago. I was a girl then, but still working for them.'

Badger looked all around. 'Did anyone else here work for them?'

'What you want to know that for?' asked the woman.

Badger gave her one of his winning smiles. 'Just curious. You all made it sound so sinister.' He gathered everyone in with his grin, as if he was about to embark on a ghost story of his own.

Another old man, his moth-eaten waistcoat left unbuttoned over his striped shirt with no collar, walked to the bar to get a refill of his mug under Badger's grace. 'I used to sell my hay to them. And they paid me below market price. No one's sorry them Abernettys are gone. They were a blight on the land. Someone should take a torch to the place and be done with it.'

'It seems,' said Badger, still cheerfully, 'that we've stumbled into a genuine mystery right out of the pages of a penny dreadful.'

'That may be,' said the man at the bar, wiping the foam from his moustache, 'but the lass is right. I wouldn't go up there. I think the weather's taken most of the roof. Been looted too.'

'And how would *you* know that, Jem?' said the old man.

The others laughed. Maybe it was well known that Jem went up there and looted it himself. Jem seemed to bristle at the suggestion. 'You think you're clever, Tom. You're not. It's bollocks.'

'Here now!' said the publican. He jerked his head towards Miss Littleton.

Jem stared at her and touched the brim of his hat. 'Beg pardon.'

She made a small acknowledging nod like the nobility she was, which they all had recognized the moment she walked in. What was it about the blue bloods, Ben wondered. It emanated off them like a halo so that it was impossible *not* to recognize it.

'Still,' said the woman, 'it's bad luck up there. Full of the evil of them Abernettys. There wasn't a soul in this whole village they didn't swindle, from the grocers right up to the local magistrate. They owed me dad money, never paid it. Watched him wither and die and was glad of it, they were. Thought they didn't need to pay the debt to his kin. But they paid their debts in prison, they did. Died, the lot of them. And good riddance.'

'They were all guilty?' asked Miss Littleton with all the innocence she could muster.

Jem nodded, even with the mug to his lips. He lowered it and wiped his mouth with his sleeve. 'Don't you believe any tales about the youngest. He swore up and down he had naught to do with it, but there wasn't a soul who believed him. *I* don't believe him.'

'Did he die in prison too?' asked Miss Littleton.

'Nah,' said the woman. 'They let him go after those ten years. Wasn't enough, if you ask me.'

'Did he come back?' asked Badger.

'Never heard he had,' said the old man. 'Never saw him m'self. He'd be run out of town, I can tell you.'

The talk finally slowed and faded to the background again, until the publican came to their table to ask them if they wanted more.

'Thank you, sir,' said Ben at last. He hadn't spoken throughout the entire exchange, letting Badger and Miss Littleton do the talking as less distracting. The publican didn't seem to want to talk to him, but talk he would. 'We need two rooms for the night, one for me and my friend here and one for the lady. We also have a horse and trap that needs taking care of.'

He scratched the stubble on his chin. 'There's a common room of several beds for the gentlemen, but for the lady . . . er . . .' He continued to scratch his chin and Ben wondered if there were fleas here. 'The maid could give up her room for her. It's small but clean.'

'That will do very nicely, my good man,' she said.

Badger was staring at her, and Ben just knew he would say something he shouldn't, so he cut in with, 'That will all do fine. Shall I take care of the pony and tack myself?'

'We don't have no stableman here.'

'Very well,' said Ben. 'Tim, I'll take care of that. And you can take care of our bill.' He smirked at Badger's look of worry. Let *him* see to it if he was going to throw their money around so freely.

As the sun lowered, the maid showed Miss Littleton to her room where, with the giving over of a coin, she persuaded the maid to help her with her clothing. The publican showed him and Badger *their* room. It had several beds crammed together, but since there were no other travellers, he and Badger had the room to themselves. Ben lit up a cheroot that Badger stayed clear of.

'I was thinking, Ben,' said Badger, sitting on the bed that lowered considerably as its springs whinged. 'We should go up to the house tonight and look round.'

'I was thinking the same thing. We'll wait till all is quiet.'

'Right then. I'll just go tell Miss Littleton.' He sprang up and Ben stopped him.

'Do we really have to tell her? It will be dangerous, Tim.'

'But she's a bricky girl. Haven't you noticed?'

'I have. Still . . .'

'Don't worry, Ben. When have I ever been wrong?'

Ben rolled his eyes, puffed his cigar, and sat back on his own bed, springs digging into his back.

SEVENTEEN
Badger

Miss Littleton had been excited at the prospect and was ready in no time. They crept downstairs, disturbing no one. Even the boy who cleaned the ashes from the fireplace, who slept on a cot in the corner, never moved except to snore.

It was decided that they would need the trap, and Watson got the sleepy pony quickly hitched to it. They led pony and trap away from the inn and up the road before they dared climb in and ride.

'Good thing there's a moon,' said Tim. None of them had a lamp, which was just as well. It would probably be a bad idea to traipse about a deserted manor house with lights streaking every which way. This way, they were forced by circumstances to be stealthy.

The little pony trotted on with soft thuds. Watson had the foresight to cover some of the noisier parts of the tack with rags so as to quieten it further. Once they reached the crossroads, he slowed the rig. They had been able to establish earlier from the men in the pub that the road they wanted veered to the right and led through the woods.

Watson clicked his tongue at the horse and it dutifully followed his direction where the moon wasn't as helpful in the tangle of branches above them. Still, there was enough light and the pony could be trusted enough to take them along the path and not stumble off on his own into a ditch.

The quiet treads of the pony's hooves were the only sounds, except for the rustle in the brush and the occasional chuckle from an awakened pheasant.

Tim expected owls and other sounds, ready to reassure Miss Littleton, perhaps even with a bracing arm round her shoulders, but he didn't have the opportunity. He frowned into the quiet wood at its lack of helpfulness.

In the distance, a dog barked.

'Hope that ain't in the house,' said Tim.

'If it's abandoned as they say,' said Miss Littleton in soft tones, 'it shouldn't be there. My goodness, that dog does not seem to even take a breath.'

'I was never one for dogs,' said Tim in the same quiet voice. 'I always like cats better. They're quiet.'

'I can picture you by the fire with a cat on your lap,' she said.

When he turned to her, she flashed a grin. Maybe he *should* get a cat. But he didn't want to offend Mrs Kelly by her thinking he needed a mouser. She kept a clean, vermin-free house. And Mister Holmes didn't have a cat. He occasionally borrowed the use of a dog for his investigations, but the man didn't otherwise seem to have a kinship with animals. He had a mind that was too occupied elsewhere, Tim reckoned.

He peered into the gloom, broken only when the canopy above thinned and moonlight could stream over their path again.

The dog in the distance continued to bark, but it did seem to recede into the woods.

'It might be a gamekeeper's cottage,' said Miss Littleton. 'Or a woodcutter. It won't be near the house, so we have nothing to fear.'

The trap moved on until the trees dwindled and the boxy manor house rose up before them. Now that they could see it closer, it did indeed appear to be derelict. The only light in the windows was from moonlight flooding in from the open roof. Even Tim could see the outline of big beams slanting into the rooms on the ground floor, an angle they surely should not be at.

'Even if the house is in this state,' said Watson, 'there is still the kitchens and cellar.'

'He's right,' said Miss Littleton. 'Those would still be intact and habitable. Well. Such as it is.'

They left the pony and trap at the edge of the woods, tying the horse's lead to a log. One by one, they bent low and rushed across the open space of unkempt lawn towards the house. Tim turned to his partner. 'I know it's a deuce of a time to ask . . .'

Watson patted his coat. 'I've got my Webley.'

'I knew you would.'

'And I,' said Miss Littleton, whipping out a small pistol from her coat pocket, 'have my Pepperpot.'

'Put that thing away, Miss Littleton,' said Tim, grabbing it by the multiple barrels. 'Do you even know how to use it?'

The Misplaced Physician

'Of course I do. My father taught me *and* my mother to shoot a variety of guns. We did have shooting parties, after all. And my father didn't give a hang what people thought of his wife and daughter taking up a gun.' She yanked it back from his hand. 'Now shush!' She put her finger to her lips.

He and Watson exchanged exasperated looks, but could do nothing in the face of her stubbornness. Instead, they walked carefully, getting used to the dull moonlight, and came up to the house. They peeked into windows and found only dust, a few broken chairs, and remnants from curtains. Tim made his way to the unprotected main entrance. The door opened easily, and he caught it in time before the breeze could pick it up and cast it against the wall.

'I'll go in alone. Less noise that way.'

'Don't be absurd,' Miss Littleton whispered. 'It can't be safe by yourself.'

'Tim knows a fair bit about breaking into houses all quiet-like.'

She turned to Tim and measured him.

Sheepishly, he returned her appraisal. 'Well . . . I wasn't always a detective. And you did know that about me. About the housebreaking and all.'

She seemed to acquiesce and he got back to looking over the room before him.

He scrutinized the floors. They looked solid enough under the layer of dust and he stepped in, motioning Miss Littleton back and to keep still.

Cautiously, he stepped on to the floor and stopped, waiting for the floorboards to squeak, and when they didn't, listening for any sounds in the rest of the house. There wasn't just Abernetty, but Mister Hobnail as well. And who knew where the latter kept himself. Of course, much as he gave less weight to it, Tim had done plenty of housebreaking in his younger days, and he knew what to listen for, and so his ears were as wide open as could be. *Not a bloomin' sound*, he thought, even though he listened double hard. He turned back to Watson and Miss Littleton and made motions to indicate that he was going to go further in.

They acknowledged him with silent nods and waited in the doorway.

He moved softly through the rooms, skirting fallen beams and plaster. More bits of furniture that looters didn't want – a table here, a chair there. The chairs' upholstery was too rat-chewed to sell, the tables too scraped and chipped to be any good to anyone. He passed light rectangles on the wall surrounded by darker shading where paintings used to hang. It wasn't a bad house, just left too long in the weather, what with its broken windows.

There was only a parlour, a sitting room, a library bereft of books, and perhaps a morning room on the ground floor. He pushed at some of the walls in the library and morning room, but there were no secret panels to hide a man or mouse, though there were plenty of the little beasties running along the edges of the walls. He recognized the look of the dirt on the walls where their greasy little bodies would scurry up and down. It made him shiver.

He found the stairs. And because the ceiling had fallen in there as well, he knew they were probably in poor shape. He made certain to use the handrail for balance as he slowly ascended the steps and saw where some of the timbers had plunged through them. If he hadn't lived in places similar to this in London's East End, he might not have been aware of how bad bad could be. Someone like Miss Littleton might have gone clean through those cracked steps and ended up with a broken neck in the cellar. And he didn't like the thought of that at all. It was a good thing he had chosen to be the one to go through the house.

After a few steps, he stopped and listened again. There was a rustling he couldn't identify . . . until it flew at him through the stairwell, full of screaming and terror.

He barely suppressed a scream himself and nearly toppled down the stairs. He grabbed for the handrail with a hand to his heart, feeling it beat hard against his chest.

Ruddy bird!

He listened, but no other sound came from above, and so he started up again.

Once he reached the landing, he stayed low as if crawling up the stairs and peered about. No one there. Not that he could see. Slowly, he rose to a crouch and continued his creeping forward, careful of the fallen beams and slate tiles scattered about. He could look upwards and see the stars through the broken ceiling. Saw a barn owl flying silently by, grateful it hadn't decided to streak through the opening at him.

He shivered.

Looking down at the floor, he reasoned that though there might have been footprints before from looters – for there was not a thing worth a toffee left in the gallery or in the rooms when he looked – they were long covered over in dust and bird droppings. There were no beds, no furniture, no lamps or chandeliers remaining. Even the wallpaper was torn from someone stealing the sconces. Broken crockery was scattered everywhere on the floors. The townsfolk did a fine job of stealing from the thieving Abernettys. But there were no footprints now except for the ones he made in the dust himself.

He found the servants' stairs and took them, and even looked in on the maid's rooms, but there was nothing there either, and no indication that it had been inhabited at all in the last ten years.

'That decides it,' he told himself.

He carefully and quietly made his way back to the ground floor and met Watson and Miss Littleton in the doorway.

'Not a living soul, save for a pigeon that scared the life out of me. So it's time to investigate the kitchens below. That's the last place left.'

They all agreed to go together and made their way round to the back stairs to the kitchens. This time, Tim led the way with Watson behind him, and Miss Littleton taking up the rear.

They obeyed him when he motioned for them to stop and listen. The corridor was dark, but the arched entry to the kitchens themselves was lit by moonlight from the clerestory windows. Tim peered around the corner into the room . . .

Everything – every stick of furniture – had vanished, just like the rooms above. He was shocked to note the blank area where the Esse had been, leaving nothing but a stove pipe in the wall and soot all around it. Only the shelves attached to the wall were left, but nothing of the copper cooking pots. The heavy work table was also still there. Perhaps it was bolted to the floor. A fish block also remained, but there were no plates, cups, cooking utensils, cast-iron pots, wash basins. Only the lead-lined sinks for the scullery were still, surprisingly, in place.

And still no sound.

Miss Littleton went ahead with her Pepperpot at the ready and climbed the stairs to where the cook and housekeeper kept a small office to oversee the kitchen staff, but when she looked down through the broken windows, she shook her head.

It was then that the world seemed to explode with an immense report of gunfire. Miss Littleton was overturned with feet flying upwards and skirts flailing. Tim hit the floor on his belly and saw that Watson followed suit. His heart was pounding in his chest like a regiment of drummers, but the single thing that beat time in his brain was 'Ellsie! Ellsie!'

Someone shot her! He leapt to his feet and took the rickety stairs two at a time. Without thinking of the danger to himself, he yanked open the office door and saw her crumpled against the corner of the room, hat fallen into her face. He fell to his knees before her. 'Ellsie! Where are you hurt, my sweetheart!'

He wanted to enclose her in his arms, but he dared not touch her. Where was the blood? Where had she been hit?

Slowly, she pushed her hat up out of her face and gazed up at him. 'You called me "sweetheart".'

'I shall so call you that a thousand times, my darling, if you tell me where you were hurt.'

She chuckled. What was wrong with the woman?

'I've only hurt my pride, Timothy. It was *my* gun that went off. Something came at me and I am afraid my finger was too quick on the trigger.'

They both saw the shadow move . . . and when it reached the stream of moonlight, it turned out to be a cat. It sauntered out of the gloom, gave them barely a look of disinterest, and left through the half-open office door.

'Ruddy hellfire,' he whispered. Maybe he had to rethink cats in general. 'Then you ain't hurt at all?'

'Only where I'm sitting. If you could help me up . . .'

He grasped her arm and pulled her to her feet. She brushed off her skirts, tried to surreptitiously rub her backside, and looked up sheepishly. 'Now I've given the game away.'

'Of all the—' Watson stood in the doorway, glaring.

'It's all right, Ben. A cat scared her and she . . . well. She took a shot at it.'

Watson said nothing but bent down to retrieve her Pepperpot. He slipped it into his own coat pocket, and when she made a sound of protest, the look he gave her dared her to argue. She wisely said nothing.

'Well, as you said, Miss Littleton. If they were here, they aren't here now.'

'But that's ridiculous.' She stomped her foot, fully recovering her dignity. 'There is plainly no one here.'

They all stopped to listen. No sounds at all. No window sashes being cast up, no doors opening, no footsteps on the run. The blast of the gun would have awakened the dead, but nothing seemed to have transpired.

Tim tucked his hands into his trouser pockets, more relieved than he'd ever been in his life now that he knew she was safe. 'There's only the cellars left.'

Watson nodded. If the kidnapper and victim were here, this was the last place they'd be. They all made their way carefully down the steps and ventured towards the cellar door.

The wine would have been stowed there, and probably a store of vegetables and preserved fruit as well. But when they reached the door, the lock had been jemmied badly, including tearing some of the door edges off, and Tim would have been surprised to find even a jar of pears left in there.

Still, he approached it, and no lamp or candle illuminated the darkness. Surely Doctor Watson would not have been kept there!

Tim saw from the corner of his eye that Ben had pulled his Webley from his pocket. He struck a match with his other hand and revealed a stark room, and it soon became abundantly clear that no one had inhabited this entire house since the Abernettys were alive and well. Looters had come for a time, but even their footprints were lost to antiquity. The cellar was not being used for housing a kidnapping victim.

It was plainly a dead end.

EIGHTEEN
Watson

They made their forlorn journey back through the woods and on to the inn again. Ben brushed down the pony and put him into his disreputable paddock once more with a bundle of hay he grabbed from a clean pile of it, and the three of them returned to the inn as silently as they had left it.

When Badger was settled into his bed, Ben turned to look at him, his profile lit by the moon still high in their view. 'Now what?'

Badger turned his head that was lying on his folded hands. His eyes glittered as they gazed at Ben. 'Cor blimey, Ben. I haven't any idea. What have we done wrong?'

The plaintive tenor of his voice made Ben feel the stab of it too. For if they failed at this – to retrieve in good health Sherlock Holmes's bosom friend – they could truly no longer call themselves detectives, and the game would certainly be up.

'I . . . I don't know that we did anything wrong,' he said slowly, thoughtfully. 'We're going to have to go back to the beginning. Look at our notes. We made a decision somewhere that simply wasn't the right path. We chose the wrong story to concentrate on maybe.'

'But it made so much sense.'

'I know. It's like we've got to erase the slate. Start new thinking in another direction.'

'Ruddy hellfire,' his friend expressed in one long sigh. 'We're losing time.'

'But we must. What would the guv have done in this situation?'

'I don't know that he's ever been wrong.'

'I've read the stories. He has been. On rare occasions.'

'You're right. Let's . . . try to get some sleep. We'll start out early in the morning.'

Ben watched Badger for some time. He lay awake, his worried

eyes open and staring at the ceiling, even as Ben leaned over and blew out the candle.

In the morning, even before the sky was grey with morning's false dawn, Badger was up, washed and shaved, and just pulling his braces up over his shoulders. Ben wasn't far behind him. 'Why don't you go and make certain Miss Littleton is awake,' he told his friend. Usually, this would have cheered Badger, but he dragged his crestfallen figure to the door and opened it. The thuds of his slow footfalls climbing the stairs to the maid's quarters reverberated through the thin walls.

Ben performed his morning ablutions and was dressed quickly. By the time he got downstairs, he found Badger sitting with Miss Littleton. Apparently, she was an early riser.

They took tea, bread, and butter from the publican and sat as morose a company as ever there was. Miss Littleton sighed. 'I suppose that you are right. There's little to be gained by staying.'

Ben sighed as he removed her Pepperpot from his pocket and slid it across the table towards her. She seemed to take it almost reluctantly and slipped it immediately into her handbag. He'd never seen her so subdued.

They finished their repast and paid and thanked the publican. Then they readied the trap and pony. It was a long, silent ride back to town. They paid the liveryman at the stables, and walked slowly back to the train station. Digging out their return tickets, the trio waited on the platform benches, just as silent and glum as they had been at the inn.

'This will never do,' said Miss Littleton suddenly, turning to them both. 'What is the next step? This is the fourth day of Doctor Watson's kidnapping and we are no closer to a conclusion. We must do something!'

Badger slumped on the bench. 'Maybe we wait for the kidnappers to send a note again and we pay the ransom this time.'

Ben shook his head. 'I still don't think—'

'What else are we to do, Ben? We've tried. And we failed. It's now our duty to simply pay the bast— er, them kidnappers and get him back. That's the important part. Get him back alive and well.'

'So they can kidnap him again when the money runs out?' Miss Littleton looked aghast. 'Surely not!'

'What's to stop them? We certainly didn't.'

'Then it's time to call in Scotland Yard.'

Her pronouncement silenced them both. In his mind, Ben railed against it. Go to the police? That was admitting defeat! But in her straightforward way, it seemed she was urging them to do that very thing. And he hated to admit it, but maybe she was right. Maybe they just couldn't solve this one.

He turned towards Badger, who was looking back at him with the same fear in his eyes. 'I reckon we really did fail this time.'

'You tried, Mister Badger. Everything made so much sense.'

He seemed to appreciate the sentiment, but it did little to appease either of them. 'We can't fail Doctor Watson again. She's right, Ben.'

He didn't want to admit it. He knew she was right in this, but he said nothing, neither acknowledging nor denying it.

A train whistle in the distance alerted them to the arrival of the locomotive. They all turned their heads to stare up the tracks. The cloud of grey smoke from the stack was visible first beyond the trees, and then the locomotive itself churned around the bend. The smell of burning coal reached Ben's nose and he recalled well his time doing the hard, hot work of a fireman.

The bloom was off the rose for the train experience for Ben. Now it was just a means of transport back to London. Back to their lodgings on Dean Street. Maybe the last time they would see them with this failure. Surely Mister Holmes would not be happy with this outcome, and his 'little experiment' – as his brother Mycroft called it – would be at an end.

When they were able to board the train and find their compartment, he dared not look at Badger. He was certain his partner was feeling as low as he was. There was a lot of chins resting on hands as they stared out of the window. He could not even bring himself to look at the ticket collector, and merely handed his ticket over without raising his head.

After a while, it was Miss Littleton who suddenly broke the silence. Again. 'Cheer up, gentlemen. We may not have had the result we desired, but I am certain Doctor Watson will be returned to us. I can easily lay my hands on five hundred pounds.'

Tim finally raised his head to look at her. 'You *can*?'

'Of course.'

He wore a pained expression, as this was only more proof that she was well above him in station. Ben couldn't even offer any solace to his disconsolate friend.

'My newspaper will foot the bill. After all, they will be getting a sensational and exclusive story.'

Badger perked up considerably, but then surprised Ben. 'I don't want Doctor Watson to be part of no story no more.'

'Timothy!'

'No, I'm sorry, Ellsie. Miss Littleton. But seeing how it is likely the end of our detecting business, I don't feel it's right no more.'

'But Mister Badger . . .'

'Leave it, Miss Littleton. If Tim don't want it, we shouldn't do it.'

'But . . . that's why I came with you in the first place. To catch that exclusive story while it happened.'

'And you got it,' said Ben. 'While it happened. Because nothing happened.' He sat back again with arms folded.

The arguments had come to an end. There was nothing more to say. No rescue. No story. If their venture as detectives was over, they certainly didn't need the *Daily Chronicle* to report on it.

The train ride seemed to take longer than their going out, but that was expected, he decided. They had nothing but worry on their minds. When the train finally pulled into Euston Station, they left their compartment, sought an omnibus, and took that to the nearest stop to Dean Street.

They climbed the stairs to number forty-nine, Ben in the lead, and opened the front door. They continued up the stairs to the first floor as Ben got out his key, fit it in the lock to flat 'B' and entered. He stopped dead.

'Oi, Ben! What did you stop for?' said Badger, who had almost run into him.

There before him, in their drawing room, was his mother . . . and Katie Murphy sitting down to tea!

Badger pushed at him and he stumbled forward, and when Badger finally noticed what had stopped him, he drew himself up with a smile. 'Mrs Watson! What are you doing here?' He strode forward and bent down to kiss her cheek.

'I worried about your friend,' she said in her gentle patois, 'and I wanted to see if there was anything I could do.' She gestured to Katie Murphy who slowly rose. 'And I met your Miss Murphy,

Benjamin.' Mrs Watson clasped her hands before her and sat as she was, cocking her head and waiting for Ben to speak.

'Don't just stand there, Ben,' urged Badger. 'Mrs Watson, may I introduce Miss Ellsie Littleton, reporter for the *Daily Chronicle* and, incidentally, my . . . my lady friend.'

Miss Littleton stepped forward and extended her hand. 'It is a pleasure, Mrs Watson.' She shook her hand, and Mrs Watson turned her head mildly to stare at Ben.

Badger looked from one to the other Watsons. 'Er . . . why don't we all sit down?'

Miss Murphy seemed poised to dart for the door. 'Why don't I get more tea?'

'Please, Miss Murphy,' said Miss Littleton. 'You are a guest today. *I* will talk to Mrs Kelly.'

'Oh no, miss. *You're* the guest.'

'Nonsense. Weren't we all sitting together only yesterday morning discussing the case? I'll go.' Without another word, she spun away through the door and down the stairs.

'Bless my soul,' the maid murmured and slowly lowered to the settee again.

Mrs Watson sat in the chair opposite her. 'Benjamin, sit down.'

'Mother, things are a bit a-jumble right now. Maybe it's best—'

'Maybe it's best we all sit down,' said Badger, gripping Ben's arm and shoving him into a chair.

It was suddenly a topsy-turvy world. His mother, sitting to tea with his . . . with Miss Murphy, while the daughter of a baronet went to fetch the tea for them all. Maybe he had fallen asleep on the train . . .

'It was kind of you to come, Mrs W,' Badger was saying. 'We've been meaning to have you here for supper. But I have to tell you both that we've had a . . . what you might call a setback in the case.'

'Oh no,' said Miss Murphy. 'Whatever do you mean, Mister Badger? It looked like we had all in hand.'

'Yes, we thought so too, but we set out to Milton Keynes and did not find Kenneth Abernetty. We think he's the kidnapper,' he clarified, leaning towards Mrs Watson. 'Nor did we find Doctor Watson. And so we're sort of back to the beginning. And because we failed, we might not be detectives too much longer after this.'

'But Timothy,' said Mrs Watson. 'Even policemen fail, but they get back up and try again.'

'Yes, but we are here in these rooms by the benevolence of Mister Sherlock Holmes, and Doctor Watson is his bosom companion. To fail at this is a mighty big fail.'

Miss Murphy seemed perplexed. 'I can't understand it. It all had fallen into place. The paper was got from Buckinghamshire, and that's where you said Kenneth Abernetty came from. So he must be there. You said so.'

She turned her expression towards Ben and his heart leapt to his throat with the look of her. 'But we must have made a mistake somewhere. That maybe he *is* in London. Or it wasn't him at all. We must go back through all the clues . . .'

'But it had to be. The notepaper. The story Doctor Watson penned. The Norfolk jacket.'

It *did* sound logical. It *had* made sense. What were they missing?

Mrs Kelly entered with a tray, followed by Miss Littleton. 'I asked Mrs Kelly to join us to discuss the situation. The more minds that work on this, the better.'

Badger helped her with the tray, set the old cups and teapot on to it, and took it himself to the sideboard out of the way. 'It did seem the best course. I can't see that it was anything other than the Abernetty case.' He poured milk and sugar and tea without thinking to all the cups, as if by second nature.

What Ben really wanted was a brandy, but he took the teacup in all politeness and sipped the strong brew.

With teacup in one hand and the saucer in the other, Miss Littleton frowned. 'Perhaps what we need to do is go back to the "why". Doctor Watson was kidnapped by this person – be it Abernetty or not – for some reason for a very low ransom. Why? What did he want him *for*? Surely not a mere five hundred pounds.'

Badger slurped his tea, and then seemed to realize that it was impolite and instead swallowed the one big gulp of the hot brew before he tried sipping instead. 'I thought it was because he couldn't get Sherlock Holmes.'

'But *is* that the case?' she reiterated. '*Is* there some other particular reason he abducted Doctor Watson and him alone? Perhaps even waiting until Mister Holmes was out of town? Tell us again what you found at Baker Street.'

Badger deferred to Ben, and Ben began. 'There was the casebook open and on the floor under his desk, enumerating several older published stories. The ash from an expensive cigar. The slipper Doctor Watson lost. The muddy footprint from a hobnail boot. That was all.'

It was Miss Murphy who asked, 'Have you the slipper here?'

Ben nodded. 'We do, but it had no meaning other than the good doctor's being whisked away so quickly.'

'I should still like to see it.'

'Very well.' He rose and went to his chemistry table where the clues were kept. He grabbed the slipper and gave it to her.

She turned it over, looking at it carefully. 'Just an ordinary man's slipper,' she muttered. 'My father had a similar one. But what of this? The label.'

'What about it?' Ben asked.

'It says *Scriven and Sons*. The manufacturer's tag. *Scriven and Sons*. Could that be a clue? The maker's label?'

Ben sat back, looking at his tea but not drinking it. 'I don't see how. What would *Scriven and Sons* have to do with it?'

But Miss Murphy was going over the slipper like a bloodhound. 'Maybe not the manufacturer itself, but . . . Am I mad? Doesn't the *word* "scriven" mean something?'

Miss Littleton rested her teacup on her saucer. 'It means "writer".'

'I thought so,' said Miss Murphy. 'Maybe the good doctor didn't *lose* the slipper, but *left* it as another clue.'

'Because of the label?' said Badger. But then his face bloomed with surprise. 'Ben! Remember what *else* was a clue? What was *not* there!'

Ben thought a moment before he snapped his fingers. 'The nibs.'

'His pen nibs,' said Badger, pointing at him. 'Not one nib or pen was left on his desk. Not one scrap of writing paper in the drawer. The kidnappers took Doctor Watson in order to force him to *write* something.'

'Oh good heavens!' declared Miss Littleton. 'I see it all now! We were right all along, Mister Watson. The kidnapper has to be Kenneth Abernetty. He had always declared his innocence in the trial of his family. And perhaps he *had* been all along. But when he was released from prison, the one thing that he wanted was to set the record straight. That's why he kidnapped Doctor Watson and not Sherlock Holmes. He wanted the good doctor to rewrite the Abernetty case to exonerate him. He made Doctor Watson take all his writing things, and the good doctor knew the label in his slipper and left it as a clue, just as he left the open casebook as one.'

Ben was suddenly lighter with the information. He almost got to his feet. But then remembered the derelict house.

'All right. It still could be Kenneth Abernetty. It makes sense with this new information. But where the deuce is he? He wasn't in his old house. No one's been there.'

Badger, too, slumped. 'Then we're still back to the beginning.'

NINETEEN
Badger

They all tossed ideas into the pot. Miss Murphy suggested calling up the Dean Street Irregulars to scour London for him.

'Then why the Norfolk jacket?' said Tim.

'Maybe that's what he went into prison with,' said Mrs Watson. Everyone turned to the heretofore silent woman. She had been listening judiciously, thinking every time someone said something. Now she took in all their expressions and shrugged. 'It may have been the only suit he had.'

'Mother, you're brilliant.'

'Thank you, Benjamin. I always told you so.'

'All the letters came from London post,' said Mrs Kelly.

'It would be easier to make those posts whenever he liked from London itself,' Miss Littleton concurred.

'Then we're back trying to figure out where in London he is,' said Tim. 'Where are them envelopes?' He sprang up and went to the evidence table, shuffling the letters in his hand. 'Look here, Ben. The postmarks all say "London E.C.". That's London Chief Office.'

'But that still doesn't mean he's in London,' said Miss Murphy.

'No, it does not,' said Watson. 'Not either way. But now we must go on this new assumption that he *is* in London. Where is the General Letter Office?' he said to the room.

Of course, Miss Littleton answered first. 'St Martin's Le Grand. It is a very big, very crowded building. If you are thinking of posting your Dean Street Irregulars, they will have a near impossible job ahead of them.'

'I was thinking that too,' said Watson.

'It's gotta be done, Ben. Here. I'll run out and get Ned—'

'He's downstairs now,' said Mrs Kelly, standing by the window and looking down.

'Then get him up here, Mrs K, if you please.'

She gave a quick nod and threw up the sash. 'Here! Boy!'

'Wotcher!' came the shouted reply.

'Mister Badger and Mister Watson need you. Could you please come up?'

'Cheers!'

They heard the slapping of feet over the pavement and the quickened tread up the stairs. The boy slammed open the front door and then the flat door and stomped up to Tim.

'Right, guv'nor!' he said, tipping his hat. 'What's wanted now?'

'Ned, take your boys over to St Martin's Le Grand General Letter Office and see if you can't find that bloke with the Norfolk jacket. Or his hobnail friend.'

The boy screwed up his face. '*Where?*'

'The Post Office,' said Miss Littleton. 'At St Martin's Le Grand.'

'Right you are, miss! Whoosh!' And he was out of the door.

'I gotta admit, Tim,' said Watson. 'Those Irregulars was a ruddy good idea.'

'Steal from the best, I say,' Tim replied. 'And there ain't none better than Mister Holmes himself.' He faced the collection of women and Watson. 'So. What's our move?'

'Take a page from your own Mister Holmes's book,' said Watson. 'We find pubs near the General Letter Office and ask round if they've seen a man in a Norfolk jacket thereabouts.'

'A country public house is one thing, Miss Littleton,' said Tim, trying his damnedest to convince her, 'but the centre of London is no place for a *lady* in a pub or tavern. It just ain't done.'

'May I remind you for the hundredth time, Mister Badger, that I am a reporter and a reporter must go where the story is, regardless of whether it is "the done thing" or not.'

Watson was waiting impatiently at the door for him, and Tim gave a great sigh. He gently took her by the elbow to the other end of the room. 'Ellsie, please. I thought I lost you back there at the Abernetty house when your own gun went off. And I swore to m'self that if you were alive, I'd do anything you say from now on. But we can't be just another couple of blokes if you come along. We'll be noticed. Just like Mister Holmes told me when I grew up and wasn't any use to him as a Baker Street Irregular. "You are too obvious now, my lad," he told me. I weren't no street kid no more. I was a youth and looked like trouble. And bless me, but it was the truth. And a lady coming into a public house is trouble. No one will talk freely.'

'But they did at The Ploughman,' she insisted.

'Because we posed as dabblers. Innocent, stupid dabblers from the city. But in London, it's just regular blokes from the parish. You won't fit in. Any woman in a pub in the city is a . . . well. Best not mentioned.'

She sighed deeply. 'I suppose I shall have to invest in disguises as you do.'

'That's a right good idea. But, er, next time. All right?'

She sighed again, glowering at him, chin nearly to her chest. 'I have no other course but to accede to it.'

'Don't fret. Now I won't have to worry over you.' He looked back at Mrs Watson chatting with Mrs Kelly and Miss Murphy, and at Ben looking at his pocket watch. Since no one was looking, he quickly leaned in and kissed her on the cheek, then gave her a winning smile. 'I'll be back later. Watch for any post.'

She couldn't seem to help but smile too. 'You are very persuasive, Mister Badger. Timothy.'

He winked. 'I hope so.'

He and Watson took a 'bus, changing routes a few times to stop at St Paul's and walking the rest of the way to St Martin's Le Grand. Watson saw a pub immediately and pointed it out. The Lord Raglan. In they went and stood in the doorway, adjusting their eyes to the dimmer surroundings.

They made their way near some older men who seemed to have set up shop there, studying them and then the rest of the room to see if it could yield what he wanted. They left the old codgers behind and Tim went to the barman to order two pints of bitter. With glasses in hand, he looked round again to get the lie of the land, and saw several groups of men that looked promising. Toffs and clerks, mostly. He motioned to Watson to move to where he was alighting.

Tim noticed other black blokes inside and reckoned that Watson wouldn't particularly stand out, and that made him feel better. He sipped the rich beer and opened his ears to the conversation nearby. He looked at Watson and decided to test the waters. Saying in a loud voice, 'I'll wager none of these gents here have seen a man in a Norfolk jacket.'

Watson was sharp and immediately picked it up. 'Not this again, Tim. No one in London wears a Norfolk jacket.'

'Three shillings says they do.'

'Here,' said one of the men at the next table. He seemed to be some sort of clerk, for Tim noticed his suit was well trimmed and the fellows he was with were likely similarly employed as they all had ink-stained fingers. 'Did you just wager your friend there that no one in London wears a Norfolk jacket?'

Tim turned the smile he had for Watson to the other gentleman. 'Well, it's just that we've been having the same argument in all sorts of pubs throughout London, and I was saying here to me friend that it ain't the kind of clothes – a Norfolk jacket and knickerbockers – that you'd see in the city. Am I right?' And he waved his glass to the man's companions.

'I could take that bet myself,' said the man. 'For I *have* seen a fellow in a Norfolk jacket in this very public house.'

Tim framed his face with just the right amount of incredulity. 'No! You haven't, have you?'

The man raised his chin. 'I certainly have.'

'Well, now. You've seen such a man here in this very pub?'

'I have. Like clockwork. He was here yesterday and the day before, and I have no reason to believe he will not be here this afternoon.'

Tim laughed loudly. 'And was he carrying a brace of pheasant over his shoulder?'

The man sat steadfast. 'If you don't believe me, all you need do is sit here for . . .' He took his watch from his waistcoat and looked down at it. 'For another two hours.'

'Crikey. Did you hear that, Ben? Should we all wait? It's three shillings to you, sir, if you're right.'

The man checked his watch again and looked at his friends worriedly. 'I am afraid I have to return to my office. Er . . .'

Tim moved to the man's table and Watson followed and sat. 'I'll stake you another pint, good sir, even if you can't stay.'

'That's awfully decent of you.'

'Not a bit of it. I appreciate a good wager.'

The beer was brought and Tim settled back in his chair, merely sipping his own. Watson watched him with a bit of admiration in his eyes. Tim preened. 'Did you ever talk to him?'

'No, of course not. He usually has some other fellow with him.

Looked a bit rough to me.' He looked to his fellows and they concurred.

'A rough gent, eh?' He elbowed Watson. 'Sounds odder and odder. I feel like asking him what he's up to. Say! Maybe he's an actor come from a play!'

'Never thought of that,' said the man, gulping down a dose of his beer. 'But then . . . wouldn't he have been wearing face paint?'

'And he wasn't? Cor. I haven't an answer for that.'

Watson straightened and used his best diction. 'Perhaps it is best we wait to observe for ourselves.'

'Right you are, Ben. Even if our companions here can't wait about to see him.'

The first man seemed to decide something. 'You're right. I want to see this thing through. My superior can hang. He'll probably not be in for the rest of the day anyway.' He slammed the table with his hand. 'I *will* wait with you!'

Tim reached over and slapped the man on the back. 'That's the spirit!'

They chatted of small matters, the price of this or that, the music hall and their favourite songs, which they sang. Loudly. Tim fabricated an occupation when he was asked, and he deferred to Watson for his own story.

Tim and Watson were careful to nurse their single pints along, and let the other fellows order several more for themselves, until the appointed time arrived.

Tim stretched his neck to look over the many people in the pub as the population waxed and waned during the next two hours. The first man at their table – by the name of Frederick Gunn – checked his watch. 'It's about that time.'

'You just point him out to me and the three shillings are yours,' said Tim, putting three shillings on the table and scanning the people in the dimly lit tavern.

Gunn took another swig of his beer and almost choked. Tim slapped his back to help him, but he shrugged Tim off. 'Bless my soul, there he is!'

As Gunn pointed, Tim looked and sprang from his chair. 'Come on!' he shouted to Watson as he pushed his way through the crowd. A man with brown hair, with streaks of grey for so young a man, stood with another man in rough clothing. The former was clean-shaven with a cigar in his mouth – a Partagas most likely – and wearing a tan tweed Norfolk jacket and knickerbockers. He suddenly glanced over at Tim threading his way through the crowd with a few shoves. The man slapped his companion in the chest and ran.

Tim had nearly reached him when the rough fellow with a dark beard stretched out his leg to trip him, and Tim tumbled forward to his face on to the dusty floor.

He scrambled to his feet and slammed open the door. The man in the Norfolk jacket was gone, but Hobnail wasn't too far ahead. Tim turned on the steam and leapt.

They tangled on the pavement, with women screaming and men shouting. The man went for Tim's throat, but Tim managed to rear back and slam his forehead into the man's bearded chin, making that gong ring in his sore head again.

Hobnail kicked and sent Tim flying, but he jumped to his feet and reached for the man. Tim managed to secure a grip of his coat. But Hobnail tore it away from him, kicked out with that big, heavy boot that Tim just barely succeeded in avoiding, and hightailed it out of their tussle. Tim tried to go after him, but some of the men on the street held him back.

'Get off, you fools! He's a criminal!'

But it was of no use. They let him go too late, and Hobnail was only a distant memory.

'Ruddy hellfire!' Tim berated the men. 'You just lost me a kidnapper!' Disgusted, he swung away and ran into Watson.

'Hold, Tim. He's long gone now.'

'No! Ruddy bastard.'

The men crowding round them glared, some with curiosity, some with annoyance. But both Norfolk Jacket and Hobnail were gone.

Tim hustled through the throng with Watson at his heels, moving quickly from the crowds on the pavement before a copper arrived.

But look all they might this way and that, they saw no one resembling their prey.

TWENTY
Watson

'It was a good try, Tim.' He laid a consoling hand on Badger's shoulder.

'Not good enough, though.'

'But you did establish that he used this post office to mail the letters.'

'And what to make of that? It didn't necessarily answer that he lived in London.'

'The both of them were here. Would they leave their captive alone all that way in Milton Keynes?'

Badger took both index fingers and pressed them to each temple. 'We've got to think. We've got to use the method.'

'Hang the method.'

'No, Ben. We've got to. Sherlock Holmes's method *will* help us. Granted, he's got to use London post because it's quick. He's got twelve times a day to send us post. And Milton Keynes is only an hour away by train. We've seen that for ourselves.'

'But the house was empty.'

'That ruddy house. It's tricking us badly.'

'There's nothing more to do. We've got to get back to Dean Street.'

'I suppose.'

He stopped Badger on the street to look at his neck and to help him snap his loose collar back into place. 'You all right?'

'Good enough, I reckon,' he answered sourly.

They waited at an omnibus stand, and when the horse-drawn conveyance arrived, they hopped on, climbing to the rooftop to sit on the knifeboard bench. They huddled in their coats as the sky darkened, threatening rain. They both pulled their hats down firmly on their heads.

Even as morose as they were, Badger smiled and elbowed Ben. 'What did you think of your mum there chatting with Katie Murphy?'

Ben's eyes widened. 'I nearly had a heart attack.'

Badger laughed outright. 'They'd have to meet sometime.'

'I know, but . . . I just barely got in good with Miss Murphy. But I'm still not certain whether she's that interested in me.'

'Course she is. She couldn't keep her eyes off you.'

He blinked at Badger. 'Truly?'

'You've got nothing to worry about, me lad. I think she's smitten. And meeting your mum sealed the deal.'

'It didn't.'

'It did. Mark my words.'

The 'bus rattled on, stopping all conversation when it dipped sharply into potholes in the street.

'A little street maintenance wouldn't go amiss,' swore Badger.

'You notice the carriages swerve round it.'

'The carriage trade. Ah, how I'm going to miss getting about in a hansom.'

'I would tell you not to give up, Tim, but . . .'

'I know. Still, for five years, we've done it. Without great success on our own, and yet . . .'

'And yet . . . it didn't seem so mad a plan after a while.'

'After Mister Holmes stepped in. Ruddy hellfire, Ben.'

They fell silent again. The 'bus rounded a corner and came to their stop. They rambled down the steps just as the rain began and they scuttled down Dean Street to number forty-nine, holding their hats on their heads, before hurrying with the key to run up the stairs.

Ned had come and gone, reporting that he had not seen the men in question. Badger and Ben were about to sit in their drawing room when Mrs Kelly made a small shriek, suggesting that perhaps they should change into dry clothes before resting on her upholstery. They exchanged glances and agreed and retreated to their separate rooms to do just that.

Ben got into his dark green suit and pulled a flannel over his hair and tamed it with a comb and some pomade before he emerged at the same time Badger did in his brown suit.

'All right, Mrs Kelly?' asked Badger as he sat with his gamin smile.

'Much better, Mister Badger.'

'Well?' said Miss Littleton. 'Did you find him?'

'Almost caught him. Don't know if he'll be in that pub again, but it clarified where he mailed his post. And by the way, did any more come today?'

'We waited for you,' said Miss Murphy, handing the letter to Ben.

Ben took it carefully and walked with it to his chemistry table. He took up a pair of tweezers and pulled the letter free from the envelope. He dutifully dusted it with the black powder to bring out the skin ridge marks.

'Ben, read it, for cripes' sake!' said an impatient Badger.

When Ben was satisfied that the marks were visible, he blew off the rest of the powder with a small rubber squeeze bulb and straightened the page.

> Last chance. Leave the ransom at the foot of Nelson's Statue in Trafalgar Square At eight o'clock tonight. No police.

'That's straightforward enough,' said Ben, looking the paper over from front to back.

'At night, he wants it.'

'Under cover of darkness,' said Miss Littleton.

'Benjamin,' said his mother, 'this sounds dangerous.'

'It can be, Mum, but I don't intend to get myself into danger. Right, Tim?'

'Mrs W, you can be sure I'll be watching after Ben, just as he is watching after me.'

'And I will be there,' said Miss Littleton.

'No, you won't,' said Ben and Badger at the same time.

'Not this again,' she grumbled. 'Gentlemen, may I remind you—'

'Ellsie. Please. It's dangerous.'

Mrs Watson stood. 'I thought you said it wasn't, Timothy.'

'Well . . . er, it's not. For men. But for women—'

'I dearly hope you do not intend to finish that sentence, sir,' said Miss Littleton with a sneer only those of noble birth were capable of.

Badger had such a look of sadness on his face that Ben couldn't bring himself to leave him on his own.

'Against my better judgement,' he said, 'I think we must allow Miss Littleton to accompany us. Again. For perhaps the final time.'

'There he goes with that "allow" nonsense,' she said, shaking her head.

'Miss *Littleton*!' He was on his last nerve with her. *And good luck to Tim*, he thought.

'Oh, very well. I see that you are being magnanimous in this, and I thank you.'

'Ben!'

'Tim, she's going to come anyway. Why fight it?'

Mrs Watson moved away from the settee and stood before Miss Littleton with her hands folded before her. 'Miss Littleton, you are certainly an unusual young lady. I don't wonder why our Timothy seems smitten with you.'

'Mrs W! Not you, too.'

'Timothy, it is obvious to even an old woman like me. You take care to see that no harm comes to her.'

Badger seemed to mellow and offered Ben's mother a gentle smile. 'That's a wager you can take to the Bank of England, Mrs W.'

It was a long afternoon. Ben and Badger talked it through, turning over thoughts and clues, arguing back and forth on it.

Mrs Kelly kept trying to leave and drag Miss Murphy with her, complaining that they had the running of the house to do, and then Miss Littleton had gone back to her newspaper to enquire of her publisher for the ransom.

As the day turned to evening, Mrs Watson suggested making a West Indian dinner for them all, and Mrs Kelly was eager to watch her cook and learn the recipes. The two of them disappeared for a while to do some shopping at the fishmonger's, grocer's, and spice merchant before Miss Murphy finally pleaded her case to return to the scullery to wash dishes for the evening's repast since there were no longer clean ones available.

It was later that they heard the downstairs entry door open and the laughter and gay talk from Mrs Kelly and Mrs Watson, and it wasn't long thereafter that the wonderful smells of his mother's recipes started to wend their way up the stairwell from the kitchen. It was his mother's dish called Golden Fish, the Spanish-sounding Pescado Dorado, since, as she had explained when he was a child, the Caribbean islands were influenced by Spanish, Portuguese, and French cooking, along with island ingredients – including olives and capers – with all manner of different elements happily combining together. There was rice too, but it smelled more like the Indian rice so plentiful at some Indian grocery shops in Soho. Tomatoes, onions, pimentos, capers, limes, olives . . . it made his mouth water with hunger . . . and nostalgia. This was his father's favourite meal. He often said how he missed papaya and pineapple with his food, but the former was not available on these shores, and the latter was too expensive and reserved for wealthier tables as an exotic fruit. He had thought to venture to the West Indies someday, but didn't really believe he ever would.

He wondered how Mrs Kelly and Miss Murphy were getting on with it, with its strange combinations and peppers.

And he decided then and there to save his money to get his mother a pineapple for Christmas.

'That smells incredible,' said Badger. His companion's tastes were wide-ranging. He reckoned that's what came of a boy growing up without much food. Every morsel was tempting to *his* palate.

'When's it going to be ready?'

Ben chuckled. 'When it is. We'll be told. I hope your Miss Littleton doesn't miss it.'

Badger checked the clock on the mantel. 'She's been gone a while.'

'Maybe she's having a harder time convincing her editor than she thought.'

The bell rang below and footsteps went to open the door. Ben thought he heard Miss Littleton's voice, and up the stairs her feet trod.

Miss Murphy opened the door for her and gave her a companionable smile. *Oh dear.* He hadn't noticed, but while the landlady and maid visited with the daughter of a baronet, something had changed between them. There didn't seem to be that deference between mistress and maid any longer. Miss Murphy had become at one with Mrs Kelly, his mother, and Miss Littleton.

What have we done?

He shot a glance at Badger, but he wasn't paying attention. Instead, he was reading the latest novel he had acquired about some ghastly spirit inhabiting a house and causing havoc among those living there.

But Badger stood when Miss Littleton came into the room and helped her to remove her hat and coat. 'Did you get the money?' he asked.

'I did. It took some convincing from my publisher, but in the end he did manage to get it for me from his safe, though I did have to tell him a bit of the story.'

'I thought we weren't going to publish that.'

Ben sighed. 'Tim, give it up as a bad job. We need the publicity. Even if we cannot continue here in Dean Street, we'll have to hang our shingle somewhere else.' And he suddenly thought of Mister Miles Smith of Tottenham Court Road. Perhaps the lawyer would be accommodating and give them a corner in his solicitor's office. That would save them quite a bit of brass, come to think of it. And perhaps they could sleep in the attic. Who needed to spend so much on a landlady and a maid? Though the latter thought gave him a chill. Would he ever entice the likes of Miss Katie Murphy again if he were a failure?

No, not a failure, he told himself. Just a step backwards that could change their fortunes if they kept at it, especially Miss Littleton's stories. Badger had told him that she was hired by *The Strand Magazine* to publish their stories there now instead of the *Daily Chronicle*. Surely that would get more attention, since Mister Holmes's stories were also published in that magazine. *Imagine, Badger and Watson right on the same pages with Holmes and Watson.* It cheered him to muse on it.

Just as the clock on the mantel chimed six o'clock, Mrs Kelly, Miss Murphy, and Mrs Watson came through the door, bringing trays of plates and lidded dishes to the sideboard. Miss Murphy began to set the table with plates and bowls and silverware, along with wine glasses. She was very careful and deliberate with her place settings, and he allowed himself to imagine for a moment that she was setting a place at *their* home for *their* guests. But then he frowned.

If he was fortunate enough to convince the pretty maid to allow him to call on her and eventually *marry* him, where would they live? Would she still serve as a maid somewhere? Would he allow that? Would they *need* to? And what about Badger? He couldn't afford to live here on his own. Would he live *with* them? Or . . . *Cor blimey,* he wondered. Would he marry Miss Littleton and move into *her* house? Would she continue to work and write up their adventures?

Suddenly, Mister Holmes's words came back to haunt him. '*Have I not told you to keep your female associations to a minimum?*'

'Female associations,' he murmured under his breath. It was certainly complicating matters.

'Oh, Mrs Watson,' crooned Badger. 'That smells heavenly.'

'I hope you like it, Timothy. Now, you sit here, and the lovely Miss Littleton shall sit beside you, no?'

Badger complied and smiled at Miss Littleton as she gracefully took her place.

'And you, Miss Murphy, you sit here beside Benjamin.'

'Oh, Mrs Watson, I think it best that I stick to my place. Earlier was the expediency of the case, but we must find ourselves back where we all belong.' She darted a glance at Ben so quickly he almost imagined it, but she was being the smarter of the two of them. It wouldn't do to blend the upstairs with the downstairs. Working on a case together was one thing. But perhaps he wasn't being as mindful as he should have been. He watched, a little mournfully, as she left.

And then he couldn't help but look at Badger making gooey eyes at Miss Littleton, and her slurping it up. Well, some things might have a chance to change.

Mrs Watson, with the help of Mrs Kelly, went to each place and served up her fish dish with a little rice, and they all dived in with sounds of appreciation all round.

Badger closed his eyes and threw his head back. 'Mrs W, you've outdone yourself. This is what you cooked back in the West Indies?'

'That and more, but with more fruit. The markets in England do not have all the ingredients. There's a very spicy dish I used to make, but the spices are not here.'

'That's a shame, that. Ben knows I like a spicy curry.'

'How intriguing,' said Miss Littleton, looking at Ben's mother. 'Mrs Watson, what made you come to England?'

'Well.' She fussed with her serviette, took a sip of her wine, and retrieved her fork and left it poised over her dish as she spoke. 'My husband had decided that England was a better chance to make a living and a home, so we came. It was a very long voyage and I was glad to get to dry land! Once we arrived, we worked hard and saved our money and eventually opened our grocer's shop in Camden. That's where Benjamin was born. But the work was hard and slow to grow. Some in the parish welcomed us, while others . . .' She shrugged.

'That's disgraceful,' said Miss Littleton. 'What possible difference could your race make?'

'Some people do not like immigrants. And so we struggled. And eventually lost the business. Which ended up killing my husband. His heart could not withstand the strain.'

'I'm so sorry,' she said.

'I am, too. But my Benjamin' – she reached over and laid her hand over his on the table – 'he supports me as he has always done. I am proud of him for his accomplishments as a detective. I read the stories over and over.'

Miss Littleton glanced at Ben and kept her gaze steady. 'I have no doubt, Mrs Watson, that Badger and Watson will continue to thrive.'

The supper things were cleared away, and after Tim had drooled over the five separate hundred-pound notes, Ben returned them to their envelope. Since Ned and the Dean Street Irregulars had quit the post office hours ago, Tim set his boys in a constantly milling circle around Trafalgar Square as the minutes ticked away.

Finally, it was time. Miss Littleton left first to get there ahead of them, and Badger and Ben sent Mrs Watson home in a hansom and bid their farewells to her, promising to let her know the outcome.

And then it was Ben and Badger who set out to leave the drop. They took a hansom to Trafalgar Square, watching the lamplights all begin to bloom in the coming darkness as the cold hit their faces in the unprotected carriage until it came to a stop by the monument.

Badger stood and looked up to the statue of Nelson staring stoically out over London, while Ben put the envelope of money into a hessian sack and tucked it in around one of the lions at the statue's plinth. Then they climbed back into the hansom and their driver moved the carriage away up Cockspur Street. And when the hansom clattered on, Badger opened the folding door, slickly rolled out of the cab, and popped back on his feet to double back.

The driver looked back with a frown, but Ben reassured him that his fare would be paid and that he would be getting out at the nearest cab stand.

Once they reached the stand, he paid the fare and sent the cabby on his way. He stuck to the shadows, but Badger was much better at such clandestine movements, and all Ben could do was hold back. With a view of the statue and the square, Ben stuck to his place behind a pillar of a private bank – closed, of course.

He looked but he knew he would never see Badger. Or his Dean Street Irregulars, for surely they were milling round along the square as well. They were just as crafty as he was.

And now to wait. He dearly wanted to light up a cheroot, but then thought better of it. The smoke might give him away. He looked at his watch and could barely see it in the dim corner he had chosen to spy the drop, but he saw the big hand click on to the twelve and knew it was now eight o'clock on the dot . . . just as the distant tones of Big Ben chimed, muffled by incoming fog. The only question was, from which direction would the kidnappers come?

He was careful when he glanced round the edge of the column. He saw no one on the street except for a crawler in the doorway of a shut tobacconist. He watched her carefully, thinking it might be one of the kidnappers, but the poor thing never moved. Probably asleep from a long day of gin drinking.

He neither saw nor heard those boys that Badger put so much store by, but neither did Badger seem to be there, and he knew he was. And no one approached the lion at the southwest of the square.

When he looked down at his watch again, only ten minutes had passed.

Where the ruddy hell are you? He never liked waiting. He was no shopkeeper like his father had been. His dad had taken to it after an adventurer's life on the seas and then as a dockworker, and finally as a man who fell in love with a woman right where he came from and took her far away to England to set up shop. The man could stand stoically for hours, a bit like Nelson on his column. But perhaps that was what killed him, such a solitary stoic life when he had been used to so much more. Ben had told himself years ago not to dwell on it, but waiting as he was and having had his father's favourite meal that his mother had cooked, he couldn't help but think on it.

A shout!

He jerked up his head. How had he missed it? The ransom had been taken, and a man in a dark coat was wrestling with . . . the crawler! There was a scream, and Ben ran forward without thinking further on it.

Was Badger the woman? No, that had been a genuine woman's scream, unless he was an incredible mimic too. Boys darted in from all directions, including one from a sewer grate. But the man wrestled himself free and ran. The boys pursued, but the man was getting farther and farther ahead of them. Another man burst out of the shadows, and even as far away as Ben was, he could hear the man's steps slap the pavement and echo off the many Georgian buildings surrounding the square. It was Badger! And just as it looked as if he might catch up to the man, a hansom cab cut in front of him. The horse reared, and Badger fell back away from the hooves. There was some shouting exchanged between cabby and Badger, and by then the kidnapper was long gone.

'Damn!' Ben stopped, breathing hard from the exertion of running. He walked back to where the woman was nursing her wounds. 'Oi! You!'

He expected her to swear at him or run. But she did neither. The woman straightened from her bent position, put her fists to her hips, dark straw hat askew, and waited for him.

He got closer and couldn't quite believe the dirt-smudged face as he stared at her. 'Miss *Littleton*?'

TWENTY-ONE
Badger

Tim ran back to the woman who had struggled with the kidnapper, slowing his steps as he heard Watson declare, 'Miss Littleton!'

Ruddy hellfire! The woman was all made up to look like a crawler, with tatty shawl and all. And he saw she was holding up the hessian sack. 'He might have got away,' she said, pushing her straw hat out of her eyes and breathing heavily, 'but I got the ransom back.'

Tim exchanged a look with Watson. 'Miss Littleton,' he said at last when his shock wore off, 'you've put us right back to the beginning.'

'If we had caught him, it would have been the beginning anyway. It was Mister Hobnail, at any rate.'

'Did you see how we tried to catch him, Mister Badger?' said Ned, running up with several of the boys.

'I did. It was a rum situation, right enough. You tried, and that's worth some brass.' He dug into his coat pocket for his coin purse and dumped out a handful. 'That should do it,' he said, pouring the coins into Ned's cupped palms.

'Right-o, guv! Thanks from the Dean Street Irregulars.'

'I tip me hat to you all,' said Tim, touching the brim of his homburg.

Ned and the others were gone before he could blink, disappearing into the gloom.

'That's all well and good,' said Watson, snatching a glance over his shoulder at Miss Littleton again, 'but what do we do now?'

'We go back to Dean Street. If he truly wants his money, he'll contact us again.'

Watson didn't look convinced, and to tell the truth, Tim wasn't all that convinced either. If only Miss Littleton had not interfered! Except that none of them could seem to catch the horse-limbed

The Misplaced Physician

Mister Hobnail. Maybe it was time to pay a call on Detective Inspector Hopkins.

It wasn't even half past eight when they climbed the stairs to flat B, and all three dropped on to their respective chairs and settee.

'The method,' Watson began, 'is not helping us find where Abernetty is hiding out in London.'

Tim shook his head wearily. 'Maybe we ain't doing it right. We never looked for any associates of Abernetty. Maybe he made friends in prison. Maybe they have family here. We have to communicate with the prison and see if he had any associates that got out at the same time. My money's on Hobnail being one of them.'

'He was in Fleet Prison,' said Miss Littleton. 'I can enquire, if you wish.'

'This is a Badger and Watson investigation, miss,' Watson reminded.

'And yet you have asked for the help of your landlady, your parlour maid, and street urchins. Perhaps it's time to use a professional reporter. May I remind you we are running short of time?'

They all stopped as the doorbell rang downstairs.

It was too late for clients, wasn't it? Was that Ned returning? But Ned never rang the bell. Tim sat up as he heard footsteps coming up the stairs, not the stomping rush of the Dean Street Irregulars, but of Mrs Kelly and someone else. A woman?

The knock on the door, and then Mrs Kelly opened it.

'Begging your pardon, sirs . . . oh, and miss. But there is a lady to see Badger and Watson.'

A tall, thin woman with a pinched face pushed her way through. Her corset seemed to be particularly starched and she stood so straight it seemed that she might snap in half under the right circumstances.

She looked each of them over with a jaundiced eye through her black-rimmed pince-nez with its black ribbon snaking down from the glasses to a jet pin on her bodice, and finally set her gaze on Tim. 'Do I have the pleasure of addressing Mister Badger or Mister Watson?' But it didn't look to Tim that it was a pleasure at all. Her accent was affected from a lower-class part of town but trying to sound as if she was from a better one.

'I am Mister Badger,' he said cautiously.

'Then you are Mister Watson?' she said, swivelling her head towards his partner.

'That's right, miss. Miss . . . er . . .?'

'I am *Mrs* Cress. And I merely wondered if the detecting agency of Badger and Watson was in the habit of completely ignoring an urgent request from a client?'

Both Tim and Watson suddenly jumped to their feet. 'Oh no, missus,' said Tim at the same time Watson said, 'It is not our policy, no.'

She straightened her shoulders and addressed each in turn. 'Then can you explain why you have not replied to my desperate plea about my missing dog?'

Watson's face was a puzzle. 'Your dog?' But Tim ran to the chemistry table where the post for the last few days had been piled, and searched through the envelopes. It was coming back to him now, the lady from Somers Town with the missing dog named Wellington, and he dug it out of the pile and looked it over again.

'I remember now, Mrs Cress,' he said, reading the letter again. 'We've just been in a bit of a . . .'

But as he read it, a fierce percussion seemed to assault his chest. 'Blimey. The *dog*! The dog that wouldn't stop barking?'

'Yes. He might be a nuisance to some, but since my dear husband died, Wellington has been my sole companion. If you could but—'

'Ben,' said Tim, ignoring the woman. He grabbed his shoulders. 'The dog that wouldn't stop barking. The dog we heard back in Milton Keynes. The dog in the wilderness.'

'Couldn't be,' said Watson.

'It's logical. Mister Holmes would say that it was a trifle, a clue dropped into our very laps. It's got to be!'

'It's too much of a coincidence.'

'But look, Ben. Suppose Kenneth Abernetty heard this dog barking in London in Somers Town while on his way to Euston Station. He got him an idea and he found it and took it to guard Doctor Watson while he and Hobnail were away. It fits!'

'Mister Badger is right,' said Miss Littleton, eyes bright and gazing lovingly at Tim. He almost lost himself in that gaze, but snapped himself out of it.

'We've got to get back to Milton Keynes,' said Tim.

Miss Littleton glanced at the mantel clock. 'It may be too late to catch a train.'

'We've got to try. Come on!'

It was only when they hurled down the steps and reached the entry that Tim heard Mrs Cress exclaim, 'What about my dog?'

They must have caught the last hansom cab to take them to Euston Station, for the traffic was decidedly thinning for the night. They quickly climbed out, paid the driver, and rushed up the steps, with Tim holding tight to Miss Littleton's elbow to make certain she kept up, and it was then he remembered she was still wearing her crawler disguise. Well, at least she wore no face paint to make her look older, and just appeared like any woman from his former part of town.

They ran to the ticket clerk and asked for three tickets to Aylesbury Vale.

The ticket clerk looked over his shoulder to the wall clock and ticked his head. 'I'm sorry, but the last train left for Aylesbury Vale ten minutes ago.'

They desperately searched one another's faces for alternatives. Miss Littleton ventured, 'We could hire a carriage but it will take us hours to get there. Maybe not even till morning.'

'What are we going to do, Ben? Should we . . . shouldn't we call upon Inspector Hopkins?'

'No. Not yet. Let me think.'

Watson began to pace, looking back at the ticket clerk who was busying himself with his paperwork, and back to the platform. A locomotive was huffing on the tracks by itself, powering down for the day, with workmen going to and fro around it and then off to other duties.

Watson looked over his shoulder once more. 'I've got an idea. Come with me, and don't say anything!' That last was a finger pointed at Miss Littleton. She gravely nodded.

He led them to the platform and they walked as if they were simply waiting for someone. But Watson was inching them closer and closer to the locomotive, still huffing with the occasional release from the steam cocks.

He seemed to be waiting for something, but Tim wasn't sure what that was. Until suddenly, with a burst of energy, he swivelled and threw himself into the train's cab and motioned for the two of them to climb on. Tim, hoisting Miss Littleton by her waist, lifted her into the cab while Watson dragged her the rest of the way by her arms. Finally, Tim glanced both ways for anyone looking in their direction, before he leapt in and they all crouched down.

'Mister Watson,' Miss Littleton whispered, 'what are we doing?'

'Well, miss, it seems we have no option. We are going to borrow this locomotive.'

TWENTY-TWO
Watson

'We're going to *what*?' hissed Badger.

'It is Mister Watson's intention to steal this train,' she explained.

'It isn't a train,' breathed Ben, 'it's a locomotive. We don't want the train. Only the engine and the tender.'

'Ben,' said Badger carefully, 'you feeling all right? Because . . . we can't steal a train or an engine or whatever you're calling it.'

'Locomotive.'

'Whatever you wish, but we cannot steal it! What would Mister Holmes say?'

'He'd say, "Why is it taking you lot so bloomin' long to rescue my friend?" That's what he'd say. Desperate times call for desperate measures.'

'But . . . but Ben! We'll end up in Fleet right along with Kenneth Abernetty. And that's the end of Badger and Watson Detecting Agency for certain.'

'It's over if we don't do it. Now are you with me, or not?'

He looked helplessly towards Miss Littleton . . . who obligingly shrugged.

'I think we're in for a world of trouble,' Badger insisted.

Ben didn't have time for Badger's whinging. Slowly, he raised his head and peered over the side of the cab. None of the workmen were lingering near them, so he climbed out on the left side away from the platform, and walked quickly to the back of the tender with its generous pile of coal within. Trying to keep his boots as silent as possible, they crunched anyway over the ballast amid the sleepers. He situated himself between the tender and the cars, carefully lifted the three heavy chain links from the hook at the back of the tender between the buffers, and, with barely a screech of metal on metal, as gently and as quietly as he could, lowered the heavy chain with a slight clanking sound to the ballast. He ran back and ducked inside the cab again.

'Forgive me for asking the obvious,' said Miss Littleton quietly, 'but do you know how to work a locomotive?'

'Course I do,' said Ben. 'I was a fireman for a few months. That's the man that feeds the firebox. I watched all the workings of the driver and figured it out. Tim, it's you that needs to be the fireman this time while *I* serve as the driver.'

'Ben, I don't know what to do.'

'All you do is take that shovel and shovel that coal into *that* firebox there' – he pointed to the heavy iron door with the glow of coals within it – 'when I tell you to.'

'Oh. I can do that.'

'That's a good lad.' *It's a good thing this engine has been working all day*, he mused. It would have been impossible to hurry the heating of the water in the boiler or even to get the firebox hot enough without hours of work.

Ben stood on the left side of the cab and measured the valves and wheels. He checked the gauge glasses and the pressure gauge, the injectors, the water valve under the driver's seat, the brass handle for the blower, amazed at how much he recalled.

'All right, Tim, now listen up. You'd better take off your coat because it's going to be hot work – and dirty too. You can't just throw coal in any which way. We've got to get it stoked but quick since it's had a chance to cool a bit. Here's what you do. You need to cover the back and sides to make it burn the way it needs to, get me?'

'Back and sides. Yes, Ben.'

'All right. Start shovelling, and when it gets hot enough, we'll be able to be on our way.'

'What if there isn't enough water in the boiler?'

He stared at the woman with incredulity. For a woman, she seemed to make it her business to know about all manner of things.

'We'll just have to hope for the best. We'll have to hope a lot of things. Start shovelling, Tim.'

Badger unbuttoned his coat and peeled it off, muttering to himself the whole time, and handed the coat and his hat to the woman. He grabbed the shovel, dug it deep into the pile of coal at the back of the cab, and as soon as Ben shoved open the door to the firebox with his foot, Badger tossed it in as far back as he could.

'That's it,' murmured Ben. 'Now put another in the back and then take turns putting it in on either side and the back again.'

As Badger worked, grunting as he shovelled, Ben checked the blower handle to make sure there was enough air in the fire. He checked the water level again and it didn't look too bad, though he wondered if it would get them all the way to Aylesbury Vale. And then, of course, they'd have to make certain the tracks weren't switched, taking them in the wrong direction. The more he thought about it, the more he realized that all the little variables along the way might scupper them, including the police catching them before they could make the rescue themselves. Maybe they *should* have talked to Scotland Yard first.

Badger wiped his sweaty forehead with the sleeve of his shirt, getting it dirty with coal dust. 'How's the fire looking, Ben?'

'It's proceeding well.' He checked a glass gauge. 'Miss Littleton, keep a watch to make sure no one has spotted us yet. But don't let yourself be seen.'

She saluted and crept to the edge of the cab's opening and slowly lifted her head to peer along the tracks. 'So far, all is clear,' she said over her shoulder. She still clutched Badger's coat and hat close to her chest without even realizing it.

Badger continued to shovel in the coal and the cab itself was warming nicely. Too bad the driver had removed the kettle for tea from the shelf above the firebox, thought Ben. He could have used a cuppa about now.

'Mister Watson.' Miss Littleton was still spying over the edge of the cab, making as little profile as possible. 'I see some gentlemen making their way towards us from the far end of the platform.'

He checked the gauges once more and decided. 'That's our cue to go.' Praying that the firebox was hot enough, he wound the reverser forward and kicked closed the firebox. The locomotive lurched forwards.

'The men are walking quickly now,' warned Miss Littleton.

A little air for the firebox, a little teasing the reverser forward, and the engine started to move with more speed. Ben looked down out of the window to the drive rod and it was steadily picking up momentum, pushing the large drive wheels, and as they turned, the engine chugged and puffed. The locomotive slowly cleared the platform and Miss Littleton informed him that the men were running now. He couldn't resist reaching up and blowing the whistle.

Through the noise in the cab, it was impossible to hear any shouting, but he imagined what the workers would be saying about now, and it was not fitting for Miss Littleton's ears.

And then it was *her* that shouted a rather offensive word! 'Mister Watson!' she added.

He could see hands grasping the side of the window. One of the workmen had obviously leapt on to the side of the engine. 'Stop this engine!' he shouted over the chugging and puffing of the trucks beneath them. He brought his moustachioed head up over the side and glared at each of them. 'What the ruddy hell do you think you are doing?'

Ben froze, trying to decide what to do when Miss Littleton grabbed a metal cup used for tea and hammered on the man's fingers. He yowled and one hand suddenly fell away. The man swore, saying some very ungentlemanly things towards Miss Littleton. She hammered more on the remaining hand and it just as suddenly disappeared.

'I am terribly sorry!' she shouted after him.

Badger leaned out of the window next to Miss Littleton with as shocked a face as Ben had ever seen him wear. He turned back towards Ben. 'He's all right. Just took a tumble but he got back up. He shouldn't have said those things to you, miss.'

'Well, it can certainly be excused. We *are* trying to steal his train, after all, and I did hurt his fingers.'

'It's still no excuse for that ungentlemanly behaviour.'

'Tim! Keep shovelling!'

'Oh. Right you are, Ben.'

We're in for the nick now, he grumbled. Assaulting a railway worker. This will not go well for any of them. They had better be right about that dog! Looking back out of the window, the station drew farther away and they quickly moved down the tracks at a good pace, even as he calculated all the laws they were breaking. What would he tell his mother?

Miss Littleton wrapped herself tight in Badger's coat and crushed his hat to her chest. 'We are away at last!'

But for how long? 'More coal, Tim!' cried Ben through the puffing of the grey smoke – just the right colour, he noticed – wreathing the cab.

Badger bent to it, opening the firebox himself by its handle, and strong-arming the coal on to his shovel and placing it with care within the firebox. *The boy learns quick*, Ben mused. Maybe he won't mind breaking big rocks into smaller rocks in prison.

Soon they were firing like a cannon into the dark countryside with only the occasional lights of lamps in windows giving them scant indication that they were making headway. It was difficult to see beyond the head lamp blazing its trail along the tracks, and the occasional flutter of sparks from the stack.

After what seemed like a long while, Miss Littleton said, 'There's a station coming up.'

Ben leaned out and looked ahead as far as the head lamp allowed. No trains or engines in his way. He pushed the regulator forward and they zoomed ahead through the approaches and past a bewildered ticket inspector standing on the platform, watching them fly by him.

'That will get someone's attention,' said Miss Littleton.

Checking his watch, Ben reckoned they had something like forty minutes ahead of them, *if* they encountered no impediments. The alarm was out, though; there was no question of that. If the attendants at Euston Station hadn't reported it – and there was little doubt they had, especially the man who had grabbed on to the cab – then that gentleman at the country station certainly would have done.

We're truly in for it now. Well, that was another short occupation, being a detective. When you steal something this grand, there was no going back. But they wouldn't have taken the chance if a human being's life hadn't been at risk, and Doctor Watson's life was certainly one worth saving. Especially since they had botched up the ransom time and time again.

Badger stood back from the firebox and closed the door with his foot. He leaned on the shovel and wiped the sweat from across his brow with his sleeve. 'Well, Miss Littleton, you'll get your chance to write from a prisoner's point of view very soon. That's a certainty.'

'It will be worth it to save the good doctor. And, I dare say, my editor will be ecstatic to get such a story.'

Her editor, thought Ben. What a strange woman. He glanced at her, posture erect, chin raised, watching the track ahead as her hair blew back in a flutter from its careful coiffure, while Badger, when he had a chance to rest between coal shovelling, gazed at her with true admiration. Maybe they *would* make a good pair. If they ever got out of prison.

After a time, Ben checked the gauge glasses again. The water was slowly getting lower, but it seemed to him that it would hold out. The coal, too, would not let them down, though Badger was getting tired. But he was a strong lad and would fare well enough. Yet the last few times they passed country railway stations, there were larger and larger gatherings of coppers. The word had gone out.

'Ben,' he heard in his ear from Badger. 'Did you notice them rozzers at the station . . .'

'I did. Before we get to Aylesbury Vale Station, we'll slow her down so we can jump out before we reach it.'

'I'm glad you're a thinking man, Ben Watson.'

'One of us has to do it.'

'Oh, very funny.'

'Of course, I freely admit that perhaps this wasn't my best idea.'

'Look how far it's got us.'

'All the way to the nick.'

'We'll worry about crossing that bridge when we come to it. But Ben,' said Badger, 'what will we do when we get there? We'll need transport to get to the woods like last time. Will we steal a horse and trap too?'

'We'll try to come by them legitimately.'

'And what does that mean?'

'It means we'll hire them, even if we have to get the liveryman out of his bed.'

Badger ran a fist over his nose, leaving it smudged black from coal dust. 'Well, there's that at least.'

'I just saw a sign for Aylesbury Vale Station,' said Miss Littleton.

'Right. Time to slow her down.'

He applied the brake, pulled back the regulator, cut off the injectors, and opened the firebox. They all felt the train slow immediately. Ben watched outside the cab carefully for the speed, before he dared use the reverser handle which slowed it further.

'Get ready everyone. Best to use my side as it will not be visible to the village.'

Miss Littleton offered Badger back his coat, but, coal-smudged gentleman that he was, he refused it. They gathered round Ben and he readied to tell them just when to jump.

'Go!' he yelled.

Badger hesitated, but Miss Littleton didn't and leapt off the side. Badger, not wishing to look the fool, followed her directly. She *was* rather bricky, Ben thought, as he leapt out too. He landed on a tilt and rolled down from the slightly raised tracks into the underbrush.

The locomotive chugged and wheezed on at a much slower pace without them. Hopefully, someone would be able to jump in and stop it completely before it rammed into something.

Lying in the dark, he assessed if he had any broken bones. Bruised, but nothing else seemed amiss. He climbed to his knees and peered round for the others. Seeing movement behind him, he heard talking, a man and a woman, and realized it must be them.

But best to use discretion, he told himself, and he waited without a sound until they neared and he could spot them in the moonlight.

Badger's face was spotted with coal, but there was the clear, pale countenance of Miss Littleton.

'Over here!' he rasped out and waved his arm. Badger saw and pointed, and they made their way through the fern towards him.

'That was one ruddy ride, Ben.'

'The best I could do.'

'I applaud your ingenuity. And your more larcenist tendencies,' said the woman.

'Needs must, Miss Littleton. Now, to get us into town without raising any alarm.'

'I suggest we head directly to the livery stable,' she said. 'I noted a cottage behind it. It must be the proprietor's.'

'Let us hope it is,' he said, and, straightening, he headed over the tracks to the road where the cottages and shops began.

TWENTY-THREE
Badger

Tim hurried ahead in long, crouching strides, trying to keep his head down. Looking left, then to the right, he saw no one along the streets that could possibly point a finger at them. Not that it mattered since that railway man got a good look at them before Miss Littleton bashed his fingers to rid them of him. He couldn't believe she had done that, but why not? She was as impetuous as they came. And he admitted to himself that he liked her even more for it.

Ahead was the livery stables and behind it the cottage, but before he could reach it, Miss Littleton stopped him and pointed to the water trough. He shook his head, not understanding what she meant when she motioned to her face. But there was nothing wrong with her face. Nothing at all.

Until he realized she meant *his* face.

Blimey. He looked down at his hands and arms and, in the moonlight and the one street lamp nearby, realized that he must have been well dusted with coal. He took a moment to sluice his face and arms in the cold water, used his coat to wipe them as dry as he could, rolled down his sleeves, and donned the coat to appear more presentable. He squared up the hat that she had crushed and put that on his coal-dusted hair as well.

The three made their way to the liveryman's cottage and rang the bell. There was one lamp lit in a far window and soon it appeared to be picked up and carried throughout the house, with a small glow moving behind lace curtains from window to window before it glowed behind the milk glass window in the front door. The lock was turned and the man opened the door a crack.

'Here. What do you want? It's late.'

Miss Littleton stepped forward. 'Good sir, we apologize for so late an intrusion, but we are in desperate need of a pony and trap.'

'Is it . . . is it Miss Littleton? You're them people from yesterday.'

'Yes, we are. It's very difficult to explain, but we truly need emergency transportation. It's to help a sick friend. Can you accommodate us? We will, of course, pay a premium for the lateness of the hour.'

That seemed to perk up the man, and he took the lamp with him to the stables as the three followed.

When the man unlocked the wide stable door and lit some lamps, the horses shuffled and nickered. 'The same pony and trap? Will that do?'

'It will do very nicely, Mister Plover.'

The man harnessed the beast in no time, and Miss Littleton paid him handsomely. Without more words exchanged, they were quickly on their way.

The moon was covered by clouds, but Watson did the driving again and remembered well the way, only they weren't going to the big house this time, but through the woods to find the barking dog.

'It must be a gamekeeper's cottage,' explained Miss Littleton. 'Since there was such a lacklustre attempt to auction the house, they could easily have missed the gamekeeper's cottage as part of the estate.'

Even as she finished speaking in her quiet tones, there was the sound of a barking dog emerging from the distance, muffled by the woods themselves.

'Such a ruddy racket,' said Tim. 'It could hardly alert them to intruders when it just barks all the time.'

'More likely, they took it to scare others away,' said Watson. 'No one wants to encounter a barking dog. He might be vicious.'

'Crikey, Ben. What if it is?'

'We'll worry about that when we get to it.'

His friend was always saying things like that. Tim liked planning ahead. Sometimes. Though, granted, when he burgled a place, he only did the most rudimentary of investigation. But he was good with an evolving situation, and he certainly knew a thing or two about escaping a bad one.

'We should have brought a sausage for old Wellington.'

Miss Littleton chuckled. 'I have every expectation that we will be able to handle the problem. Since the dog always barks, it won't alert our culprits to our presence, now will it?'

'That's good thinking, Miss Littleton.'

'Not at all, Mister Badger. And I'm certain your Mister Watson still has his Webley handy.'

Watson patted his coat pocket. 'That I do. For dogs or miscreants.'

'You can't shoot the dog!' said Tim. 'What will Mrs Cress say?'

'I would think that her neighbours would cheer.'

The trap continued over the stony path, and Tim listened as they drew closer to the barking. 'I think it's that way, Ben.'

His friend halted the trap near a narrow path and cocked his head. 'I think you're right. Let's take this road, and keep your eyes peeled for a cottage.'

'I just need me *ears* peeled, don't I?' said Tim, as the barking persisted deep in the wood.

Tim's pride at Watson's abilities knew no end as the man teased the pony just a bit further and then stopped him at the very point he wanted him stopped, just so he could look round and pinpoint where the dog was.

'I think we should get out here,' he said from the driver's seat.

He swung down and tied the lead shank to a branch. He pointed through the undergrowth between the trees to a light in a squat cottage beyond.

And to where a dog was barking.

Tim gathered the three. 'So, what's the plan?'

Watson glanced over Tim's shoulder to the dark outline of the cottage. 'We'll walk round it, taking measure, peering into the windows to see what we can see and make sure that we've got the right place, and decide from there.'

'I can knock on the door,' said Miss Littleton. 'I can tell them I am a tripper and lost my way.'

'Then they'd kidnap *you*,' said Tim.

'And what if they do? I'll fight them and you two can rescue me as well.'

'Now, Ellsie . . .'

'Wait, Tim. She might have something there. Her being at the front door can surely serve as a distraction for us to get Doctor Watson. But only after we have identified that he is there.'

Tim stared at his friend aghast. 'You'd put Miss Littleton in danger as a distraction?'

'I volunteered, Timothy. I see nothing wrong with it.'

'My gawd, woman!'

'Mister Badger, control yourself and focus on the case at hand.'

Tim glared and then threw his hands up in surrender. The ruddy two of them. Agreeing. There was no getting round that.

They crept forward, and the dog's barking never grew louder and never fainter. It was a constant barrage of the same barking over and over. It turned out that Wellington was a beagle and tied to a rope, now taut at the end of it, continually barking into the aether.

That dog's gone crackers, thought Tim. *He's not facing us. He's barking at nothing at all.* He reckoned living with pinched old Mrs Cress would do that to man or beast. *What did her husband die of?* he wondered.

They made it to the edge of the clearing and carefully watched the cottage. There was a light in the window at the back and a smaller one in the front. Watson directed Tim to go round one way and then indicated that he would go round the other and they'd meet in the middle.

Tim nodded and crept towards the back, while his friend went round to the front. This was Tim's speciality, after all. He certainly had employed stealth when he was a lad and as a Baker Street Irregular. Mister Holmes himself had remarked at how like a shadow he was. So he watched where he stepped to make sure he wouldn't crack any twigs or kick about any dried leaves and got to the back window at last.

The cottage itself was in poor repair. An old, thatched place with a bowed roof like an old horse's swayed spine, with half-timbered walls and a decided lean to one side as if a mere breath would tumble the whole thing over. He came up close to the window smelling of mildew and raised his head ever so slowly and quietly. Even though it had some shabby curtains, he could see well enough through them. And crikey, there he was! Doctor John Watson himself, still in a smoking jacket and cap, sitting at a desk and writing on page after page. There was already a pile of written pages sitting under the flickering oil lamp.

So they had been right. He was kidnapped to do writing and probably to set the record straight, though only in the eyes of Kenneth Abernetty, who must have been just as mad as that dog.

Tim's heart soared. *It won't be long now, Doctor Watson,* he thought to himself, much cheered by this discovery. Oh, how he wanted to get that window open and get him now! But he knew the wisdom of following Ben's orders and continued around the building. There was a broken wattled fence that he easily stepped over, with no traps planted round the perimeter. He paused at the barking dog and made a wide swathe around it and met up again with Watson where they had both started and inched back to the place at the edge of the clearing in the shadows.

'He's in there, all right,' said Tim.

'Thank God,' said Miss Littleton. 'Then, shall we proceed with my plan?'

Watson nodded. 'Let Tim and me make our way to the back of the hut where Doctor Watson is, count to ten slowly, then approach the door.'

'As you say, Mister Watson.'

'Be careful, Ellsie.' Tim paused before he leaned in and kissed her petal-soft cheek. She smiled prettily up at him and backed into the shadows.

'Shall we?' said Watson, brandishing his Webley.

Tim agreed and crept low like his companion to the back of the house again, where they positioned themselves under the window. They waited. Until the dog . . . fell silent. And then there was a knock on the door.

Tim looked at Watson. What in the world happened to the dog? Did Miss Littleton . . . dispatch it?

The light at the front window suddenly extinguished and there came a gruff voice through the door. 'Who's there?'

'Excuse me, but I've been travelling and I've lost my way. Could you possibly see your way to help me?'

'What . . . what have you done with the dog?'

'I told it to be still. You have to be firm with dogs.'

'I'll be blowed,' whispered Tim. And then he checked in the room. The doctor stopped writing and turned in his chair towards the closed door. It was then, when the front door opened, that Tim rose and tapped on the window. Doctor Watson turned.

Tim waved. 'It's me, Doctor,' he rasped. 'Tim Badger.'

The doctor rushed to the window and pushed open the casement, but it was clearly blocked from opening wider. 'Great heavens. Badger!'

'We've come to rescue you, Doctor. This is *my* Watson, *Benjamin Watson.*'

'Doctor,' said Watson with a nod.

'Benjamin Watson! I am much relieved, gentlemen.'

Tim put a finger to his lips. 'No time to talk. We'll have to force this window and then it's quick business for you to climb out. Ready?'

The doctor nodded, and Tim gripped the opened window tightly and yanked hard. The nails came loose and the window opened wider and then fell out. Tim put out a hand for the doctor just as the door opened to the room.

There was a blast of the Webley in noise and a flash, and Hobnail fell back, wounded. Tim tugged the doctor through the open hole and they both tumbled to the ground. Untangling himself, he looked to Ben. 'I'm going to help Miss Littleton.'

Tim left the doctor in his friend's care and ran round to the front just in time to hear Abernetty exclaim, 'You're the blasted street woman who took my ransom!'

'I am nothing of the kind. I am a reporter for the *Daily Chronicle*, Miss Ellsie Moira Littleton, and you, sir, are a vile kidnapper. Get him.' Tim realized in a blink that she wasn't ordering *him* . . . but Wellington the dog.

The beagle leapt. It hung on the man's arm and growled and tore as if he were a fox on the chase, until the man yelled and tried to hit the beast.

And before Tim could do anything about it, Miss Littleton grabbed the lead and said, 'Heel, Wellington,' with quite an authoritative tone, and the dog obeyed. He stopped gnawing on Abernetty and sat next to his new mistress, and Tim was never so happy that she was who she was.

'It's over, Abernetty,' he said. 'You and your vile companion have been caught by Badger and Watson Detecting Agency. And it's time to get you back to the authorities and to prison for good this time.'

Hobnail revealed himself to be Tom Clifford, late of Fleet Prison. He had a bullet in his shoulder; the wound was ministered to and staunched with a tied rag by Doctor Watson – who seemed to tie the rag with a bit more vehemence than necessary – before both prisoner's hands were bound behind their backs and they were forced nose to nose into the trap, while Ben and Miss Littleton squeezed together on the driver's bench for the ride back to town.

Tim and Doctor Watson walked behind. 'I'm sorry there's not room for you in the cart, Doctor.'

'I do not mind it at all, Badger. I haven't had any exercise for some days and it is good to get to walking again.'

'We deduced – Ben and me – that they kidnapped you to write a new story proving Abernetty's innocence.'

'That's extraordinary, Badger. I must confess to you that though I have been friends with Sherlock Holmes for a good number of years, I have never quite mastered his method of deduction. However did you discover it?'

'Well . . .' Tim puffed up a bit and walked with surer strides behind the trap. 'You see, we discovered the casebook you had carefully placed under your desk, ingeniously opened to a page that included the title of the story we needed to see.'

'How glad I am you worked that out. I had so little time. I wondered at all that Scotland Yard would understand it.'

'Ah, but Mrs Hudson came directly to us. We never did call upon Scotland Yard. They said no police, and we feared for your health, sir.'

'But how did you deduce that I was being forced to write a new version of events?'

'It's elementary, ain't it? Number one, all your writing things were gone. And number two, we established that it was Kenneth Abernetty's case. And finally, number three, he wanted too little in ransom. We deduced from that that it was not for money he wanted you, but another purpose. And then there was the slipper you left behind. It was an understated but good clue.'

'Ah, I knew that was taking a chance. I did not think that anyone from Scotland Yard would see the maker's label and put two and two together, though on the off chance that Holmes had returned . . . But by Jove, I am glad that Badger and Watson did!'

They walked a bit more as the doctor shook his head. The man had not stopped grinning since being rescued. 'I am astonished. And very pleased. I must say, I had my doubts about Holmes's experiment with you Dean Street chaps, paying for that Soho flat and the money expended to you both. I warned him against it. How wrong I was! I freely admit that his faith in you was entirely justified.'

'I'm only sorry we didn't figure it out sooner, sir. That it took so long.'

'After the initial unpleasantness, I realized I was no longer in any immediate danger. Though when the men were out of the house, they tied and gagged me and had that damnable dog guard me in my room. But I knew I had only to wait it out. And write as instructed, of course. I was penning a quite amusing piece of rubbish,' he said proudly.

They wandered through the woods, and Tim suddenly remembered that the good doctor had on only one shoe and that his stockinged foot was getting damp. Tim touched his sleeve. 'Doctor, perhaps you'd care to change places with Ben and drive the trap. Even after talking about it, I quite forgot your, er, shoe difficulty.'

'Not a bit of it. The town is not that far.'

'You're a sport, you are, sir.'

'Just enjoying my freedom,' he said with a wide grin . . . even as he began to limp a bit.

The gas lamps of the town soon came into view and his friend drove the trap through to the police, whose blue lamp was lit outside the modest brick structure.

He pulled up the trap and leapt out, helping Miss Littleton – who was holding the dog Wellington in her lap – down from the cart. Then Tim and Ben muscled the two kidnappers out of the rig and marched them up the steps to the police.

And when they entered, several rozzers were gathered and turned to look, and someone said, pointing, 'There they are!' and the police descended upon them all.

TWENTY-FOUR
Watson

All six of them found themselves sitting behind bars in the small cell at the police station. Doctor Watson pleaded with them to telephone Scotland Yard and to contact Inspector Lestrade to explain his identity, but Badger piped up with, 'Please get Inspector Stanley Hopkins, sir! He'll know us all.'

But he was laughed at, as he might expect he would be. Then the rozzers discussed the theft of the locomotive, and Badger slumped, retreating to the back of the cell to sit next to the woman.

Abernetty and Clifford were still bound and sat glowering in a corner of the cell by themselves.

Badger glared at them. 'Just what did you think you were doing, Abernetty? What would be gained by kidnapping a man like Doctor Watson?'

'Vindication, you fool! I was innocent, and ten years of my life were ripped away from me. I wanted the world to know. I wanted them to read from Doctor Watson's own hand that he and Sherlock Holmes had been wrong!'

'You'll get more than ten years for this, you rotter. Kidnapping and assault? You'll be lucky if you ever get out ever again.' He shook his head. 'And why on God's green earth did you ask for a ransom? You had what you wanted.' Abernetty's glance slid towards Clifford. 'You needed money for this blighter?' Badger pivoted towards Clifford. 'You just got out of prison. Why'd you do a fool thing by putting yourself in with Abernetty?'

He scowled. 'The money.'

'Oh, the money!' he chortled. 'Got a lot in your own hands, did you? That wasn't going to be enough to last you. All this and it's back to prison for you.'

Clifford jerked to his feet and tried to lunge at Badger, but forgot that the coppers had left him tied up. Badger laughed at him harder, and he fell back into his seat again, commiserating silently with a glum Abernetty.

Doctor Watson seemed to ignore their conversation and instead sat next to Ben, looking him over. He suddenly extended his hand. 'Mister Watson, I am pleased to officially make your acquaintance, sir.'

He shook his hand. 'And I you, *Doctor* Watson.'

'I do not suppose we are somehow related,' said the doctor with a chuckle.

'I don't see how, sir. My father, Peter Watson, was born in the West Indies.'

'I have no people there.'

'I didn't think so.' He adjusted his bowler. 'I wish this was under better circumstances. I have wanted to talk with you, sir, about scientific things.'

'Medical things?'

'I was only a chemist's assistant, yet I learned much. But I have taken to the other scientific things that Mister Holmes is fond of for solving crimes.'

'Have you now? Self-taught? I am impressed.'

Ben felt his cheeks flush at the compliment. 'Well . . . I get by, certainly.'

'I can only help with medical matters, I am afraid. It is my colleague who is expert on a number of scientific disciplines. Also self-taught.'

'Oh, indeed?'

'Yes, he studied chemistry at school, but he picked up the rest either by experiment or by inventing crucial ways of discovery himself. Holmes is an unusual man.'

'He is that, sir. He's mentored us with extraordinary patience.'

'Patience?' He chuckled. 'There may be hope for Holmes yet.'

They sat as they were for hours, until the rozzers – tired of Miss Littleton insisting on telephoning her editor – grudgingly relented at last. She was escorted to the front desk and patted Wellington's head as he obediently lay on the floor by the sergeant in blessed silence. The number was requested and they waited another short while for the exchange to return the call.

'Mister Massingham!' she said loudly into the telephone when they handed her the instrument. 'This is Miss Littleton. Yes, sir, I am aware of the time, but this is vitally important. It concerns an extraordinary story I am working on, as we discussed. Yes . . . Yes . . . That one. If you could be so good as to contact Inspector

Stanley Hopkins at Scotland Yard and tell him it concerns the kidnapping of Doctor John H. Watson and that he and I and Badger and Watson are incarcerated at the police station in Aylesbury Vale, it would be most appreciated.'

She listened attentively before replying again. 'Yes, Mister Massingham, you heard that correctly. Your writer is in gaol. Along with *Doctor Watson* of Sherlock Holmes fame, whom we have rescued under great duress from his kidnappers. And I am making note of all those officers and their names who are holding us unlawfully, including the man in charge, one Chief Inspector Martin Walker. That is *Martin Walker*, sir. W-A-L-K-E-R. Oh, er . . . and there may be an issue or two with the railways. I shall inform you in more detail later. If you could please telephone Inspector Hopkins, all will be revealed. Thank you, sir. Oh, I shall.'

She handed back the telephone apparatus to the constable at the desk. 'Inspector Hopkins from Scotland Yard should be on his way shortly.'

She was escorted back to the cell by a considerably more sober police force.

Miss Littleton had fallen asleep on Badger's shoulder, and Badger had nodded off beside her. The good doctor lay on the cot asleep, but Ben was restless. They saved the doctor, but at the expense of Badger and Watson. There was that little matter of making off with a locomotive, and he knew that that would not go down well with the authorities. Try as he might, he couldn't find a way round it. They could, of course, employ Miles Smith of Tottenham Court Road, and he would be glad to do it, but Ben wasn't certain that would make any difference. He was only sorry that his mother had to see her only son incarcerated. Who would support her then? It was his hubris that was their downfall. It was bad enough that Badger skirted the edge of the law, but it was Ben this time – quiet, resolute, logical Ben – who had tipped them completely over it.

By morning, he was exhausted and had got no sleep. But it was he who heard the first clamourings of more people arriving at the entrance of the police station. Wellington awakened and began barking.

Miss Littleton arose from Badger's shoulder and shouted, 'Wellington! Quiet!' And the dog once again obeyed.

'How'd you do that?' asked Badger.

'Simple. I am well acquainted with hounds from our country estates. They merely need a firm hand to learn obedience.'

Badger made a face that formed into a sly smile and a twinkle in his eye, and that's when Ben rolled *his* eyes and turned away from them to stand at the cell's bars.

Two Scotland Yard constables in their dark blue tunics, silver buttons, and custodian helmets had come through first and made way for Inspector Hopkins, looking a bit worn and rumpled from his early rising and long journey to Aylesbury Vale. His tan suit under his long Ulster coat of herringbone tweed appeared wrinkled from the train ride. 'Where's your chief inspector?' he demanded.

'Right here, sir,' said the man in a smart dark blue tunic, silver buttons, a swag of a chain over his shoulder, and heavy boots. 'Do I have the pleasure of meeting Inspector Stanley Hopkins from Scotland Yard?'

Hopkins shook his hand quickly and let it go. 'And you are?'

'Chief Inspector Martin Walker, Aylesbury Vale Police.'

'Well, Chief Inspector, you've put your foot in it, haven't you?'

His moustached ruffled. 'I don't know your meaning, sir.'

'You've apparently incarcerated Doctor Watson, companion to Sherlock Holmes.'

The white-moustachioed chief inspector shook his head, posturing with hands behind his back, his tunic straining against his round belly. 'I had no way of knowing that the gentleman wasn't lying to me, sir.'

'No way of knowing,' Hopkins muttered disgustedly. 'Take me to them at once.'

'Now, now, sir. There is a lot to sort out here regarding his companions. And as you well know, we have jurisdiction here. Two appear to be the prisoners of the others.'

'Then I suggest you take me to them now, Chief Inspector, so that *Scotland Yard* can sort it out *for* you.'

The copper hesitated, his full moustache fluttering from his high dudgeon, but he seemed to know that this bout would not be worth the battle. He pivoted on his heel and marched through the doorway where the cells were and stood.

'Badger and Watson indeed!' said an exhausted Hopkins. 'And ... *Doctor Watson!*'

'How good it is to see you again, Inspector.'

'Get this cell open now!'

Chief Inspector Walker nodded to one of his men, who stepped forward with a large ring of keys. He summarily unlocked the door and opened it wide.

The two kidnappers rose with anxious looks on their faces.

'Who are those men?' asked Hopkins.

'They're the kidnappers,' said Badger. 'They took Doctor Watson from his Baker Street flat five days ago.'

Hopkins aimed a scowl towards the chief inspector before returning a gentler glance towards Doctor Watson. 'Sir, is this true?'

'It certainly is. That' – the good doctor pointed to Abernetty – 'is Kenneth Abernetty, recently released after ten years in Fleet Prison, convicted of conspiring with his family to commit fraud and theft. He claims he was not guilty and imprisoned unfairly, so the moment he is free, he conspired to kidnap me to force me to write a new version of events to exonerate him. He did not favour my original story published in *The Strand Magazine*, apparently.'

Hopkins's scowl deepened. 'Oh, you did, did you? I hope you enjoyed Fleet, my man. For you will surely be enjoying the queen's pleasure there for an uncertain length to come. And this other?'

'His companion,' Ben interjected. 'Tom Clifford. Abernetty met him in prison and they worked together.'

'Well, isn't that pretty. You two didn't learn your lesson, did you?'

The prisoners both frowned.

'Chief Inspector,' said Hopkins, turning towards the reddening copper, 'we will be taking them back to London to face charges. These others are free to go, having rescued the good doctor. That is Miss Ellsie Moira Littleton, reporter for the *Daily Chronicle*, and these gentlemen are Timothy Badger and Benjamin Watson of Badger and Watson Detecting Agency, Dean Street, London. I can personally vouch for them.'

'I am afraid that is impossible, Inspector Hopkins,' said the chief inspector, with perhaps too much glee at getting one over on Scotland Yard. 'Those three stole a locomotive and shall be charged accordingly.'

Hopkins turned slowly back to the three, his hand hiding his eyes as he kneaded his forehead. 'Tell me, Mister Badger, that this isn't true.'

'Well, Inspector, it's like this. The trains stopped running to Aylesbury Vale from Euston Station by the time we discovered where they had been keeping the good doctor, and we didn't feel it safe for Doctor Watson to wait till morning, so we . . . er . . . commandeered the train—'

'Locomotive,' said Ben.

'Locomotive,' Badger continued, 'in order to rescue Doctor Watson. You see, sir, it was imperative. What would *you* have done?'

'A stationmaster was injured when he tried to stop them,' said Chief Inspector Walker, rocking on his heels. Though his moustache hid his mouth, he was clearly smiling.

'But I looked back to make certain he was all right,' said Miss Littleton, as if that would make it better.

Hopkins merely stared at her in disbelief. 'The three of you stole a train?'

'A locomotive,' said Ben again. 'Erm . . . we are sorry for doing so. But, er, needs must.'

'You. Stole. A. Train?'

Ben opened his mouth to correct the inspector again, when Badger jammed him in the ribs with his elbow. Ben decided to keep silent.

Hopkins walked in a tight circle, head down, thinking. 'Why didn't you contact Scotland Yard as soon as you discovered the doctor had been abducted?'

Badger stepped forward and raised his finger to explain. 'Oh, we were specifically told not to contact the police, sir. And, after all, we *are* detectives.'

Hopkins's face darkened. He did not seem to find that much of an excuse.

It was at that moment that a rather dishevelled boy who looked as if he had just tumbled out of bed, and likely had, stepped through the police station door. 'I have a telegram for Inspector Stanley Hopkins!'

'Here, boy!' said the inspector, appearing relieved for the interruption. He took the envelope and then dug in his pocket for a coin for him.

He tore open the paper and read. And then he laughed, shaking his head at Badger and Ben before handing the paper over to Chief Inspector Walker. 'It appears you have friends in high places, gentlemen. That is a telegram from the Home Office, pardoning any infractions of theft by Badger and Watson and Miss Littleton in this railway business during the course of their investigations. It is signed M. H.'

'Mycroft Holmes,' murmured Ben.

TWENTY-FIVE
Badger

Miss Littleton was asleep again on his shoulder while the train clattered over the rails back to London, but Tim didn't mind a bit. Wellington the dog was lying at her feet, perfectly content, and perfectly quiet.

He watched as Doctor Watson talked excitedly to Ben Watson, getting on like a house on fire. Who knew? Tim himself was slightly intimidated by the doctor, just as he was of Mister Holmes. But he reckoned that Ben didn't have the experience that Tim had with Holmes and Watson. *Ben always said he wanted to meet Doctor Watson*, he mused. It was natural that they would like and respect each other. Scientific men were like that.

Tim had the presence of mind before they left Aylesbury Vale Station to send a telegram to Mrs Hudson to let her know all was well. It made him smile to think of the merry face she'd wear after receiving that. And then sent another to Mrs Cress to tell her that they had recovered her dog and not to worry.

He was also relieved that Mycroft Holmes came through at last, and that Mrs Watson wouldn't have to see her son in prison. He'd have to write a letter of thanks to him as well.

He settled into the cushioned seat, listening to the soft breaths of Miss Littleton asleep on his shoulder. He gazed down at her in wonder. *My girl!* And to think that at one time he hated the sight of her! She had written some horrible things about him in the past, saying that he was a thief and ne'er-do-well and cheating clients out of their money, not that it had been much money when they began. And never mind that some of it might have been true. It still wasn't nice to see it in print. And then she'd turned right around and become their ally. And more, he thought with a smile. Much more. She was 'his girl'. She'd said so. That meant more kisses to be had. More cuddling. Celibacy was all right for Mister Holmes but certainly not for him. He could detect *and* have his girl at the same time, he reckoned. Why not? Plenty of Scotland

Yard inspectors had wives. He was ashamed that he did not know if Inspector Hopkins was married and looked towards him in the seat beside him.

'Inspector, I am loath to admit that I do not know more personal things about you.'

Hopkins narrowed his eyes. 'What personal things?'

'Oh, such things that friends would know about one another. And I consider us friends, especially after this incident.'

'Oh, you do?'

'Oh, yes, sir. For instance, I don't know whether you are married or not.'

His face softened and he smoothed out his well-trimmed brown moustache. 'As it happens, I am. Three years now.'

'That's lovely. I'm sure the missus is a kind and beautiful helpmate.'

'Well . . . that's . . . that's very kind of you to say, Badger. Yes, she is. Understanding when I am called out of bed in the middle of the night to rescue . . . my friends.'

Tim gave him a wide smile and touched the brim of his hat. 'Any time you need help, sir, Badger and Watson are ready as ever.'

'I've no doubt,' he muttered and went back to reading his paper.

One of the train attendants walking down the corridors beside the compartments announced that they'd be in Euston Station in five minutes. Hopkins rose and folded the paper, setting it on his seat. 'It's time I joined my constables in the next compartment with our prisoners.'

'Very good, sir,' said Tim. 'Do keep us informed. I reckon we'll be called as witnesses to the trial.'

'Most certainly.' He tipped his hat. 'The three of you . . . keep out of trouble.'

'I can't guarantee that, sir,' he replied with a laugh.

Hopkins did not seem to share in his jollity and left the compartment quickly.

The door sliding back into place woke Miss Littleton, and she wiped her eyes and patted her hair which was in much need of her maid Cynthia's skilled devotions.

'Are we nearly there?' she asked with her hand over her yawn.

'Yes, five minutes.'

'I apologize for using your shoulder again as a pillow.'

'I don't mind at all,' he said softly.

She smiled, glanced at their companions who were still busy talking, and leaned in and kissed his cheek. 'You are gallant, sir. And quite my hero.'

'Aw. That's not needed. But, er . . . I like hearing it from you just the same.'

She slipped her arm in his and leaned against him. He felt as if his good cheer was making the train speed on its way, for it suddenly felt as smooth as a silken trail.

Inspector Hopkins said his farewells on the platform at Euston Station. The two constables manhandled the scowling prisoners towards the exit, where the thin ropes that bound them had been exchanged for iron manacles. 'Well done, Badger and Watson. But remember, despite the criminals' admonishments, it's always better to consult with Scotland Yard.'

Doctor Watson chuckled. 'I doubt *my* colleague would make any different decision that these dear fellows made.'

'Yes. And see what trouble they got themselves into.' His moustache twitched.

Miss Littleton, still in her beggar's clothes, stalked up to him, holding tight to the dog lead. 'And they got themselves out of it, too, Inspector. I would not dismiss these gentlemen so cavalierly.'

'Wasn't it you, Miss Littleton, who used to disparage Mister Badger in print?'

'Oh! I am gratified to hear that you read my articles, Inspector. I have since changed my mind on the matter, witnessing for myself their competence and successes.'

He eyed Tim stepping forward to offer his arm to Miss Littleton.

'So I see,' muttered Hopkins. He tipped his hat to all of them and strode away with his constables and prisoners.

Doctor Watson turned to them and rubbed his hands together. 'Shall we depart for Baker Street? I'm sure Mrs Hudson will greet us with a hearty breakfast. I, for one, can certainly use a good meal.'

They agreed and hailed a four-wheeler so that all of them could sit comfortably within. 'Two hundred and twenty-one Baker Street, if you please,' said Doctor Watson to the driver.

'Very good, sir,' he said, barely glancing at his strange fare of a beggar woman with a dog, two rumpled men, and a gentleman in a smoking jacket and cap with only one slipper.

The coach lurched into traffic and wove in and out of omnibuses, wagons, and hansom cabs, vying for the best route with shouting, horses' hooves clattering on the cobblestones, and cartmen pushing into and through the confused lanes of traffic with loud oaths and obscene gestures, even as a pale yellow sun bravely shone through the morning fog.

Doctor Watson breathed deeply with a smile.

'It's good to be back in London, eh?' offered Tim.

'It certainly is, Badger.' He turned to look at him anew. 'You've grown, you know. Since the last time I saw you.'

'To tell you the truth, sir, I wasn't certain if you even knew who I was.'

'Oh, I knew. I knew well. You were, more often than not, there in the morning when I arose. Sleeping on the settee.'

Tim knew his cheeks were flushed, but he refused to turn away. 'Mister Holmes . . . was kind to me,' was all he managed to say.

'He saw a spark in you that those other street urchins didn't seem to possess. In all truth, I think he was flattered that you, too, wanted to be a detective as he was. It reflected well on him. Until you seemed to fail miserably at it, that is.'

Tim flicked a glance at Miss Littleton, but she was looking at the passing carriages and absently stroking the dog's head and pretending, at least, that she hadn't heard Doctor Watson's words.

'Well, as Mister Holmes explained it, there's no use in trying to get paying clients when you live in a hovel with tatty clothes. Or some such, he said. And he was right. You need the right trappings to convince the punters . . . er, clients. Just like a play on the stage. The right costume convinces them.'

'How right you are. Holmes taught himself how to use theatrical make-up and costume. I never managed to convince anyone when I tried it. It is a specialized skill, to be sure.'

'Right, sir. I tried it m'self in this very case. I convinced the queen's own guards that I was a feeble old man.'

The doctor laughed, full of good cheer now that his ordeal was over. 'Truly? I would have liked to have seen that!'

The barouche turned at Marylebone Road, and Baker Street was just in sight. Doctor Watson was alert and anxious, and Tim spoke to him no more, just happy to see the man safe and content.

Tim's colleague paid the driver when he pulled up in front of 221 Baker Street while Doctor Watson fairly flew out of the conveyance and up the steps, unlocking the door.

Tim helped Miss Littleton to the horse block and down to the pavement. The three heard Mrs Hudson's shriek and weeping when they hurried up the steps and into the foyer, where Doctor Watson embraced her and gently patted her back.

'Dear Mrs Hudson. I thank you profoundly for procuring the help of Badger and Watson.'

'I knew they could do it, sir.'

'I am ever grateful to them for doing so. Would you be so kind as to fix the four of us a good English breakfast?'

'I'll make that kitchen sing!' She blew a kiss to Tim and scurried away to do her best. It made Tim's mouth water to think of it.

They followed the good doctor up the stairs to the 'B' flat and waited as Doctor Watson unlocked the door. And when he stepped inside, he halted. 'Holmes! What the devil are you doing here? You are supposed to be out of the country.'

'Watson. Pleased to see you. I understand you got yourself into a spot of trouble.'

'A *spot*? My good fellow.' He stepped forward and took his friend's hand, pumping it heartily. 'I missed you.'

Mister Holmes scanned the company. 'Badger. Watson. And Miss Littleton. Do come in.' He flashed a smile at the good doctor. 'I dare say you could use a wash and a change of clothes. I do not suppose walking about on one slipper is preferable on the streets of London.'

'It certainly is not. If you all will excuse me.' He turned to go down the hallway to his own room.

Tim's company walked through the doorway, and all of them seemed to be aware of their own shabby and slept-in clothes.

'Well, gentlemen. Sit down where you will. My brother Mycroft has informed me of the doings of your detecting agency and alerted me to Doctor Watson's predicament. He said that you came to him to ask for the dubious ransom. Naturally, I rushed back to London, only to find my services were not needed.'

'I apologize, sir,' said Tim, scooting forward to the edge of his seat. 'It was my idea to see him. And he was right that we shouldn't have paid it.'

Mister Holmes sat and picked up the tea cup sitting on his side table amid a clutter of papers and, for some reason, a small bird skull. 'Indeed not. You should have deduced instantly that such a small ransom meant that the money mattered little to the kidnapper.'

'Oh, we did, sir,' said Watson.

'Then why, gentlemen, did it take so long?'

Tim had seldom seen the guv this cross. It was bubbling just below the surface of his civilized veneer, but Tim recognized it just the same. It was in the lowering of his brows, the subtle squint of his eyes, the beak-like nose aimed at them like a piercing spear. And further, Tim knew they deserved it. It took far too long to work it all out. 'I don't blame you for being angry with us, sir. We worked as hard as we could. And with the help of Miss Littleton here and the Dean Street Irregulars, we—'

Mister Holmes raised a long, tapered finger and Tim silenced immediately. '*Dean* Street Irregulars?' A smile flickered at the edge of his mouth as he said it.

'That was my idea,' said Tim proudly. 'I took a page from your book, sir, and me own experience as one of your Irregulars, and got our own gathering of street boys. They do good work, sir, just like me and my fellows did when I was a lad.'

'Did they, indeed? Well, it should interest you to know that—'

'You've got a new batch of Irregulars. Yes, I know it, guv. And I told my boys to steer clear of yours. Them boys are a good lot. It wouldn't surprise me if one or two of them became detectives when they grow to men.'

'It would not surprise me either,' muttered Mister Holmes. 'But it did take you nearly a week.'

'Mister Holmes,' put in Miss Littleton. He frowned at the presence of the dog. Or was it the woman, Tim wondered. 'I can assure you, that Mister Badger and Mister Watson have been at it night and day. They called upon me to help them acquire the stories from *The Strand Magazine*'s archives that were mentioned in the casebook pages that Doctor Watson left as a clue. They questioned those in the flats directly across from these apartments as to whether anyone had witnessed the abduction, and those witnesses helped identify the hired livery and thence the information that the culprits took Euston Station to the country. And by ferreting out the *right* story, they deduced that it had to be the Abernetty case, which led them to Milton Keynes.'

'And to stealing a locomotive.' He couldn't seem to help the lopsided grin that softened the severeness of his face. 'That was well done, Mister Watson.'

'It was *ill* done, Mister Holmes,' he replied.

'Yes, well. My brother was good enough to make certain that the three of you suffered no consequences for that. But I must confess . . . I would have done the same thing.'

'You see!' said Tim, pointing a finger at his friend.

Watson sat up, indignant. 'You're the one who tried to talk me out of it.'

'Never mind, gentlemen. All's well that ends well. The culprits are in custody, my dear friend is back home at Baker Street where he belongs, and none of you are the worse for wear.' Though at that last, his eyes raked over Miss Littleton and her inappropriate attire. His eye sparkled, but he refused to ask. Perhaps, Tim reasoned, he already deduced it.

'And here I am refreshed and renewed,' said Doctor Watson, striding into the room with a soft grey suit and *both* shoes on his feet.

It was then that Mrs Hudson entered with an enormous tray. She set the place for *five*.

'Mrs Hudson,' said Mister Holmes, examining the place settings. 'How in the world did you know I would be here?'

She smiled at him, cheeks rosy and round. 'Mister Holmes, you've been a tenant here for over fourteen years. In all that time, I have learned a thing or two. Naturally, I deduced it.'

He laughed heartily and sat in his place, picking up the lids to the dishes and peering inside to see what was on offer.

TWENTY-SIX
Watson

They took another carriage back to Dean Street after they finished Mrs Hudson's excellent meal and felt the need for their own wash and refresh.

Miss Littleton lingered only to talk to Badger on the pavement below their flat with Wellington sniffing at the street, and Ben watched them out of the window, standing closer and closer. Since the window sash was open, he couldn't help but hear their conversation.

'Timothy,' she was saying, 'I have more news for you. You recall my telling you that *The Strand Magazine* offered me a ridiculous sum to publish my stories with them?'

'I do. And I have to say how proud I am of you.'

She blushed prettily but brushed it quickly aside. 'Yes, but my editor, Mister Massingham, got wind of it, and he insisted on paying me *more* for the stories. More than *The Strand Magazine*. And so I am still with the *Daily Chronicle*, and fortunate I am to be there.'

'That's great news, Ellsie, me love. You're going to own that paper someday.'

'The thought hadn't occurred to me . . . until now.'

And then Badger leaned in and planted a chaste kiss to her cheek and she in turn offered him a shy smile.

'What about this dog here? Old Wellington.'

'I'll take care of him until you can contact poor Mrs Cress. I'm sure she'll be glad to get him back. He's a very good boy.'

On cue, the dog gazed up at her lovingly with ears twitched into arches and tail wagging furiously against the pavement.

Badger helped her and Wellington into the hansom and paid the driver to take her back to her house a few blocks away.

Well, Ben supposed it was inevitable. What a strange couple they were. He imagined he'd have to accept it now. Truly, she bore the whole thing exceptionally well, even being in gaol, though he was certain it appealed to her sense of adventure as a proper journalist. He was equally certain it would be a prominent part of their story when it appeared in the *Daily Chronicle*.

He left the window with the intention of heading for his desk when he encountered Katie Murphy standing patiently behind him with her hands crossed over her apron. Her face was hopeful.

'Mister Watson, did you solve your case?'

'We did indeed. Doctor Watson is now home and safe with Mister Holmes again, and we caught the culprits, who are currently in gaol at Scotland Yard.'

'That's a grand thing.' Her cheer that was so prominent on her face seemed to abruptly melt away and she worried at the apron's hem. 'I wonder, Mister Watson, if we could take a moment to talk.'

'Certainly, Miss Murphy. Would you care to sit down?'

'No, sir. It wouldn't be proper. Oh, Mister Watson. That indeed is the crux of it. You see, I think you are a fine gentleman.'

A rock suddenly appeared in the pit of his stomach. He knew he was often a dour man, always sensing the negative, but he somehow knew what she was going to say.

'A fine gentleman indeed, and your mother is a grand lady. But . . . I've been thinking and talking to Mrs Kelly, and we believe that it would not quite be the proper thing for you and me to become . . . well, more than employer and employee. If we were not in this situation, it might be different. I do regret it, but it has to be. There must be no stain of impropriety on you or Mister Badger.'

He cleared his throat. 'Not to mention your own reputation, Miss Murphy.'

'Well . . . that's as may be. No one truly trusts a maid and an Irish maid at that. But it's your reputation and the reputation of Badger and Watson Detecting Agency that propels me to this decision. I hope . . . I sincerely hope that you can forgive me, sir.'

'Oh, Miss Murphy. There is nothing to forgive. You made a considered decision. And you have always been honest with me.'

'As I ever shall be, sir. Now, if it would suit you better for me to find a different situation, then I will—'

'Oh no, Miss Murphy.' How he wanted to go to her and take her hands! 'That would be a terrible inconvenience to you.'

'It's not me I'm thinking of.'

'But you should. Dear me.' He rubbed at his forehead. 'I was advised against this, and now I see the truth of the matter. Do forgive *me* for creating this very situation.'

'There's nothing to forgive, Mister Watson. If you think we can both work professionally together, then I can perform my duties as I have before.'

'Yes, of course. Do you wish me to discuss it with Mrs Kelly?'

'Not necessary, sir. Mrs Kelly agreed to abide by whatever you said.'

Ruddy hell. He nodded. He realized he was still holding his hat and now suddenly didn't know *how* to hold it. He fiddled with it until she took it from his hand and hung it on the peg by the door.

'Will that be all, sir?'

Wasn't that enough? 'Yes, Miss Murphy. I apologize for any inconvenience this might have caused you.'

She smiled her usual cheery smile. 'Not a bit of it.' She curtseyed and opened the door. Badger was standing there with a strange look on his face. She passed him by as he entered.

Sheepishly, he hung his hat next to Ben's. 'Erm . . . I couldn't help but hear . . . Ruddy hellfire, Ben, I heard her talking and I waited on the landing.'

'Oh.' Ben sat on the settee and sighed.

He laid his hand on Ben's shoulder. 'Listen, old son. You'll be all right. She's a good girl. And she knows what's right. More than we do about scandals and such.'

'Yes. I reckon she's right.'

'But your heart is broke. I know how it feels.'

But you've got Miss Littleton, he longed to say. Yet he well knew Badger had had many exploits with women, and some *had* broken *his* heart a time or two.

'It's for the best,' Ben admitted sadly.

'Look, why don't we both get washed and shaved,' and here Badger ran his hand over his own stubbled chin, 'and we'll go out for a pint or three, eh? Forget our troubles and celebrate another case closed.'

'That's a good idea, Tim.' Ben rose to retreat to his room. He wondered if Miss Murphy would bring the hot water, and then he decided it was best not to think about it further. There would be other cases to solve, other fights for justice to be won. Of that, he was certain.

AFTERWORD

'Is there any point to which you would wish to draw my attention?'
'To the curious incident of the dog in the night-time.'
'The dog did nothing in the night-time.'
'That was the curious incident,' remarked Sherlock Holmes.
      'The Adventure of Silver Blaze' (1892),
           Sir Arthur Conan Doyle

Of course, our dog *did* do something in the night-time. It barked incessantly, unlike in the incident Mister Holmes cites.

I'm doing my best not to toy too much with the canon. I want it to remain just as if it were historical fact. And indeed, the canon has been most helpful for me to identify certain things that were ordinary in the day for Conan Doyle but are quite removed in time and use from us today. What Holmes and Watson ate and where, for instance, and timetables of trains and such.

So here we have Doctor Watson kidnapped when that didn't happen in the canon, but I think this is entirely possible, since he didn't write down *all* his escapades. But you might have noticed that a big clue in this book came from some of those 'untold' stories in the canon. They are mentioned in passing in the Doyle stories, and probably the most famous of these is *The Giant Rat of Sumatra*. It's certainly my favourite title. Doyle wanted to give his characters a life past the pages of the written word, and to mention cases that happened for them both together and before they met certainly expands their lives beyond the stories and beyond the covers of a book.

I made good use of them. They were *The Case of the Darlington Substitution Scandal, The Case of Old Abrahams, The Arnsworth Castle Business, The Case of Mrs Etheridge,* and *The Dreadful Business of the Abernetty Family.* These were stories mentioned in passing by Holmes, and it should also be noted that these were not actual titles as such. The plots of these stories were also not fleshed out and it was up to me in this instance to create brief plotlines with character names and motives. Don't get frustrated trying to find them in the canon. As I said, they are only mentioned in passing.

In this tale, Miss Littleton contacts her editor, Henry William Massingham, the real editor at that time for the real *Daily Chronicle*. It was a very left-leaning paper, and after he departed the *Daily Chronicle*, he wrote for *The Nation* from 1907 to 1923, considered a very radical paper. He was also responsible for giving George Bernard Shaw his break by hiring him as a deputy drama critic for *The Star* when he edited there. I do love including real people in the drama, even though Massingham doesn't actually make an appearance this time.

In London, communication was surprisingly dynamic. Yes, telephones were beginning to be part of the landscape and we of this modern era can't even imagine life without the instant gratification of that phone always at hand in our pockets, ready to call or text and Google information we require. Telegrams were as instant as it came (because making a phone call took sending the number through one or more exchanges before they called *you* back to connect you). But in London, you also had mail or what the Brits call 'post' that was available *twelve* times a day. Think of that! How ingenious. Almost better (and cheaper) than sending a telegram. So it was entirely possible to send a letter detailing that you had kidnapped someone, and later in the day send the ransom note.

I'd also like to mention that, when I can, I write about real pubs that existed in this time period, and more often than not, they still exist in the same location today. The Porcupine on Charing Cross Road and The Lord Raglan on St Martin's Le Grand, for instance. Pop in and look around. Send me a photo!

Nellie Bly was indeed a real American journalist. Her real name was Elizabeth Cochrane Seaman, and she is best known for the mental institution spying that Miss Littleton cites, and for her trip around the world to best Jules Verne's book *Around the World in Eighty Days* . . . by eight days! Her penchant for taking chances spawned a new kind of investigative journalism that is still with us today.

In this book, we have a little adventure outside of London. Indeed, Mister Holmes and Doctor Watson frequently found themselves travelling some distance from London on a regular basis for their cases. Now Badger and Watson get their chance too, and more so in future volumes.

And they definitely have more adventures ahead for them. The next in the series is *The Vampyre Client*, a gothic tale that Badger would be glad to read in one of his penny dreadfuls on a stormy night . . . and one that also harkens back to one of Doyle's canon tales, where Badger and Watson are hired by a man whose neighbours are convinced he is a vampire and have threatened him and his home. He wants the detectives to prove to them that he is just an ordinary scientist. But when tragedy strikes, Badger and Watson find they have a case they can truly sink their teeth into.

See all my books and other keen stuff at JeriWesterson.com. And, as always, if you like a book, please review it! Cheers.